The Chronicles of Vladimir Tod

TWELFTH GRADE KILLS

THE CHRONICLES OF
Vladimir Tod

TWELFTH GRADE
Kills

Heather Brewer

> DUTTON CHILDREN'S BOOKS <

AN IMPRINT OF PENGUIN GROUP (USA) INC.

DUTTON CHILDREN'S BOOKS
A division of Penguin Young Readers Group

Published by the Penguin Group
Penguin Group (USA) Inc., 375 Hudson Street, New York, New York 10014, U.S.A. ▾ Penguin Group (Canada), 90 Eglinton Avenue East, Suite 700, Toronto, Ontario M4P 2Y3, Canada (a division of Pearson Penguin Canada Inc.) ▾ Penguin Books Ltd, 80 Strand, London WC2R 0RL, England ▾ Penguin Ireland, 25 St Stephen's Green, Dublin 2, Ireland (a division of Penguin Books Ltd) ▾ Penguin Group (Australia), 250 Camberwell Road, Camberwell, Victoria 3124, Australia (a division of Pearson Australia Group Pty Ltd) ▾ Penguin Books India Pvt Ltd, 11 Community Centre, Panchsheel Park, New Delhi—110 017, India ▾ Penguin Group (NZ), 67 Apollo Drive, Rosedale, North Shore 0632, New Zealand (a division of Pearson New Zealand Ltd.) ▾ Penguin Books (South Africa) (Pty) Ltd, 24 Sturdee Avenue, Rosebank, Johannesburg 2196, South Africa ▾ Penguin Books Ltd, Registered Offices: 80 Strand, London WC2R 0RL, England

CIP Data is available.

Published in the United States by Dutton Children's Books,
a division of Penguin Young Readers Group
345 Hudson Street, New York, New York 10014
www.penguin.com/youngreaders

Designed by Jason Henry

Printed in USA ▾ First Edition
ISBN 978-0-525-42224-2
3 5 7 9 10 8 6 4 2

▼ ▼ ▼

To my agent, Michael Bourret, for believing in Vlad—and
me—from the very beginning, and for continuing to believe.

And to the Minion Horde, for being the most fangtastic
bunch of outcasts on the planet. Without you,
Vlad would not be.

ACKNOWLEDGMENTS

An enormous amount of thanks should go to my incredible editors, Liz Waniewski and Maureen Sullivan, for their brilliance and immeasurable amount of patience. Big, well-deserved thanks to Team Vlad at Penguin Young Readers: Don Weisberg, Lauri Hornik, Felicia Frazier, Scottie Bow-ditch, Erin Dempsey, Jennifer Haller, Andrew Harwell, Shanta Newlin, Christian Fuenfhausen, Emily Romero, Courtney Wood, Allison Verost, Rosanne Lauer, Jason Henry, and many more I'm sure I'm forgetting to name here.

Thanks to my sister, Dawn Vanniman, for keeping my sanity (relatively) intact and for being there whenever I need her. And a big shout-out to MTB, who truly get it.

Paul, Jacob, and Alexandria, I could not have written and published an entire series without your unfailing support. Nor could I continue to write, and continue to feel happy, safe, and loved without the Brewer Clan behind me every step of the way. You've helped me reach "The End." And this is only the beginning.

CONTENTS

The Chronicles of Vladimir Tod

TWELFTH GRADE KILLS

PROLOGUE
A BRIEF DETOUR

D'ABLO'S FLESH had almost completely healed from his blistering battle with the sun a year and a half before, but his hand . . . his hand was gone for good. He was eternally scarred and the honor of his name forever stained, all because of a teenage boy by the name of Vladimir Tod.

Now D'Ablo dropped to his knees and shook his head, his wide eyes locked on the man before him, his voice trembling slightly. "But . . . why? I've done nothing wrong!"

The man standing before D'Ablo remained silent. His features were draped with shadows, as if even the lights cast by the office lamps were afraid to touch him.

The air was thick, full of a warning that D'Ablo could not deny. And even though the office window was open and a slight breeze was ruffling the curtains, the air felt heavy, stale, stagnant, old. It was difficult to breathe in.

"I've . . ." D'Ablo began his thought, but then closed his mouth again, fearing the repercussions his words might bring.

He looked at the man—the familiar face, features he knew all too well—and held his hands up in a pleading gesture. Or more exactly, his *only* hand . . . and the stump that had been left behind after Vlad had taken that hand with the Lucis.

But his pleading would not be enough to stop what was coming.

Suddenly, the Shadow Man leaped across the room, knocking D'Ablo onto the floor. With his fangs bared, the Shadow Man thrust his hand forward. The tips of his fingers pierced D'Ablo's flesh. D'Ablo howled and thrashed in torment, gnashing his teeth, struggling to get free. The man pushed hard, forcing his hand deeper inside D'Ablo's chest. With a bitter purse of his lips, he whispered into D'Ablo's ear, "I have put this off for far too long. You have served your purpose."

He gripped D'Ablo's still beating heart and pulled, freeing the organ from his chest. Standing, the man squeezed until what he had held was no more than a mushy pulp. The light left D'Ablo's eyes.

He was dead.

The door opened and a second man entered. The man in shadows stood and shook D'Ablo's blood from his hand. "Remove the head and burn the body. I want to make sure he stays dead."

1
An Unexpected Reunion

D AD?"
The word trembled, perhaps even more than Vlad's lips were trembling as he spoke it aloud. He searched the man's eyes, scrutinized his laugh lines, dared to seek out some flaw that would show him that the man standing in front of him was anyone but his father.

But there was no flaw to be found. It was Tomas. Or maybe his twin. Not that he had had a twin. Even if he did, the odds of him and his twin brother both becoming vampires were astronomical. And the man standing before him was definitely a vampire. Vlad could smell it on him.

It smelled like blood. And wisdom. And youth. All rolled together.

There was nothing else like it in the world.

Vlad's vision blurred with tears, his heart filling with

impossible doubt. This couldn't be his father. His father was dead. He knew. He'd seen the charred corpse, smelled death in the room. Tomas Tod was dead.

And standing right in front of him.

Doubtfully, almost angrily, he croaked, "Dad?"

Tomas nodded, his mouth shrugging, sorrow and pain and loss lurking in his eyes. When he spoke, it removed only a portion of Vlad's doubt. "Yes, son."

Vlad turned at the shuffling noise behind him. Joss, bleeding, broken, was scrambling for the stake, struggling to stand.

For a moment, Vlad had all but forgotten him, had all but forgotten that he was about to kill Joss. His friend. His betrayer.

Joss stumbled, collapsing on the ground. Vlad flicked his eyes between Joss and his father, but remained motionless, in complete, captured awe of the man before him.

"Are you . . ." Vlad gulped, the taste of Dorian's blood still on his tongue, the memory of Dorian's madness still racing through his thoughts. Dorian had been brilliant, but insane. Had Vlad inherited some of that insanity by drinking his blood? Had his worst fears been realized? He'd known that doing as Dorian had asked and drinking from him would be a terrible risk, but he'd done it anyway. Otis had drank from Dorian's son, Adrian, and now had telekinetic powers, so it's not like the warning of bizarre consequences hadn't been there in front of him the entire time. And yet, he went through with it. Just before Dorian died, Vlad had drank his blood.

And maybe now he was crazy. Maybe now there was no going back at all.

He took a deep breath and forced the words from his lips, already knowing that the answer to his question was no. It had to be. Because he *was* like Dorian now. He was crazy. Completely, utterly insane. Not to mention hallucinating. "Are you real?"

The vision of his father merely smiled. Tomas stood in silence—a memory, something looming over Vlad's every thought, every nightmare, every action. His father. His dead father.

Here. Now.

Vlad closed his eyes briefly, haunted by the memory of the fire that took his parents, wondering if it was to be his punishment to see visions of his father now. Growing more and more certain that feeding from Dorian had poisoned his mind, Vlad sighed and opened his eyes again.

The man that looked like his father, his crazy vision, whatever it was . . . was gone.

Only he and Joss and Dorian's corpse remained in the clearing.

Vlad spun around, searching the surrounding area, but saw no one. Not even so much as a broken twig, indicating movement. His heart sank. Crazy or not, it had been nice to see his father's smiling face again.

Then there was a noise. Vlad whipped around to see Henry racing into the clearing, his face ghostly pale. "Vlad!

Are you okay? I had this horrible feeling. Like . . . like you needed me."

And Vlad did need him. He'd just beaten Joss within an inch of his life, and had just witnessed the impossible. He may have just made the biggest mistake ever—drinking from a madman—and right now, the only person in the world he felt he could count on was his drudge. His best friend. "Henry . . . everything is so messed up."

Henry's eyes went wide as they dropped to Vlad's mouth. "Dude, is that blood? Who have you been feeding on?"

Vlad's eyes moved to Dorian's corpse. Henry's followed. He shook his head. "You fed on the creepy vampire stalker guy? No offense, Vlad, but I imagine there are tastier options out there."

"I had to. He . . . he told me I had to. And Joss . . . oh man, Joss!" Vlad took a deep breath before rushing to where the Slayer lay, the memory of his father still burning on the edge of his thoughts. But he couldn't tell Henry. Not yet. It was too fresh, like an exposed wound.

Joss was lying on his back, his forehead smooth, his eyes closed, his chest rising and falling in shallow, pained breaths. Breaths that rapidly slowed until it seemed there were no breaths at all. Vlad knelt beside him, trepidation taking hold of every cell in his body. "Joss?"

But Joss couldn't answer. He was unconscious. Or worse. Had Vlad killed him? It was possible. Hell, with Vlad's vampire strength, not to mention his unleashed fury, it was likely.

Henry swore under his breath and knelt beside his cousin,

his heartbeat racing. Vlad listened to the steady thumps pounding in his ears, drowning out any sign that Joss was still alive. "What happened, Vlad? What happened between you two? What did you do?"

Vlad put two shaking, terrified fingers to Joss's neck and sighed in relief at the steady beating of a pulse.

He hadn't killed Joss. And felt strangely both relieved and disappointed by that fact.

Henry went into action. Without meeting Vlad's eyes, he pulled Joss's cell phone from his pocket and said, "We have to get him to the hospital. I'm calling an ambulance. You head back to Nelly's. I'll meet you there."

"No, Henry." Vlad shook his head slowly. "I'm staying here with him until the ambulance comes. It's the least I can do."

Henry set his jaw. "The least you can do is get out of here so we don't have too many questions from the cops. I got this, Vlad. Let me handle it."

"No." Vlad's tone became darker and gravelly, full of determination. He couldn't leave Joss. Not now. Not after almost killing him. "I need to stay."

Henry sighed heavily. "Fine. But once the ambulance takes him away, you're going to tell me everything that happened here tonight."

Time flew in a series of moments and emotions, but Vlad didn't feel present in it. He was there, but not really there at all. He was the cause of this. Just as Joss had been the cause of Vlad's near death just a few short years before.

He waited by Joss's side, whispering apologies. Apologies

that he wouldn't have meant only moments ago. Apologies that he never would have dreamed he would utter to the boy who had betrayed him in so many ways.

He was sorry. Even if Joss had deserved every blow. He was sorry.

Henry was at his side, quiet and aloof.

Then, before the cops came, Vlad and Henry retreated into the woods, hiding, so that no one could see them. It seemed like only moments—mere breaths—before they saw the lights flashing as the ambulance approached. Lights so similar to those that he'd seen in his feverish memories after Joss had stabbed that damn stake of his through Vlad's back, through his heart. Lights that had convinced him he was dying. He wondered if Joss was convinced of that now, or if the pain had dragged him under already.

Vlad's eyes locked on Dorian's corpse. The EMTs approached Joss, and Vlad knew they'd see Dorian. He knew there would be questions. Then, as if Dorian wasn't even there, the two men stepped over his corpse and headed straight for Joss.

Once the lights from the ambulance had faded into the distance, Vlad turned away, leaving the scene of his crime behind. Leaving the man who looked like his father behind. Leaving his anger toward Joss behind. Leaving everything, perhaps even a bit of himself, behind for good. Nothing mattered now. Only his friend, the boy he put into the hands of doctors and nurses. Only Joss mattered.

Because Joss was his friend. Because after everything

they'd been through, he knew that fact more than anything. If Joss had mistakenly killed Dorian when trying to kill him, there had to be a reason for it.

Because they were friends.

And all that mattered right now was making sure Joss was okay. Nothing else. Not even Vlad's dad. If it was his dad. It might have been a ghost, or something weird cooked up by Vlad's imagination. It was something, for sure.

Something. Something not real.

Something Dorian's blood had put inside his brain.

2
BITTER TASTES

A WARM SUMMER BREEZE brushed Vlad's black bangs from his eyes as he and Henry made their way back to Nelly's house. As soon as the ambulance had pulled away, Henry had demanded answers from Vlad, and, after covering Dorian's body with some fallen, leaf-covered branches, Vlad had given them.

Even though they were hard to say. Even though the truth of it all wasn't very pretty.

Vlad had been walking away, away from everything. He was going to clean out his parents' room and then leave Bathory behind forever. He was going to run from Elysia's brand of justice like a coward. But something had stopped him, and that something was Joss. Or, more accurately, Joss's stake.

He had no idea what had made Joss attack him. In fact,

he'd thought they'd come to a sort of understanding in their unusual friendship. But Joss had attacked, and if it hadn't been for Dorian stepping in the way, Joss would have killed Vlad.

Then Dorian had told Vlad to do the impossible: drink from him. He'd said it was the only way for Vlad to know the prophecy of the Pravus. So, moments before Dorian's death, he drank. And then he'd turned his fury on Joss, but was stopped.

And now . . . now everything was messed up and nothing would ever be the same again.

"What made you stop?"

Vlad blinked, slowing his steps some. "What do you mean?"

Henry was still right beside him, keeping his pace, his eyes occasionally finding Vlad in the darkness. "What made you stop beating Joss? What made you not kill him?"

Vlad chewed his bottom lip for a moment, mulling over Henry's possible reaction to the news that Tomas Tod was alive and well. At least in Vlad's fevered imagination, anyway. "If I told you, you'd think I was nuts."

"I already think that, so come on. Out with it, Vlad." It was the same tone he'd used to get Vlad to do . . . well, anything, ever since day one of their friendship. Vlad knew he couldn't resist. He also knew he needed to confide in someone before he lost it completely.

"A voice stopped me."

"Ominous, creepy, and weird rolled into one, dude." Henry

slowed his steps and stopped Vlad by grabbing his sleeve, tugging him to a stop. "Whose voice was it? The tooth fairy? Principal Snelgrove? Was it the voice of Glob? These details make a difference, man."

Vlad swallowed hard, and then forced the words from his lips, his eyes on Henry the entire time. "It was my dad, Henry. I saw him. He was standing right there in the clearing. And then he was gone. Just . . . gone."

Henry's eyes had gone wide, but he nodded. "Okay. So. You saw your dad."

Vlad shrugged and wished very much that he could sink into the ground and disappear.

Henry gulped. "Alive?"

Vlad readied a glare to show Henry exactly how stupid that question was, but he stopped himself. After all, it wasn't stupid. But Vlad didn't know how to answer exactly, because his dad may or may not be alive. He wasn't sure.

Henry was doing his best to be supportive, even if he was looking at Vlad as if he'd lost his mind completely. He slapped Vlad on the shoulder and said, "Run that whole story by me again, would ya? I just wanna make sure I'm hearing it right."

In the few minutes they had left before they reached Nelly's house, Vlad went over every detail again, this time explaining more about why he drank from Dorian, and every bit of detail that he could remember about seeing his dad. By the time they stepped onto Nelly's porch, Henry looked frazzled. "Whoa. That is messed up."

Vlad nodded as he opened the door. It *was* messed up.

And the worst part was that Vlad had no idea if the person standing just inside the door was really there, or just a nightmare coaxed into his reality by Dorian's tainted blood.

"Vladimir Tod. It's so good to see you again." Em smiled and held up a cookie that she'd clearly helped herself to in the kitchen. "Would you like a cookie?"

Vlad glanced at Henry and then looked back to Em, shaking his head in shock. She was early. Way early. Vlad wasn't ready for his trial yet. Not by a long shot.

Her presence filled him with disgust, but it was countered by his utter relief that Nelly was working double shifts at the hospital all week. She, fortunately, would miss out on the pleasure of Em's company.

Em was dressed in a black corset and black baggy Tripp pants, with purple stitching. On her feet were Converse, not unlike the ones Vlad was wearing. She smiled a superior smile and perched on the arm of the couch, breaking the cookie in half. She held out the other half to Vlad, who shook his head in refusal. Frowning, almost pouting, she forced the cookie into his hand.

Vlad grimaced at her touch, but after a near-glare from Em, took a bite. The chocolate chips tasted bitter.

Em finished her half of the cookie and licked her fingertips clean. "I suppose you're wondering why I'm here."

Beside her stood Enrico, who looked ashamed to be her escort. Vlad nodded to him, ignoring Em for the moment. "Enrico, it's good to see you again."

Enrico—the owner of V Bar and Dorian's father—moved

forward, shaking Vlad's hand and smiling warmly, though something dark lurked in his eyes. "A pleasure, as always, Vladimir."

Vlad didn't have the heart to inform Enrico of Dorian's passing. Not yet, anyway.

The steps creaked as Otis made his way downstairs. He was shirtless, his hair still dripping from a recent shower, a white, damp towel draped around his neck. "I thought I heard voices down here. Enrico? To what do I owe the honor of your company?"

As Otis's eyes found Em, his shoulders slumped some, his demeanor darkened.

Vlad wondered if anyone was ever happy to see her.

Enrico glanced at Em, who nodded. Then he looked back to Otis. "I'm afraid there's been a tragedy. It seems a member of Elysia, an important vampire figure, has been assassinated."

No one spoke.

Vlad's heart thumped twice, hard, then returned to its quiet race. Dorian. They knew about Dorian after all.

The air thickened. But still, no one spoke.

Finally, as if unable to handle the silence, it was Henry who broke it. "Some of us don't have telepathy, y'know. Who died?"

Em glared at him, as if seeing him for the first time and hating him on sight. Vlad winced. Henry didn't even blink. Vlad was beginning to think that nothing could scare a Mc-Millan.

Through clenched teeth, Em spoke, but not to Henry. She

would only speak to the vampires in the room. "It would seem that D'Ablo has been murdered."

Vlad whipped his eyes back to Em in shock. D'Ablo? Dead? The vampire who had been a thorn in Vlad's side for four years, the vampire who Vlad was certain would never cease trying to kill him, the vampire who Vlad counted on to be the big bad evil in his life . . . was *dead*? By someone else's hand? It wasn't possible. It couldn't have happened. There was no way D'Ablo could be dead. The guy had survived having a giant hole shot through him with the Lucis, for crying out loud.

Vlad looked at Enrico. "You're . . . sure?"

Enrico nodded. "Two piles of ash were found. When we tested them for DNA, both matched D'Ablo, which meant that his head had likely been removed before burning."

"It could be a trick." Henry's voice sounded so foreign in a room filled with vampires. But he was right.

"It's no trick, *human*." Em's tone was biting. Which was probably what she was about to do to Henry if he didn't shut up. "We're well versed in how many ounces of ashes a burned vampire leaves behind. D'Ablo is dead. Do not doubt that for a second."

Vlad felt oddly hollow. It was almost as if a friend had been stolen from him before he'd had the chance to say good-bye.

A horrible, evil, maniacal friend who wanted nothing more than to see Vlad suffer.

Otis stood at the foot of the stairs, his expression blank.

Em stood and Vlad had to fight the immediate urge to step back. Folding her arms in front of her, she said, "Needless to say, your trial's been compromised, as a portion of the charges against you have been dropped due to D'Ablo's convenient passing."

"Convenient?" Henry snorted, drawing Em's hate-filled eyes. "What are you saying? That Vlad killed D'Ablo? Fat chance. He hasn't been very successful at that in the past."

Vlad was about to warn Henry that if he valued his life at all, he'd zip his lips. But it was too late. Em shot across the room until she was almost nose to nose with Vlad's drudge. She scraped a long, purple fingernail down his cheek, drawing blood, but Henry didn't wince. Vlad thought he might have gone into shock. Either that, or despite everything Vlad had told his best friend about Em, Henry hadn't quite put two and two together, that the ancient, evil being known as Em was also the cute girl standing in front of him, her eyes like daggers. Poor Henry. Poor stupid, stupid Henry.

Her voice was almost a purr. "Human, you have no idea the pain that I can bring you. I suggest you keep your thoughts to yourself, lest I give in to the overwhelming urge to skin you alive."

Vlad glanced at his uncle, who was watching the scene with some interest, but still not speaking. Then he turned back to Em. "So what are you implying, exactly? That I killed D'Ablo? Or that I had someone kill him?"

Otis spoke, his voice quiet, somber. "Neither is true."

Em stepped back and turned on her heel to face Otis.

After silently gauging him for a moment, she flicked her eyes back to Vlad. Before she could speak, Henry whispered, "Dude, the evil chick is kinda hot."

Vlad rolled his eyes, but stopped once Em had returned her attention to him. She didn't even glance at Henry again. "One charge still remains against you, little one. The charge that your father entered into a romantic relationship with a human."

Henry shot Vlad a telling glance, but Vlad was already on the case. "I'm only standing trial for that because my dad is dead, right?"

She nodded once, suspicion and doubt lurking in her eyes.

Vlad took a deep breath. "What would you say if I told you that I saw my dad tonight, alive and well?"

Otis spoke, but inside Vlad's head, away from the prying ears of the company they kept. *This is not a game, Vladimir. You cannot fool Em in order to gain more time.*

I know. I'm not trying to fool anyone, Otis. I really saw him.

Otis fell silent for a moment, then nodded to his nephew and stepped back, looking deeply disturbed. *We will discuss this at length once Em is gone, yes?*

Of course.

Em seemed to mull this over for a moment before replying. "Are you willing to testify to that fact, little one?"

Vlad set his jaw and nodded once.

"Then it seems a trial is coming, after all. A trial for Tomas, if you can produce him by the final day of December. We'll hold it right here in the quaint little town of Bathory. However, if you cannot produce your father, alive and well, then you will stand trial for his crimes. And you will die for them. Slowly. And as painfully as possible. I'm sure I don't have to remind you that his romance with a human falls on your head if he has perished." She met Vlad's gaze, and though her voice sounded kind, there was no kindness to be found in the depths of her eyes. "It is only because of my fondness for Tomas, and our history, that I am giving you or your father any time at all to say goodbye to the world. Consider it a kindness, and respect my decision by not running. If you run, if you attempt to hide, I will make it much worse for you . . . and for your father, if he really is alive."

Otis's voice was low and wondering. "And what of D'Ablo's murder? Have you any leads?"

She turned to face him, and something unspoken passed between them. Vlad didn't know what it was, but it was unsettling, to say the least.

Vlad said, "What history? How did you and my dad know one another?"

Em clucked her tongue. "Tomas and I were well acquainted. You see, I am his grandmother. Mother to Ignatius."

She paused a moment, waiting for her words to sink in. When they didn't, she said, "I'm your great-grandmother, Vladimir."

Vlad's chest felt oddly hollow. Like someone had dug an enormous hole through his rib cage without him being aware.

Great-grandmother. The girlish monster whose eyes

reflected a hunger to witness his demise was his great-grandmother?

No.

She couldn't be.

He shook his head, refusing to believe Em, and trailed his eyes from her to his uncle, who looked both nauseated and disturbed. "My great-grandmother?"

After a moment of silence, perhaps to gather his words carefully, Otis said, "It's true. Em is my grandmother, your father's grandmother, and Ignatius's mother."

Then Otis stepped closer. "And it's absolutely no reflection on you, Vladimir. We can't choose our parentage. Or our grandparentage."

Em smiled, but it never quite reached her eyes. She stood, brushing the cookie crumbs from her clothes. "We can, however, choose our children. Though sometimes we choose poorly."

Her eyes fell on Vlad then, burning with hatred that she couldn't hide. "Our great-grandchildren, on the other hand . . . well . . . I suppose sometimes our children and their children choose poorly as well."

An awkward silence fell over the not-so-happy family then. No one spoke or moved until Em turned toward the door. As she stepped outside, she said, "You have until December thirty-first to collect your father and deliver him to the Council of Elders. And so help me if you are lying about his still living, which I suspect you are. But know that you've only prolonged your life by a few short months, as death is the only punishment for the charges that remain against you."

Vlad released the breath his lungs had been clinging to for what seemed like an eternity.

He'd just saved his own life. At least for a little while.

The problem was that now he had to do the impossible.

He had to find his father.

3

UNDER SUSPICION

THE EMERGENCY ROOM WAS CROWDED and loud and, though he waited for what seemed like forever, no one stopped moving to give him some answers, to tell Vlad whether his friend was going to live or die.

Henry had driven them as fast as he could once Em had left Nelly's house, but only after they'd stopped back at the clearing, to look for Joss's backpack—or more importantly, Vlad's father's journal. The book meant something to Vlad, and now with the possible miraculous return of his father to life, he wondered if the journal would offer him answers that he hadn't seen in its pages before, or if the journal might lead him to his dad. But all they found was a patch of grass, stained with Dorian's blood, nothing more. Confusion enveloped Vlad—where was Dorian? But as hope that Dorian had somehow survived began to fill him, Vlad recalled Dorian's last moments and knew that he was dead. Where his body went was another question. Vlad tried not to look at the spot where Dorian had perished, tried hard not to think about his final moments. Then he cursed himself for not thinking to grab the journal earlier. But it would be at the hospital, with Joss. It had to be.

Otis had insisted that he had some important business to take care of first, but that he'd grab Nelly and meet them in the emergency room.

Finally, after way too long, a man in a white lab coat approached, his muscles tense, his mouth pursed. He knew. Somehow he knew that Vlad was responsible. "You came to see the boy who was beaten?"

Vlad nodded, swallowing his guilt like a bitter pill. "Joss McMillan."

The man in the white coat—Vlad couldn't get a good look at the name on his badge—flipped through some papers on the chart he was holding and made a note in handwriting that reminded Vlad of Otis's chicken scratchings. Then he met Vlad's gaze, his eyes hooded, his expression guarded. "He's awake now, but just barely. The pain medication we administered is keeping him fairly groggy. Can you tell me what happened?"

"I . . ." Immense and immediate guilt seeped into Vlad's muscles, into his bones, into every organ—mostly his heart. Following it was the realization that revealing anything to anyone at this point would likely land him in a lot of trouble, maybe even jail. It was this thought that had just entered his mind when he laid eyes on two uniformed police officers who were crossing the room, their eyes fixed on him. Vlad's next words came out muttered, distant, lost. "No. I can't."

Henry stepped forward. "Look, Joss is my cousin and Vlad's friend. We just want to know if he's okay."

The taller cop, the grumpy-looking one, said, "Vladimir Tod?"

Vlad looked from one cop to the other as if he didn't know that they were here to arrest him for putting Joss in the hospital. Vlad would've bet his life on that.

His life. That thing that Joss had tried to take twice now.

But no one would focus on that. Mostly because Vlad couldn't tell them without revealing the fact that he was a vampire.

Well, half vampire, if they wanted to get technical.

The shorter cop, the one with a friendly smile, said, "We'd like to have a word with you, please."

Vlad gulped, the lump in his throat the size of a grapefruit, and managed a nod. They coaxed him away from Henry, who was looking more than a little tense.

The friendly cop didn't miss a beat. "How well do you know Joss McMillan?"

"Pretty well. We're friends." Vlad shrugged, his heart breaking over what he'd done to Joss. For the life of him, he'd never seen it coming. Not after they'd patched things up, not after their long, nightly sessions where they'd mock-fight. Tonight it had been self-defense. But admittedly, it was also a bit of vengeance on Vlad's part—something that now sat in the pit of his stomach, fermenting. "Or, were, I guess."

Friendly cop smiled warmly. Vlad was glad he was the one doing the talking. Grumpy cop just looked ... well ... grumpy. "Not so friendly anymore, eh?"

"We had a fight."

"About a girl?"

"No. Just ... I'm not sure what it was about. Joss has been acting really different lately." Vlad's thoughts whirled inside his brain like a tornado. Why would they think a girl was involved? Did they know about Meredith? Is that why they thought Vlad beat Joss so badly? He raked his bangs back from his eyes with a trembling hand. "Look, am I in trouble?"

Friendly cop leaned in closer, lowering his voice as though they shared a deep, dark secret. "Has Joss ever mentioned his uncle to you? Abraham McMillan? Said anything at all about him?"

Vlad blinked. What did this have to do with him putting Joss in the hospital? "No. Not that I can remember. Why?"

The two officers exchanged looks and Friendly gave Vlad's shoulder a light squeeze. "That's all we needed to know, Vlad. Thanks for your cooperation. We hope your friend recovers quickly. An accident, was it, that put him here?"

Vlad looked him dead in the eye, and before he could stop himself, complete honesty spilled out over his tongue. "No, sir."

Friendly paused then, his eyebrows furrowing, understanding lighting up his eyes.

This was it. This was the part where the cop slapped cuffs on him and dragged him off to prison. Vlad knew it. He could feel it. The cop understood he was admitting to committing a violent crime and was seconds away from reaching for his handcuffs.

Friendly frowned, then gave Vlad's shoulder another squeeze. "Even so."

As the officers walked away, Vlad stared after them, stunned and not at all certain why he hadn't been arrested.

Vlad saw Nelly rushing down the corridor, looking both frightened and concerned. Otis was at her side. Nelly said, "Are you okay? What happened between you boys? Is Joss okay?"

Vlad lowered his voice, and even though the words he chose were the right ones, he couldn't help but feel terrible about uttering them. Terrible, because while they were true, they didn't change the fact that he'd come too close to killing the one person on the planet he really counted as a friend on the same level as Henry. Even after what Joss had done. "Joss tried to stake me. I had to defend myself."

Otis's eyes narrowed as if to say *I told you so.* At the same time, Nelly's widened.

The door to Joss's room opened and his mother stepped outside, followed by his father. Vlad hadn't even seen them go in. But then, he'd been a little distracted by that whole possible arrest thing. "Mrs. McMillan, are you okay? Is Joss?"

Joss's mom sniffled into a wrecked tissue and glared at Vlad. "Don't talk to me. And stay away from my son."

Vlad searched his mind, but couldn't think of anything that was appropriate to say. So instead, he did as instructed and closed his mouth.

Joss's dad looked at Otis, an almost apologetic gleam in his eye—one that Vlad couldn't understand. Vlad couldn't help but notice that Joss's dad didn't look at him even once. "He'll be okay. It's just that we've been dealing with Joss in and out of hospitals and in and out of fights for a few years now. It's . . . it's a lot to take."

Nelly parted her lips to say something, but Otis shot her a look that begged her not to. Otis followed the McMillans into the family waiting room, where Matilda and Big Mike were now waiting with Henry. Vlad thought he should say something to them, but wasn't sure what to say. He thought of pulling Henry to the side to explain what had happened between him and the cops, but that would mean walking by Joss's parents again—something he was certain would be a really bad idea.

After several minutes, Otis returned and said, "They're taking Joss to a special medical facility to recover, but won't say where. His parents, especially his mother, blame you, Vlad. Joss told them you got in a fight and he lost, but he didn't mention what really happened, that you're a vampire and he's a Slayer. At least we can be thankful for that."

Vlad met his uncle's eyes and spoke with his thoughts. *"Otis. There's something I forgot to tell you earlier. Dorian is dead."*

Otis looked troubled, but strangely relieved, as if he were

free now. *"I know. I smelled his blood and hurried to investigate. I've hidden the body a bit better. Later, Vikas and I will dispose of it. What happened exactly?"*

"He saved me from Joss. He took the stake for me. And then he told me to . . ." Vlad's thoughts trailed off. He wasn't sure exactly how much of what happened he should reveal to his uncle. For now, it was probably better not to mention that he'd also drank from Dorian, but rather to formulate a plan for what to do next. First thing first: he had to determine if Dorian's blood had actually made him crazy, and that meant confronting the specter of his father before telling Otis about any of it. If he could find his dad, he wouldn't have to tell Otis about drinking from Dorian.

Because it's not like he hadn't known that Dorian's blood had been tainted in some way. After all, Uncle Otis developed the bizarre ability to close doors with a single thought, just by drinking from Dorian's son. And Dorian always seemed to know what was about to happen . . . right up until the very end. Otis had seemed afraid of Dorian, which had made Vlad afraid of him. If Vlad admitted to Otis what he'd done, he was in for the lecture of his life. The last thing he needed was more supervision.

Otis raised a sharp eyebrow. *"To what?"*

Vlad shook his head, ignoring the fact that Nelly looked increasingly uncomfortable during their silent conversation. *"Nothing. You took care of the body?"*

"I did for now. It's fortunate the EMTs didn't see it. But I imagine that was a bit of subconscious control on your part."

Otis held his gaze, raising an eyebrow. *"You're sure there's nothing else you want to tell me?"*

Vlad furrowed his brow a bit at Otis's casual mention of subconscious control—whatever that was—and made a mental note to ask his uncle about it later. Then he chewed his bottom lip for a moment, reconsidering his decision not to tell Otis about drinking Dorian's blood. After all, keeping secrets from Otis had never helped him in the past. Still, this felt important. This, he needed to figure out on his own. *"Not at the moment."*

Nelly patted Vlad's arm. "I don't mean to interrupt your telepathic conversation, but let's get you home."

Vlad nodded slowly, very much wishing he could see Joss at least once before he left. He also wanted a peek inside Joss's backpack, to grab the journal before it fell into the wrong—meaning Slayer Society—hands. But it didn't look like that was going to happen. Not tonight, anyway. Tonight Vlad had to let Joss's parents fret over him, and trust that he and Joss were still friends, despite what Joss had tried to do to him. The way that he'd trusted him during their late-night mock-fights. The way he felt driven to trust Joss, even now, despite what he had done.

Nelly hugged him tightly, her caring words a whisper in his ear. "You look shaken. Don't worry, Joss will live. I'd bet my nursing degree on it."

Vlad shook his head and whispered back. "It's not that."

That sweet, mothering concern entered her gaze. "What is it?"

"I saw . . ." Vlad caught himself, shook his head. He couldn't tell Nelly about his dad. She couldn't know what he thought he saw until he'd confronted the crazy demons himself and proved to himself that his father wasn't really alive, and that he really was just as nuts as Dorian had been. "Never mind. I must have imagined it. I could use some fresh air, actually. I'll meet you guys outside when you're ready to go."

As he passed by the door of the family waiting room, Vlad glanced inside. Grumpy cop took notice, nodding toward him and nudging Friendly cop. Apparently, he was still on their radar, but there wasn't much he could do about that.

He stepped out a side door and into the night, to the alley where a coolness greeted him that promised that while summer was here officially, spring had not yet loosened its grip entirely. At the end of the alley were two cops, dressed in uniform, standing by a Toyota Prius. Vlad figured they were discussing giving the absent owner a ticket. That is, until one cop opened the door and dropped a pile of paperwork on the front seat.

Weird. Very weird that two uniformed police officers would be driving a Prius and not an official police cruiser.

Vlad slowed his steps to a quiet halt. He was considering going back inside, but couldn't put his finger on exactly why the scene seemed so wrong to him. It was just an unsettled feeling in the pit of his stomach—probably brought on by the sight of more cops, when he'd just been questioned by two.

Guilt. Plain and simple.

One of the cops turned toward Vlad. He had a thin scar

running from the corner of his left eye to the corner of his mouth. When he saw Vlad, he nudged his friend and both turned toward him. "Excuse me, son, but are you Vladimir Tod? We have a few questions to ask you."

Vlad frowned and shrugged. "Talk to your friends inside. They already asked me questions."

The cops exchanged glances and moved down the alley toward Vlad.

Vlad cursed himself for not keeping his mouth shut and waited.

The scarred cop smiled as they approached. "You have a mouth on you, son. Better watch that. It'll get you in trouble some day."

The other cop, the slightly bald one, grunted.

Vlad sighed. "You have questions for me?"

"Just one. I'm just curious." Scar looked Vlad in the eye and held his gaze. "Why didn't you finish him off? I mean, your buddies wouldn't have stopped until they got the job done. So why did you let Joss live?"

Vlad's heart picked up its pace in confusion. He furrowed his brow and shook his head slightly. "What are you talking about?"

Baldy reached for his nightstick, and Vlad's eyes shot to its tip as it left its holster.

Its sharp, silver tip.

It wasn't a nightstick. It was a stake. The cops standing in front of him were Slayers.

Vlad held up his hands and stepped back slowly. "Listen, guys, we don't want to do this."

His back met with something fleshy behind him. Friendly cop—who wasn't looking so friendly anymore. "We do. We really do."

Grumpy cop was standing beside Friendly, still looking peeved. Now Vlad knew exactly why.

They were here to finish the job that Joss had started. That was why Vlad wasn't going to jail. Because they'd been waiting until this moment to put him somewhere far worse.

In his grave.

Vlad watched Friendly from the corner of his eye, his heart racing when Friendly's hand dropped to his night stake. With a deep breath and a set jaw, Vlad realized what he had to do. He had no way out of this situation but through it.

Before the Slayers could act, Vlad jammed his elbow back into Friendly's ribs. Friendly bent forward, making an *oof* sound, but Vlad didn't hesitate. He spun around with vampiric speed, whipping quickly around Friendly. He was thankful—thankful that he'd worked so hard with Vikas to train himself in how to move, how to defend himself if necessary. All of those hours in the old barn had been worth it. He knew what he was doing, despite his utter surprise that he knew what he was doing.

As he moved, he snatched the stake from Friendly's hand. He stopped behind the Slayer and shot his arm forward, the Slayer's back cracking audibly as bones snapped, and Vlad sent him flying. Moments later, Friendly hit the pavement behind Scar and Baldy, moaning, but unmoving.

Grumpy growled and swung his stake at Vlad, but Vlad ducked back, then grabbed him by the arm and whipped him to the side, where Grumpy bounced off the wall of the adjacent building and landed in an unconscious heap. As he turned back to the remaining Slayers, Vlad swore he heard one comment on his eyes, which meant they'd probably turned iridescent purple again.

He wasn't exactly surprised.

Vlad raised a sharp eyebrow at Scar, and quipped, "Still sure you wanna do this?"

By the look in his eye, Vlad was certain that not only did Scar want to engage him, he wanted to kill him. Vlad shook his head, sighing. "All right then, cupcake. You better bring it."

Insult crossed Scar's eyes and he stepped forward. As he did so, Vlad jumped up, planting his foot on the Slayer's thigh. He flipped his body backward, and as he turned completely over in the air, he brought his foot up hard, kicking Scar in the jaw. The crack of breaking bone silenced all noises around them. Vlad flipped over, then focused on his body, willing it upward, until he came to land on the side of the building—feet flat against the wall, body parallel to the ground—perfectly perched on the bricks there, held in place by his newfound mastery of his hovering abilities.

It. Was. COOL.

Even Vlad didn't really believe he was capable of all of these moves, even if Vikas had worked with him all during his junior year to get him used to the powers he now possessed.

He only wished Henry had been there to see all the Slayer butt he was kicking.

Then Vlad saw something that stole the smile from his face.

Baldy had withdrawn his stake from its holster. He whipped it up at Vlad and Vlad bent back, but almost too late. The silver tip tore through the fabric of his shirt—right over his heart. His skin was scratched and stung like crazy, but Vlad couldn't focus on that. He was too angry, too furious that these Slayers didn't know when to quit.

Just like Joss.

Maybe all Slayers were alike.

He jumped from the building's side and came down hard, pulling Scar's and Baldy's heads down with him, cracking them against the pavement. In one fell swoop, he'd knocked them unconscious and walked away, as if nothing had happened.

Three steps out of the alley, Vlad stopped and looked back at the wounded Slayers.

What was he becoming? What on earth was he becoming?

4
A Taste of Insanity

VLAD SANK DOWN IN THE BACKSEAT of Otis's car. His thoughts were clouded with the knowledge that he'd just kept two secrets from his uncle in a single day. He hadn't mentioned the Slayers, he hadn't told him about drinking from Dorian, and he wasn't exactly certain why he'd kept those details from Otis.

Otis pulled into Nelly's driveway and had just barely come to a stop before Vlad was out the door and inside the house, up the stairs, and pacing back and forth across his bedroom. Vlad was stressed, but more than that he was afraid. Afraid of what he was becoming, afraid of the immense powers that he now possessed.

On one hand, he didn't want these powers, didn't want anything at all to do with freaky Pravus powers. But on the other . . . it was really cool knowing that he was capable of almost superhero moves. Still, it scared him to think that he might lose himself in the moment, that he was truly capable of causing someone real harm. It was enough to make his head spin.

Enough to make him crazy.

He waited for a good hour, pacing back and forth as quietly as he was able, until the house had gone quiet and Vlad was certain that Nelly was in bed and sleeping. Then he put his plan into action.

He was going back to the clearing to find his dad.

It wasn't much of a plan, not really, but it was all that Vlad had, so he went with it. He cracked open his bedroom door, his ears perked for any sound, any sign that his guardian would catch him sneaking out, but the only noise he heard was Amenti mewing softly downstairs—probably at a mouse, or, more likely, out of boredom. He crept out of his bedroom and cringed the moment the floor of the library squeaked beneath his feet.

But Nelly didn't respond.

Vlad breathed a very soft sigh of relief and moved forward, promising himself that he'd be more careful. To his disbelieving horror, his toe caught the corner of the rug and Vlad flew forward, crashing into the small Tiffany lamp on the table, sending it flying. In slow motion, the lamp toppled forward. Vlad stretched out his arm to catch it, but he was still falling. It became a race to what would hit the ground first—him or the lamp.

Time picked up its pace just as each of them were mere

inches from the floor. The lamp shattered and Vlad landed with a string of curse words. Pieces of colorful glass flew everywhere, and Vlad scrambled to his feet, hastily snatching up the base of the lamp. He set it clumsily back onto the table, cursing and grumbling.

Now he'd never be able to sneak out and see if the image of Tomas he saw was flesh and blood. Because even a deaf person in a coma would have heard the commotion he just caused.

He looked at Nelly's door and readied himself for her questions as to what on earth he was doing up so late smashing her favorite lamp.

But to his shock and wonder, Nelly didn't make a sound. Not so much as a peep.

Vlad raised worried eyebrows and headed to Nelly's bedroom door, his feet crunching on bits of broken lamp. Knocking lightly, Vlad listened for any sign of Nelly moving within. "Nelly? You okay?"

When there was no answer, Vlad opened the door a crack to check on his aunt. She was lying in bed, covers bunched all around her, sleeping peacefully, as if the sound of breaking glass and clumsy thumping hadn't just happened right outside her door.

Vlad furrowed his brow. He knew she was a heavy sleeper, but this was ridiculous.

"She'll be furious that you broke that lamp, Vladimir." Otis was behind him in the library, a small plate of warm chocolate chip cookies in hand.

He held it out to his nephew, but Vlad shook his head and turned his eyes back to his snoozing aunt. "Why doesn't Nelly ever hear me sneaking out? I mean, I'm pretty loud. But she never catches me."

Otis bit into a cookie and licked away the warm, gooey chocolate from his bottom lip. "It's a subconscious order, otherwise known as subconscious control."

Vlad stared at him, then blinked. One day, Otis was going to realize that Vlad still wasn't a hundred percent educated on all things vampire. Until then, he was going to have to deal with a lot of questioning glances from his nephew.

Otis popped the rest of the cookie into his mouth and chewed before he answered. "A subconscious order is control over a human that you don't even have to think about in order to execute. For instance, you've never wanted Nelly to wake up and find you sneaking out, so you told her sleeping mind to keep sleeping."

Vlad gawked at him. If Otis had made mention of that trick years ago, Vlad wouldn't have thought twice about sneaking out, wouldn't ever have hesitated. "Can all vampires do that?"

Otis shrugged. "Not all, but some."

"Why isn't it in the *Compendium*?"

"No book has all the answers, Vladimir. Not even a book as comprehensive as the *Compendium*."

Vlad sighed. If only the *Compendium* did have all the answers . . . and if only Vlad had any idea at all where it now was. It had disappeared from his possession at the end of his junior year and, despite his search efforts, it didn't seem to be resurfacing any time soon. Which sucked, because the *Compendium* knew more about Elysia than Vlad dared to dream. "That sucks."

Otis shrugged again and picked up another cookie.

After stealing one more protective glance at his sleeping aunt, Vlad closed Nelly's door and looked hopefully at his uncle. "Are you going to tell her I was sneaking out?"

Otis gauged him for a moment before speaking. "No. I assume you have your reasons."

"Thanks, Otis." Vlad turned, ready to head down the stairs, but Otis stopped him with a word.

"Vladimir."

When Vlad looked back at his uncle, he didn't need Otis to tell him why he'd called him back. Otis was waiting for an explanation. Otis wanted to know about the return of Vlad's father.

Vlad sighed, his shoulders slumping. "I saw him, Otis. I saw my dad. One minute Dorian was saving my life, and the next I was beating Joss to a pulp, ready to kill him, and then . . . then my dad told me to stop."

"And then?"

"Then he disappeared."

Otis took this all in for a long, silent moment, then nodded. Vlad couldn't read his expression, exactly, but he was fairly sure that Otis believed him. "I trust you're off to find him then?"

"Yes. Alone for now. If I don't find him on my own, though, I'll need your help."

"You are going to sweep this mess up first, yes?"

Vlad cringed. "I was planning on blaming Amenti for the mess."

Otis flashed him a look that screamed *get the broom*, before he chuckled and looked around the room. "Where is that cat, anyway?"

Vlad shrugged. "Probably chasing mice. Really fat, really slow mice."

After sweeping up the shattered remains of what once was Nelly's favorite lamp, Vlad headed out the front door.

He hurried across town, to the place where Joss had attacked him. The memories of what had transpired flooded through his mind, through his very soul, until Vlad's heart felt heavy and hollow.

Joss had tried to take his life. Again.

Dorian—crazy, strange, knowing Dorian—was dead. By Joss's hand.

And one other thing was decidedly missing from the area.

His dad.

Which meant Vlad probably was crazy, after all.

Vlad's shoulders slumped and he turned back toward town, determined to search every inch that was accessible even into the nighttime, until he either found his dad or accepted the insanity that he was now plagued with. As stupid as it was, he'd really, really been hoping against hope that he wasn't crazy, that maybe—just maybe—the vision of his father had been real, and that he'd been miraculously given a second chance.

He walked along the outskirts of Bathory until he came to Long Road Cemetery. Stepping under the gate, his eyes swept over the shadowy stones and unkempt lawn in a search for the impossible, in search of his dad. But he found no one. Just tombstones, trees, rocks, and grass.

And memories.

Exiting the cemetery, he made his way across town, walking along Lugosi Trail until he came to his old house. His dad wouldn't be inside—he could guess that much—but Vlad wanted to search every bush, every tree, in hopes that his father had, in some small way, come home again. He had to be there, had to be somewhere in Bathory. Vlad had seen his dad with his own two eyes. He knew it. He wasn't crazy. He hadn't been infected by Dorian's blood in the worst way imaginable. Had he?

He reached out with his blood, focusing, hoping for a hint that any vampire, aside from those he already knew about, was in town, was anywhere that he could reach. But he sensed nothing. He stretched out with his abilities, further than he'd ever done before, but there was no one to find. So he went back to searching the town, hoping he'd find at least minor evidence that might point to his dad actually still being alive.

Five hours later, Vlad stumbled home.

His search had been fruitless.

5

THE LONG SEARCH

A WEEK HAD PASSED since the first night Vlad had searched the town over for any sign of his father, any sign that he might not be completely crazy.

At least he wasn't alone in his quest. Sometimes Vlad's searches were conducted with Henry, sometimes with Otis. Sadly, each night, Vlad came home completely convinced that Dorian's blood had infected him with bizarre hallucinations.

But he couldn't stop searching. It was—real or not—his dad, after all.

He'd reached out with his blood a hundred times or more, to no avail. The only vampires besides himself in Bathory were Otis and Vikas.

It was as if his dad had vanished into thin air. Thin, empty, nonexistent air.

Vlad had told only Em, Enrico, Otis, Henry, and Vikas about what he thought he saw the night Joss went to the hospital.

With his head swimming from thoughts and theories about who and what he'd encountered that night, Vlad moved his fork around in his spaghetti and sighed heavily.

After a moment, he looked up from his plate to find Vikas, Otis, and Nelly staring at him expectantly. Blinking, he said, "What?"

The three exchanged looks, and then Nelly reached over and patted his hand. "You were just muttering, dear, something about not being crazy. Is something wrong?"

Vlad blinked again. Had he been muttering? He'd been so lost in his thoughts, he wasn't really sure. Maybe this was what crazy felt like. Maybe first you start seeing dead people, and second, you start mumbling things under your breath without realizing.

A hard knock on the front door echoed throughout Nelly's house. Then the doorknob turned and the door opened.

Henry poked his head inside. "Hey, Vlad, are you ready?"

It was time. Time for another search. Vlad sighed and pushed his chair back from the table.

Nelly looked worried. "Where are you going?"

Otis patted her on the hand. "It's nothing, dearest. Just some guy time, I'm sure. What's for dessert?"

After casting Otis an appreciative glance, Vlad followed Henry out the door.

Henry met his eyes as they made their way back to the

car. "So have you spoken to Snow lately? October mentioned something when I ran into her at the park the other day."

Vlad swallowed hard and opened the passenger door. "No. No, I haven't spoken to her. In fact . . . I released her as my drudge."

The words left his mouth so easily, almost casually, but they sent a bolt of pain through the center of his soul. He missed Snow, missed her deeply, and totally regretted releasing her. But nothing could be done about that now.

Henry's jaw hit the ground, but Vlad flashed him a look that said not to inquire further if he wanted to live out the night. After a moment, Henry closed his mouth.

Vlad didn't want to talk about Snow. He could barely think about her without his heart breaking. So he looked at Henry and struggled with his words. "So how's Joss doing?"

"Much better. They say he's up and walking around now. His parents still won't say where they've taken him. It's kinda weird, actually." Henry glanced at him. "You shouldn't worry, dude. He'll be fine. Besides . . . he kinda had it coming, right?"

A lump formed in Vlad's throat and, no matter how hard he tried, he couldn't seem to swallow it. "Right."

As they were getting into Henry's car, Vlad said, "So did you notice if he had my dad's journal or not? It was in his backpack. Did you check?"

Henry slid the key in the ignition and turned the engine over. It rumbled to life. "As far as I can tell, Joss doesn't have that journal, man. Would you stop worrying? It'll turn up. Just like your dad."

Hours later, Vlad stared down at a crudely drawn map of Bathory on the table with hopeless, helpless eyes. He'd searched every square inch of the town he called home, a dozen times over. His dad was nowhere to be found. And Vlad was beginning to wonder if his dad wanted to be found. If he was still really alive, that is.

After hours of fruitless searching tonight, he and Henry had returned to Nelly's in the wee hours of the morning. Nelly had already left for work, much to the comfort of Vlad, who was sitting at the table, trying to calm his frazzled nerves.

"What apout vhe cemepewey?" Henry pulled his head out of the fridge, a leg of 'chippen' barely held in his teeth, his arms loaded with what Vlad could only assume would soon become a sandwich.

"C'mon, the cemetery? Really? Try to be a little more stereotypical." Vlad continued to stare at the map, his head resting on his hands, pushing his hair back out of his eyes. "Besides, I've already checked there . . . three times."

"Oh yeah, we were there Thursday, weren't we?"

"And Saturday." A heavy sigh flew from Vlad's chest.

"Well, there has to be somewhere we haven't tried." Bread and mayo and cheese and meat were being thrown together, confirming Vlad's initial suspicions. The strawberry yogurt was a surprise, but when you've spent as much time with Henry as Vlad had, you learned not to ask questions.

"No, there isn't. We've been over the whole damn town!" Vlad pushed himself away from the table, moving it as he did so. He walked over to the window above the sink, stared out for a moment, then returned right back to the place he'd started. Flopping down in the chair, he stared at the map again.

He was never going to find his dad. Because his dad was dead. And he was just a hallucinating lunatic.

"Calm down, man. We'll find him." Henry took the first bite of the monstrosity that he had built between two slices of bread. As toppings spilled out onto the plate Vlad marveled at the fact that his friend hadn't shouted, "It's ALIVE!" before digging in.

"You mean if he's actually out there. If I haven't lost it completely." Grumbling his frustrations, Vlad crumpled up the map and threw it across the room.

Otis caught it effortlessly in midair. He looked from the wad of paper in his hand to his nephew. "I take it you haven't had much luck in your search for Tomas."

Vlad glared, but he wasn't mad at Otis. He was mad at his situation.

He sighed heavily, and winced slightly at the hunger pain that shot across his stomach. "No. No luck at all. What about you, anything?"

Otis shook his head, his face drawn, and returned the

crumpled map to the table, smoothing it out as best he could. "Nothing. Not a trace. If Tomas is really out there, something tells me he doesn't want to be found."

Vlad stared at the map again, but didn't really see it. All he could see was the invisible clock that was ticking away the remaining minutes of his life. His uncle had said aloud just what he was thinking. What if his dad was hiding from him? What if he had no plans to come forward again at all? It was almost worse than the idea of his dad being dead.

"Otis . . ." He met his uncle's eyes, lowering his voice to a whisper. "Should I run? I mean, they'll kill me either way, right? If I find my dad and hand him over they might kill us both, or if I don't find him at all, I'm probably still as good as dead, aren't I? So what's the difference? Why make it easy on them?"

"They'll torture you for months before killing you if you run." Otis shrugged, as if this was an everyday occurrence. Maybe, Vlad thought with a shudder, it was. "That being said, it is an option. But not one without a price."

Vlad chewed his bottom lip for a moment before speaking again. "They'd go after you and Vikas, wouldn't they?"

"And Nelly. And Henry. And everyone you've ever known and loved." Something foreboding was lurking in Otis's gaze, but Vlad couldn't quite put his finger on what it was.

"They didn't come after me when they thought my dad was on the run."

Henry looked up from his monster sandwich and nodded.

He didn't speak, but only because his mouth was full of the yogurt-coated monstrosity.

Otis cocked an eyebrow at Vlad, as if what he were about to say were painfully obvious. "That's because of who you are, Vladimir. Much of Elysia fears you, fears what you are capable of."

"What am I capable of?" The room grew silent. Vlad was taunting his uncle on purpose, baiting him, trying to get Otis to admit that there was even a tiny smidgeon of possibility lurking within the Pravus stories that Otis had deemed fairy tales. When his uncle refused to respond, Vlad met his gaze and said, "Otis, do you believe in the prophecy . . . even a little bit?"

Obvious tension filled his uncle. He paused for a moment, as if summoning the courage to speak, or perhaps just putting the words together in his mind before speaking them aloud. "I cannot deny what I've been witness to over the past few years, but I refuse to believe that you are capable of enslaving the human race."

"Dorian said I'll do that out of charity."

"Dorian was a madman."

Vlad's jaw tightened. It was time to come clean and tell Otis the truth about what happened the night Dorian died. No matter what Otis might have to say about it. "What if I'm a madman now, Otis? What if you are?"

Otis met his gaze, his forehead lined with confusion. "What do you mean?"

With a deep breath, Vlad released words from his lips, words that he'd been holding in all summer long. "I drank from him. I drank from Dorian."

Otis pursed his lips. He seemed angry, but Vlad wasn't sure why exactly. Vlad had never promised his uncle that he wouldn't feed from Dorian. In fact, Otis had never said anything about the subject at all. Still, his uncle looked like he'd been betrayed in the worst way. "And you wonder why you're seeing visions of your father?"

Vlad tried hard to ignore that. Even though it stung, especially coming from his uncle.

He counted two heartbeats, then a third. After a deep breath, he met Otis's eyes again, calm.

Well, mostly calm, anyway.

"We both drank his blood, in some manner. I drank his, you drank his son Adrian's. What's the difference? Because I really don't see it. If it's so bad that I did it, then you're just as guilty." He hadn't raised his voice, not quite, but his tone was defiant. Otis was acting like he was ashamed of Vlad's actions. But really, when it came down to it, crazy or not, Vlad was glad he drank from Dorian, glad that he honored a dying vampire's final wish.

Even if it did make him hallucinate things that could not possibly be.

Otis's face flushed pink, but only for a second. He tossed the wadded up map into the recycling bin. "I made a huge mistake, Vladimir. A drunken, stupid, imbecilic mistake born of pain and loss. I was mourning your father and blood-drunk and stupid enough to listen to Dorian. But you . . . what were you thinking? You're better than me—so much better than me. And now . . ."

Otis shook his head sadly. "His blood . . . it taints people."

"He told me to do it." Vlad held his uncle's gaze, determined. "And I trusted him. So I drank."

Otis's eyes widened in surprise. Something else lurked there too. Betrayal, maybe. Maybe regret. But Vlad wasn't certain why. He knew that Otis hadn't trusted Dorian and that Otis had wanted to protect Vlad from him, but he wasn't at all certain he trusted his uncle's motives. In fact, he was a bit concerned that maybe Otis had wanted him to stay away from Dorian to ensure that Vlad wouldn't entertain any idea at all that he was the Pravus. After all, to this day Otis was still in denial about Vlad's status. Maybe he was afraid of it. And if that were true, then maybe he was afraid of Vlad.

Otis sighed in frustration and defeat. "But why? Why did you listen to him? How could you trust Dorian?"

Vlad chose his words carefully and spoke them crisply so that Otis could not shut them out of his doubting, fearful mind. "Because he's the Keeper of the Prophecy, Otis. And I'm the Subject of that prophecy."

Otis turned away, throwing his arms up, muttering something in Elysian code that had to be a curse word. Henry winced at the sound of it, even though he—like Vlad—had no idea what Otis was saying. When Otis turned to Vlad, Otis began pacing back and forth across the room. "Who told you that? Who told you those words? Who told you that there was such a thing as a Keeper and a Subject?"

Vlad wet his lips and tried hard to keep his voice calm, even though it sure felt like Otis was trying to fight with him. "Dorian did."

"And you believed him."

It wasn't a question, but Vlad offered a single nod in response.

Otis stopped pacing and shook his head slowly, sadly—as if he'd failed at saving his nephew from something truly frightening. He placed his palms on the table, closed his eyes, and simply breathed deeply for several minutes before speaking again.

The silence was deafening, and droned on for what seemed like an eternity.

"Have you experienced any . . . strange effects . . . since feeding from him?"

"Only if you count seeing my dead father." Vlad sighed, his eyes flicking to Henry and back to his uncle. "Dorian said I could know the prophecy if I drank from him. That's why I did it, Otis. Because he said that it was his job as the Keeper of the Prophecy to deliver the prophecy to me, and that the only way to do it was for me to feed from him. The prophecy . . . it's in his blood. Or was. Now it's in mine."

Otis released a sharp, disbelieving breath—one that immediately filled Vlad with shame. "And have you complete knowledge of this so-called prophecy now, Vladimir?"

Vlad's heart slid up into his throat.

Otis didn't believe him.

He swallowed hard and met his uncle's gaze, certainty and confidence filling him to the brim. "Otis, I've *seen* the prophecy, and whether you believe me or not, it doesn't matter. It's real. As real as the blood in my veins."

Henry had finally finished his sandwich and joined the conversation with something Vlad had expected to come from Otis's mouth. "What if Dorian was lying?"

"He was not lying." Vikas's voice rumbled into the room as he entered. "Dorian was mad, this is true, but he was an honest man. An honest madman. And I happen to know for a fact that he did indeed carry the prophecy in his veins."

Vlad *really* looked at Vikas for the first time since he'd drank from Dorian. His voice was quiet, and tinged with a strange sense of disbelief. "You were there that night. You killed those men—the Foreteller and Transcriber—once Dorian knew the prophecy."

Vikas offered a single nod. "That I did, Mahlyenki Dyavol, as it was to be Dorian's task, but the boy was too weak, and far too gentle to commit such an act. As twisted as his mind was, it was only out of reaction to all that he had been faced with. I rather liked Dorian and was sad to hear of his passing. Apart from his madness, he was a kindly vampire."

Vlad nodded in agreement, relieved to learn that he wasn't the only one who'd come to understand Dorian, to like him. Otis was staring at them both as if they'd lost their minds, but he didn't speak.

Vikas stepped closer, his smile warm. "Have you had any visions, Mahlyenki Dyavol?"

Vlad sighed. In fact, he had. Right after drinking Dorian's blood, he'd had a vision of himself ruling over vampirekind and enslaving the human race. But admitting that was admitting that he would one day soon be the evil thing the prophecy had foretold. So he lied. "No. Nothing yet."

Vikas sighed and patted Vlad on the shoulder. His eyes sparkled with encouragement and support—nothing like what Otis had been offering. "Perhaps with time."

Changing the subject to a more comfortable one, Otis said, "Any luck with your search for Tomas, Vikas? We haven't had much luck here in town at all."

Vikas shook his head and took a seat at the long plank table, eyeing a bottle of bloodwine. "No luck as of yet, my old friend. Dyavol is nowhere to be found. For a moment I thought I found a trace, but the trail has gone dead, it seems."

Vlad's eyes shot to meet Vikas's, hurt and anger warring inside them.

Dead.

How could he use that word?

Vikas clucked his tongue and flashed him an apologetic glance. "Forgive me, Vladimir. I have forgotten my candor. I am a fool."

Vlad sank back in his seat. "You may not be the only one, Vikas. If I don't find my dad soon . . . then maybe Otis is right. Maybe I am crazy."

They all looked at Vlad then, wordlessly, as if gauging his

sanity level. After a moment, Vlad stood and headed for the front door, Henry in tow behind him.

Otis stopped him with a hand on his shoulder. Quietly, he said, "Whatever you decide to do, we will support you. If you decide to run, we're prepared for whatever comes. But please, tell us before you go so that I can make arrangements to hide Nelly from Elysia."

Vlad cringed at the very idea of bringing down Elysia's brand of justice on his family, his friends, but he met Otis's eyes and nodded. Then he was out the door. He had a lot to think about, and there was only one place to do it. With a brief goodbye to Henry once they were outside, Vlad was on his way to the only place he could truly be alone to think.

The belfry. His sanctuary. The only place in the world he felt safe.

Vlad moved through Bathory effortlessly, his mind clouded with troubled thoughts. A slight breeze danced through the air, bringing a bit of cool to the lingering summer heat. He was grateful for it. Too much of his summer had been spent outdoors, in the sticky heat. So he slowed his steps and allowed himself a moment to enjoy his walk—something he hadn't done in months.

Once he reached the school, he floated effortlessly to the arched windows of the belfry and stepped inside.

Only . . .

The room wasn't dark.

The room wasn't empty.

Vlad wasn't alone.

A candle was lit on the small table beside his father's chair, illuminating the space with a flickering warmth. The photograph of his father was no longer in its space on the wall.

It was being cradled by hands.

Familiar hands.

Hands that had caught Vlad when he fell off the roof. Hands that had bandaged his elbow when he tumbled from his bike. Hands that he knew well.

Tomas Tod was sitting in his chair, holding his framed photograph, looking up at Vlad with an expectant, albeit worried, smile. "Vladimir." He breathed, standing. "Son. It's been too long, and this meeting is overdue."

6
Unexpected Company

HIS DAD.

Alive and in the flesh and standing less than ten feet in front of him.

Which meant Vlad really was crazy. After all, he only seemed to see his dad when no one else was around, and all other evidence pointed to no additional vampires being in Bathory. Even now, he couldn't sense Tomas's presence when he reached out with his blood. It was as if his father wasn't really there.

Vlad was insane. He was off his rocker, for sure.

"No, you're not, Vlad. You're perfectly sane, I assure you." Tomas—the man who looked like Tomas, anyway—shook his head. He set the photograph down on the table next to the candle and met Vlad's eyes, his gaze pleading. "Trust me. The reason you can't detect me by reaching out with your blood is because I burned my Mark away. I'm not surprised Otis or Vikas didn't realize that would be an effect of having removed my Mark, as so few vampires have survived the task. Doing so hasn't seemed to harm my abilities, though. Telepathy, speed, mind control—all intact, it seems. I suppose I should count my blessings."

Vlad jolted at the sound of that voice. He swallowed the growing lump in his throat. Either it was his father, or his imagination was brilliantly creative.

They watched one another for a moment but as Vlad started to speak, Tomas held up a hand, his eyes kind, sympathetic, full of an immense, overwhelming guilt. "As for my disappearance . . . son, I owe you an explanation—"

As the words began to leave Tomas's lips, Vlad's eyes snapped to him in a glare. "You owe me a hell of a lot more than that. If you're real, that is."

Tomas lowered his eyes apologetically. "Indeed. And I'd meant to come forward sooner. But I had to wait until I was certain we'd be alone. I am being hunted, as it were."

Vlad tightened his jaw, his heart racing—racing with fear and panic and upset and doubt and something else too. Anger. Immense and immediate anger.

Through clenched teeth, he growled, "I don't give a damn if you're being hunted. I don't care if the entire Slayer Society is on your heels and all of Elysia is thirsting for your blood. All I care about is where you've been for the last eight years. What happened the day of the fire. What happened to you, what happened to Mom, and why. And you're going to explain everything to me. But first . . . before you say another word, before you refer to me as your son again, before you take another breath . . . prove to me that you're really my dad. Prove to me that you're really . . . here."

Tomas nodded and furrowed his brow, his features almost too similar to what Vlad saw in the mirror every day. After a moment, his apparent distress eased some—if only a little, and he met Vlad's guarded eyes. "Did you get my note? The one I scribbled in the margins of the *Compendium of Conscientia*, directing you to my journal?"

That was something only Tomas would know. But it was also something only Vlad would know, so he still had no real evidence whether or not the man he saw before him was flesh and blood, let alone his father.

He couldn't trust his possibly poisoned mind.

Not one bit.

Vlad stood there, looking at the man who'd created him, the man who'd taught him to read, who'd been there for him every day until a fire had torn them apart. Let the madness take him. At least he'd see his father again. At least he wouldn't be alone anymore.

His bitter anger remained, but it was instantly overshadowed by a mingling of both immense relief and dire need.

Need for family. Need for his dad.

Without warning, he grabbed his dad and gripped him tightly in an embrace. His dad was warm, solid, real. He was back. His dad was back. Somehow, against all the odds and everything that Vlad had understood to be reality, somehow his dad was back from the dead.

And if he wasn't, Vlad didn't want to know.

If he was crazy, Vlad wanted very much to stay that way, to enjoy every single moment of his insanity.

Tomas hesitated—as if taken aback for a moment—then put his arms around his son. He breathed words into Vlad's hair, words that Vlad very much needed to hear. "It's all right now, Vlad. Everything is going to be all right. I'm here now. And I can explain everything."

7
EVERYTHING

VLAD SAT ON THE COUCH, but he couldn't sit still, no matter how he hard he tried. So instead, he stood and paced some back and forth across the living room of his old house—Otis's current house—his eyes expectantly on his father the entire time.

They'd left the belfry at Vlad's insistence and after an argument—Tomas had been reluctant to go somewhere he might be seen by someone other than his son. But Vlad had dug his heels in. If he was going to hear details of his mother's death and his father's miraculous escape, he wanted to hear them where it all happened, in the place where his life had taken a dramatic, downward turn.

Home.

He was waiting for answers, answers that his dad had

assured him were coming once they got there. And the waiting was killing him.

He'd lived for years not knowing what had transpired the day of the fire. Now he would know. Now he would know everything.

Tomas looked about the room, his eyes somewhat troubled by what he saw. "I see Otis redecorated."

"It needed a lot of work after staying empty for so long." Vlad's words were curt, but he didn't mean for them to be. He was just so angry that all of this time he'd been led to believe that his dad was dead, and yet here he was, alive and in the flesh. And it didn't help that his dad just wouldn't get to the point. "So about that explanation . . ."

Tomas met his eyes before releasing a troubled sigh. "I suppose I should begin with the day I disappeared, and your mother . . . your mother . . ."

Vlad swallowed hard, tearing his gaze away from his father's eyes. The sorrow there was almost too much for him to bear. "So Mom really is dead?"

His dad nodded, a heavy air about him. After he did so, Vlad nodded too, a familiar ache forming at the center of his chest. He'd known for years that his mom was gone forever, but seeing his dad again had sparked the hope that maybe, just maybe, it had all been a horrible misunderstanding. Foolish, he knew, but no amount of reason or good sense could have doused the spark of hope within him.

"I awoke that morning to find that my alarm clock had been turned off, as had your mother's. That was good of you,

Vlad, to want us to sleep in, to show us that you were more than capable of getting yourself off to school on your own." He looked at Vlad, an apology lurking in his eyes that would not leave his lips, not until he'd explained everything he needed to. Still, Vlad appreciated seeing it there, knowing that it was coming soon enough. "I slipped out of bed, leaving Mellina still resting, and stole away to Stokerton. It had become common for me to spy on Elysia, you see, and more common still for me to do so without telling your mother. So I left. Unable to resist the urge of being near vampirekind. I'm sure you've realized since you've come to know Vikas and your uncle that being away from our kind for too long is painful."

It was painful. Vlad hated being away from his uncle for very long, and it hurt beyond hurt to leave Siberia a few years ago. He absolutely understood the loss of Elysia.

"So, I left. When I returned home hours later, my need for vampire contact satisfied for the moment, I saw smoke billowing out of my bedroom window and Nelly cradling you in her arms in the front yard. I knew that what had happened could only be my fault."

It was his fault. He'd said it. Whatever it was that had happened, whatever it was that had taken his mom away from him, it was his dad's fault. Not Vlad's.

Not Vlad's.

Vlad watched him, waiting, a strange sense of relief filling him.

Tomas sat on the arm of the couch, his forehead lined with

tension and guilt. When he finally resumed speaking, it was with a hushed tone. "It's no secret that I am a wanted man in Elysia, or was, before my presumed death."

"You were after too." His dad shot him a glance, and Vlad said, "I mean, lots of vampires didn't believe you were actually dead."

Tomas sighed. "Ahh . . . This is true, son. But what you may not know is that I am also wanted by another group, though they are also vampires. A secret society who believe that one day a vampire will be born, not made."

Vlad tensed. His voice was gruff. "You're talking about the Pravus."

With a nod, Tomas said, "This group believes that he—you—will lead them in a revolt against the nonbelievers and that you will lift vampirekind to its proper place, where we live openly amongst the humans and feed on them at will. These vampires . . . they are the reason your mother is dead, and they are the reason that I disappeared that day and have stayed hidden for these seven years. They were there watching when I got home that day, among the crowd. That is why I couldn't come to you until now. That is why I had to leave the moment I did. I had to run, Vlad. I had to hide. If there was any hope of my keeping you alive, it was in my keeping my distance from you. If I'd stayed in contact with you, I shudder to think of the painful death it would have brought you."

"Why did you come to me now? And why wait for so long

after that night in the clearing? You could have told me all of this then? Why wait? Why make me wait?"

Tomas paused then, a look of trepidation crossing his features, as if what he was about to say next was difficult for him. "Every vampire I have come into contact with since that day has been killed, and I myself have only barely escaped death by their hands a number of times. After seeing you that night I questioned whether or not I was doing the right thing. By the time I'd decided that I was, you'd begun searching for me with other people. I really wanted our first conversation to be just between the two of us."

Vlad took this in and then nodded slowly. It made sense, he supposed. In a really stupid way. "That group you mentioned? I've heard of them, actually."

Tomas raised an eyebrow, but said nothing.

Vlad cleared his throat. "Why do they want you dead?"

"When you were born, I knew something was amiss. Vampires don't bear children. It just doesn't happen. There have been others who have broken the law of separation in the hopes that they might be able to bring about the Pravus. I broke the law for love. Perhaps that is what made your birth possible. However, we knew that your very existence would give that group special interest in you. That's why your mother and I stole away to Bathory—so that we could raise you in peace, and so that I could discover the reason for your existence. Through spying on Elysia and stealing away into their libraries, I hoped to know everything I could about this prophecy. While the word Pravus is spelled simply enough, its meaning is far more complex. There were theories in the books I read, but they were just theories, nothing concrete that stated exactly why the Pravus would come." A far away expression came into his eyes. Then, as if coming back to the present, he continued. "Through my trials, I learned the truth. The Pravus—you, my son—will bring peace to the world. You will unite us all and rule over all with your good sense and generosity, traits that I know you are well acquainted with. But the members of this group . . . this secret society . . . they seek to use you for their selfish gain. They tried to kill me to stop me from revealing what I know to the world and to you. They will try again. We can trust no one, Vlad. Their group is full of liars and con men."

Vlad listened for a moment, filled with so many questions, but first, he had to know. "Who was in the bed with Mom? How did the fire start?"

"I don't know. I can only assume it was one of the vampires who were after me. And I don't know how the fire started."

"This group. D'Ablo was part of them."

"Was?" His dad raised a sharp eyebrow, curiosity ebbing from him.

Vlad shook his head. "Dead now."

"D'Ablo . . ." Tomas rolled the name over on his tongue, as if he hadn't spoken it in years. Something crossed his eyes that looked like regret, or maybe loss. "I've known D'Ablo for nearly two centuries. He may have been ambitious and at times a fool, but I didn't think he'd be involved with a group like that. You're certain?"

Vlad nodded. "Positive. And Em."

"I've known of Em's involvement for some time. However, hers is more of a position to guarantee that she is not supplanted as leader. She wants to prevent the coming of the Pravus more than anything. Anyone else?"

Vlad searched his memory, but no one else in his life came across as suspect. "Not that I know of."

Tomas leaned closer and spoke with his thoughts—even though his words were locked safe inside Vlad's mind, he whispered. *"Listen, Vlad. These vampires are sly and under-handed. They could appear to be your best friend and you wouldn't even know they were plotting against you. I need to know every vampire you've been in contact with since I left."*

"Besides D'Ablo and Em, there was the rest of the Council of Elders, a small group that met here at the house—I don't know their names—and Jasik, but he's dead now. There was Ignatius . . ." Vlad flicked his eyes to his father, guilt filling him. "I mean, my . . . my grandfather. He's also dead. Otis . . . killed him. He had no choice. I'm sorry."

"No need for guilty feelings, Vlad. He was an abysmal monster." His dad squeezed his shoulder and smiled a small smile. Vlad relaxed some at the sight of that smile. "None of those sound like members. Hmmm . . . perhaps they haven't infiltrated your life. Can you think of anyone else? Someone close to you, perhaps, someone you feel you can trust?"

Vlad searched his memory, sighing. "Let's see. There's Vikas, of course. And the vampires in Siberia."

"I trust Vikas completely. But others in Siberia . . . well, let's just keep an eye out for familiar faces, shall we?" Tomas looked troubled, but determined. "Anyone else?"

Vlad chewed his bottom lip for a moment before answering. "There was Dorian . . ."

His dad's eyes widened in instant shock. "Dorian? You . . . met . . . Dorian?"

Flashing through Vlad's mind was every encounter that Vlad had ever had with Dorian. From their initial meeting, where Dorian had tried to force him to give his blood, to the strange conversations in the oddest places, to their last meeting, when Dorian had saved his life by sacrificing his own. Try as he might, he could not block out how Dorian's blood had tasted on his tongue. He wet his lips and met his father's gaze. "Um . . . yeah. You could say that. You didn't see him in the clearing that night, the night you came back?"

Tomas shook his head, filling Vlad with dread. Dread because he had to be the one to share the news—news which pained him and would forever. "He's dead too."

So much death, all surrounding him. Vlad's heart sank as he wondered if those vampires would still be alive had they not come into contact with him.

Sometimes he felt like he was poison, infecting everyone around him.

"He jumped in between Joss and me, taking the stake for

me. That's why I was hitting Joss when you came up. I was going to kill him."

"I know you were. I could see it in your eyes."

"You stopped me. Why?" Vlad swallowed the ever-present lump in his throat. "I mean, Joss is just a Slayer, right? So why save his life? Why stop me from killing him?"

His dad grew quiet for a moment before speaking. "I stopped you because I thought if you'd killed the boy, you'd never forgive yourself."

"For all you knew, we were enemies in combat."

Tomas shook his head. "Wrong. Enemies don't fight with such determined passion. That kind of focus is reserved for friends at odds with one another."

After a long, silent moment—one filled with the realization that his dad still understood him, even after all of those years apart—Vlad sighed, returning to the former subject. "Anyway. That just leaves Otis, and Otis would never plot against me."

There was a pause before Tomas spoke in a distracted, suddenly worried voice. "No . . . not Otis. He wouldn't . . ."

Frustrated, Vlad ran a hand through his hair. If what his dad was saying was right, his problems had only begun to surface. "What are we going to do?"

Tomas met his eyes. "I need my journal, Vlad. Within it, I've contained some useful tools that might help us. Where is it?"

"I think Joss has it. But there might be a problem getting it back. I forgot to grab it from his backpack in the clearing that night, and I couldn't get it from him at the hospital. And now his parents have taken him away for the summer. So this could take some time."

Tomas muttered an Elysian curse under his breath before patting Vlad reassuringly on the shoulder. "We'll get it back. But for now, until we know who we can trust . . . this is all between us, okay?"

The back screen door banged shut and Vlad and Tomas lifted their eyes to Otis as he moved through the kitchen. He paused when he saw them in the living room. Otis was frozen in place, his disbelieving eyes locked on Tomas.

The wondering silence stretched on forever.

Otis didn't move, didn't even blink. Then the corner of his mouth twitched slightly.

Tomas darted a glance at Vlad before turning awkwardly back to his brother. "Otis . . . it's . . . it's so good to see you."

Otis stood there, silent as stone. Then he set his jaw and went back out the door, slamming it behind him. After a single heartbeat, Tomas followed.

Two heartbeats after that, Vlad strode out the door, determined not to be left behind.

Even though he knew that he hadn't been invited to this conversation.

When he finally caught up to Otis, Tomas reached out, grabbed Otis by the sleeve. "Otis, stop. Let me explain."

Seemingly against his own good sense, Otis stopped and looked back at his brother. "Explain what? Explain why Vlad has spent almost a decade without a father? Explain why you chose to let him feel guilty of your death all this time? How about you explain why the hell you decided to come back now, and why, rather than just coming out of the shadows, you've let that poor kid walk around here thinking he was crazy for seeing you that night in the clearing? Well, you're clearly alive. You're clearly back in Vlad's life and I'm sure everything will be just great from now on. What more is there to explain?"

Vlad winced. He'd always known his uncle to be straightforward with his opinion, but those remarks were meant to burn. To bleed, even.

Tomas looked like he'd been slapped. "Perhaps why I left in the first place?"

Otis sighed. "I am in no mood for fairy tales, Tomas."

Vlad looked at his uncle. "Did it ever occur to you that he might be telling the truth? You've already judged him, Otis. Without even hearing a word about why he was gone. Why not listen? Or are you afraid that you might do the unthinkable and forgive him?"

Otis held Vlad's gaze wordlessly, and Vlad didn't need to ask why he wasn't speaking. Otis was quiet because he knew that Vlad was right. And Vlad was right because he was afraid of the same thing, that he might forgive his father for causing him so much pain if he listened soundly to Tomas's excuses. Only *he* was willing to work past it.

Tomas pursed his lips, looking more than a little berated, frustrated, and embarrassed. What's more, the look in his eyes said that he knew he'd wronged Otis, had wronged everyone, and he wanted to make amends. "The truth, then. The complete and utter truth, which is all I'd intended to give you, Otis. They were going to kill me. They were going to kill me and kidnap Vlad, turning him to their own hateful purposes if I came into contact with him. With my absence, Vlad had a chance. I distracted them with mind control and confused them with glyphs. I led them away from my son so that he would have a chance at a fulfilling life, a normal life. If I hadn't fled, who knows what might have happened? His blood might have been spilled all over the playground."

Otis dropped his eyes to the ground and his voice became lower, quieter, overflowing with disappointment. "That's why you left, but why did you stay gone? Why did you stay silent all these years? You could've reached out. Through me. Through Vikas. But you did nothing. You abandoned your own son."

"To protect him!"

"To protect yourself."

Vlad's jaw hit the ground, shocked. "Otis . . ."

Tomas looked hurt. "What are you saying, Otis?"

"I'm saying you're a coward." Otis slanted his eyes, his words turning bitter. "You left him, Tomas. When your son needed you the most, you left him. Don't deny it. And don't you deny it either, Vladimir. He left. When things got rough, he left. Just to protect himself. He's selfish. He's always been selfish."

The air was thick with tension. Vlad reached up and

squeezed Otis's shoulder, but Otis shook it away. "Forgive him if you want, nephew. I have better things to do."

Vlad's heart felt heavy, hollow. Here he was, standing between the two men who meant the most to him in this world, and he'd never felt so unhappy before. It wasn't supposed to be like this. "Uncle Otis, please don't leave."

Otis turned away then and Tomas took a step after him, desperation filling his tone. "So what you're saying is that I left him . . . like I left you, when you needed me the most?"

With barely a pause beforehand, Otis whipped around, shoving Vlad out of the way. His fist flew through the air, connecting with Tomas's eye. Tomas flew back several feet, landing on the ground with a thump. Dazed, Tomas sat up and touched his eye gingerly.

Otis walked away without another word.

Tomas sighed, his shoulders sagging. He watched after his brother, so quiet, absolutely overwhelmed by the severity of his mistake.

And it was just that. A mistake, a poor decision that he had made, hoping to protect his son. Even Vlad could see that.

After a moment, Tomas looked up and met Vlad's eyes, his cheeks flushed. The puffy bruise around his eye was already healing with vampiric speed, turning from purple to blue to green to yellow right before Vlad's eyes. In seconds, it looked as if the punch had never happened. "Your uncle is a difficult man. Stubborn. Terribly stubborn."

After a pause, Vlad helped his father to his feet and turned to follow Otis back to the house. "He may be, but he does have a point."

The walk back to Vlad's old house was short, brisk, and quiet . . . too quiet. He could hear his father's footsteps behind him.

One thing was sure. If Otis could see Tomas too, then Vlad wasn't crazy. The thought made him breathe a sigh of relief. But his uncle had raised some good questions. Questions that sent a prickle of angry electricity over Vlad's nerves. Why had his dad waited so long to reveal himself? And where had he been this entire time?

Vlad pulled open the back door and walked in, surprised to see Otis having a frantic conversation with Nelly, who cut him off the moment she noticed her ward. The door behind Vlad opened and Tomas stepped inside. Awkwardly, almost sheepishly, he smiled and approached Nelly with open arms. "Nelly."

Nelly's face paled. For a moment, Vlad thought he spied the glimmer of tears. "Tomas. You're . . . you're . . ."

"Alive, yes." Tomas looked reproachful. "I'm sorry, Nelly. So very sorry."

"You should be. You've ruined that boy's life, Tomas. He blamed himself for your death. And for Mell—" Nelly's trembling hand found her mouth and covered it in hopeful sorrow, her engagement ring twinkling in the low light.

But Tomas shook his head in reply to an unasked question. Mellina was dead.

Tears welled in Nelly's eyes, spilling over onto her cheeks.

She shook her head. Her tone remained calm, but Vlad could tell that she was furious. "Damn you, Tomas Tod. Damn you for every tear you made that boy shed. Damn you for every worried thought in his head. Mellina would never have—"

"I did it for him, Nelly. I left to protect Vlad." Tomas's words rang true, but even so, his reasons didn't sit well with Vlad's guardian. Or Vlad.

"Did it ever occur to you that he might have been better off with one parent than with neither?"

"He *was* better off. He had you." A small, charming smile tugged at the corners of his mouth, and Vlad wondered how anyone could resist that charm.

But then Nelly slapped his dad so hard that the sound echoed across the room. She moved out the door, Otis on her heels, without another word.

Tomas stood there, looking hurt. His cheek had flushed pink, but quickly paled again. "I suppose I deserved that."

Vlad was still angry, but he felt guilty for feeling that way. His dad couldn't have intended any harm in doing what he did. And then when he finally comes back, to right his wrongs, and to help any further complications, he's greeted with nothing but fury and rejection. Vlad swallowed hard. "They're just angry. We've all been through so much."

Tomas's eyes shimmered. His pain was evident. Vlad couldn't help but wonder what had hurt him more, their words or the punishment he was putting himself through. "Did no one miss my presence enough to overlook the pain I've caused you . . . even for a moment?"

Vlad was about to say that he had missed his father terri-bly, but just was so overwhelmed with everything that had happened. But his words were cut short while still poised on the tip of his tongue.

"For a moment, my friend." It was a familiar voice. Warm and friendly and thickly accented in rich Russian tones. Vlad was glad to hear it.

Judging by the sound in his dad's voice, so was he. A smile lit up his features as he turned to face his old friend. "Vikas, you old dog."

Vikas embraced him and patted his back roughly, letting out a relieved laugh. "You've been missed, my old friend. That, I assure you. It has been too long, Dyavol, and it seems you've already made such a stirring with your return from the dead."

The look in Tomas's eyes was a pained one as they moved to the door and back. "Otis—"

"—will be fine. Give him time." Vikas smiled, looking back and forth between Vlad and his father. "Now, let's toast to this happy reunion, and you and your son can catch up some, eh?"

8

A Celebration Interrupted

Za Vas!" Vikas's voice was jubilant, even if it was slurring slightly. In the last hour, the three of them—Vlad, Vikas, and Tomas—had emptied three bottles of bloodwine. Vlad's portion had been exactly one glass . . . one glass which had remained untouched and sitting in front of him the entire time. He stared into it, trying to wrap his head around his father's miraculous return. He should have been happy.

He wasn't. And he was feeling more than a little ashamed about it.

After all, here he was, with his dad. Together again, at last. But all Vlad could think of was how he was supposed to turn his dad over to Em's monstrous whims. By the end of the year, he was going to have to say goodbye to his dad again. This time, forever.

Tomas raised his glass with a bleary grin. *"Za Vas!"*

Vlad set his goblet on the table. "So where were you? This entire time you were gone, I mean. Where?"

Tomas took another drink and said, "Everywhere and nowhere, my son. I traveled the globe, visited my home in London, stayed unseen. It was lonely, Vlad. More lonely than you can ever imagine. I couldn't speak with many vampires, since I'd risk revealing myself to Em and others who cry out for my blood. So I had a lot of time to think. By happy circumstance, I traveled to Siberia one day, and as I was spying on my vampire brethren there—out of loneliness, I suppose—I witnessed a funeral pyre. A curious thing, with no body to be found."

Vlad took in a sharp breath. His dad's mock-funeral. His dad had been there, after all.

"Imagine my surprise to see a younger version of myself, standing before the pyre."

A lump formed in Vlad's throat at the memory. "It was a tribute to you. But I couldn't say goodbye."

His dad squeezed his hand and held his gaze. Warmth and compassion ebbed from him. "I know. Thank you for that."

Vikas took another swig from his goblet. "You have a good son, Dyavol. And he has a good father. I hate to taint our conversation with bad news, but we have yet to discuss the foreboding shadow of Em and what has transpired in your absence."

Tomas nodded and refilled his glass. "Of course. Please."

Vikas met Vlad's eyes for a moment, and Vlad was almost certain that he was going to use telepathy, to ask Vlad what he wanted his dad to know and what he might not want to discuss on his dad's first night officially back from the dead. But then Vikas shook his head, as if indicating that Tomas had the right to know all of it. Fortunately, Vlad agreed. Then Vikas began. "Vlad traveled to New York to accompany his uncle to his trial. But in a rather shocking turn of events, Vlad's own pretrial was announced. It was unexpected and completely against any context of law that the Council of Elders has ever acknowledged. It was shocking to hear his name fly from Em's lips. Of course, now . . . your return changes all that, Dyavol."

"How, exactly?" Tomas's eyes grew wide, almost fearful. For a moment, the bloodwine released its bleary hold on him.

Vikas and Vlad exchanged knowing glances. At their silent response, Tomas darted his eyes to his son. "Vlad. Tell me."

Vlad pushed his chair back silently, and stood. He didn't know how to tell his dad that he had to choose between turning his father over to Elysia or facing his own demise. He moved to the sink and tossed the contents of his goblet into it. The bloodwine splashed against the sink's insides and swirled down the drain. Crimson against stainless steel. Down the drain—just as Vlad's everything was about to be. He couldn't turn his father in. So death would come for him. He had no choice.

Vlad leaned against the counter for a moment, taking a deep breath. He blew it out slowly before turning around and meeting his father's gaze. Then, like a coward, he turned to

Vikas. "What good will telling him do, Vikas? No one can stop this; no one can help me."

Vikas held up a calming hand. "One man can help you, Mahlyenki Dyavol. Your father. Now tell him. Tell him what it is that Em expects you to do."

Tomas paused briefly at hearing Vlad's nickname, then turned to face his son. "What can I do, Vlad? I'll do anything."

Vlad's hands were shaking. He looked from Vikas, who nodded encouragement, to his father, who was waiting on edge. There was only one thing that Em wanted. "Em says that I should turn you in by New Year's Eve, or face my trial and expect death. But I can't do that, Dad. I can't turn you over to her. She's a monster."

Tomas returned his goblet to the table with a thump. His tone shifted slightly, as if he was losing patience with his son. "You should have told me. The moment you saw me, you should have said something."

Vlad's voice dropped to a whisper. "Why do you sound angry?"

"Because I am angry. Not at you. At myself. For running away in fear, for putting you through hell, thinking that I was helping you, thinking that I was protecting you all this time. But no. I was making it worse!" Tomas's voice had risen, his eyes growing moist with anger and sorrow, regret and frustration. "Up until this point, I have failed you as a father, Vlad. But no more. I will face Elysian justice this December, and nothing will change my mind about that."

A long silence passed. His dad held his gaze, and Vlad's heart sank with understanding. His dad would rather die than hurt him again. No matter what Vlad said or did, he was going to lose his family all over again. "Don't. Don't do that. I'll be damned if you're going to take my dad away from me again after all of this time."

The room grew terribly quiet.

Vlad set his jaw and glared at his dad, the man he'd missed so much since the day of the fire, since the day he'd lost everything. His words were sharp, like dagger blades, and aimed straight at Tomas.

Tomas, who'd left him behind.

Tomas, who'd made him believe that his parents were both gone forever.

Vlad shook his head, overwhelmed with emotions. Anger at losing his parents. Anger at the possibility of losing his dad again. "Don't. Just don't. I don't want to hear another word."

Vikas clucked his tongue. "Vladimir, that is no way to speak to your—"

Tomas raised a hand, silencing Vikas's chastising interruption. His eyes never left Vlad's, but he didn't speak. He was waiting, waiting for Vlad to have his say.

"I hate the idea of losing you again. But what's worse is that I hate you for being gone in the first place. I hate you for not telling me where you were and that you were okay. I hate you for endangering my life, Nelly's life, and Otis's life with your lies. And I hate you for letting Mom die, for not protecting her. I hate you." Vlad crossed the room and gripped the doorknob. It was only then that he realized that his hands were shaking. Before stepping out the door, he whispered, because it was all he could bear to do. "But the worst part is that I hate myself for hating you."

Vlad stepped outside. He wasn't sure where he was going, he only knew that wherever it was, it had to be away from here, away from his dad, away from the pain that had seeped into his chest, into his soul. He had no idea what had come over him. He'd forgiven his father for being gone, and was so undeniably happy to have him back. He had no explanation for the barbs on his tongue. Except . . .

Except for the fact that he didn't want to lose his dad again. Not after everything he'd been through.

"Mahlyenki Dyavol . . ." Vikas's words followed him out the door and hung in the night. Vikas came too, grabbing Vlad's shoulder gently, stopping his escape. But Vlad knew what he was going to say. He was going to tell Vlad that he was wrong, to urge him to apologize.

Vlad bit his tongue for a moment before speaking. "Nothing you can say will take away how I feel, Vikas. So don't bother."

Both were quiet for a long time. Then, just as Vlad had lifted his foot to step off the porch, Vikas spoke again. Calmly. Almost serenely. "Did it ever occur to you what it must have been like for your father? He lost his wife and his son and all of Elysia in one day. In one fell swoop, he lost all sense of family—and was forced to keep his distance from his only son, in order to protect him, not knowing if it really would. Can you imagine the pain that he's experienced? We've all been through a lot since that day, Vladimir. But who has suffered more? You had the love of Nelly and then later, Otis. I had Elysia. Your father had no one. No one and nothing to quiet the ache in his heart."

Vlad released a shuddered breath. Selfish—that's what he'd been. Vikas was right. He'd had it bad, but Tomas . . . he'd had it far worse. At least Vlad had a family in Nelly and Otis. At least he had Elysia with Vikas and the other vampires, if only for a moment.

Vikas squeezed his shoulder, urging him inside. "Come, Mahlyenki Dyavol. I believe the guilt that Tomas feels for leaving you is punishment enough for his wrongdoing. Don't you?"

With sagging shoulders, Vlad moved back into the house, where Tomas was waiting.

Tomas was still sitting at the table, his eyes lowered, his expression subdued. He waited a moment, pausing, as if to form just the right words in the forefront of his mind. Once he had them, he spoke, his voice soft, soothing. "You didn't give me a chance to respond."

Of course Vlad didn't. Giving him that chance would've opened Vlad up to more heartache, and he wasn't exactly in the mood. He had no choice now but to listen. Because Vikas was right. Vlad was pushing away the father who he loved, who he'd missed for so long. And all because he was scared to death of losing him all over again.

A pensive look crossed Tomas's face. One full of meaning, and regret. "Perhaps you should hate me."

A soft breeze blew through the open window, rustling the drapes. It was the only sound until his dad spoke again.

"I like to think that I left Elysia to protect your mother, and that I left Bathory to protect you, but the truth, Vlad—the real truth—is that I was afraid, *am* afraid, and it is because of my fear, my cowardice, that your mother is gone and your life is in continuous danger. I can't deny it. I can't take it back. But I am more sorry for my cowardice than you could ever believe, more filled with regret than I have ever been in my four hundred and twenty-three years on this earth. And I promise you, I will spend the rest of my days making it up to you however I can. If that means doing the right thing this time around and *not* running, then so be it." Tears shimmered in his eyes. His voice grew gruff. "I'm sorry, Vlad. More sorry than you'll ever know, son. I was wrong."

Vlad felt his resolve melt away. Swallowing the threat of tears, he met his father's eyes. He was about to tell his dad that everything was going to be okay, that as long as he stuck around and they figured out what to do about Em's looming deadline, everything would work out.

But then the door opened, and Otis stepped inside.

The air thickened with tension.

Vikas gestured with his eyes to the stairs, but Vlad shook

his head. He wasn't leaving. Not now. Not while his dad and Otis were at odds.

Otis took a step, then another, as if he hoped to quietly move past Tomas, and end the conversation before it had a chance to begin. But Tomas would have none of it. He spoke with a raspy, hushed voice. "Otis, please. Sit. Let's talk about whatever's troubling you."

"I think you know very well what troubles me, Tomas."

"My presence, though I admit, I'm confused by your reaction. I had thought—"

"Whatever you thought doesn't matter, because the fact remains that you are just as selfish as you ever were." Otis's tone changed then, still stern, but open to hearing what Tomas had to say. "I want answers, Tomas."

He flicked his eyes to Vlad and back. "We all do."

Vikas parted his lips and Otis snapped, his voice rising in venomous upset, "And I want them from Tomas, Vikas."

Tomas was quiet for a while, then said, "So much anger coming from my brother—"

"*Half* brother, remember?"

"Yes. As it seems you will not let me forget," Tomas whispered. "So much anger coming from my *half* brother and my son . . . an explanation is warranted, for certain. But, Otis, I'm not arrogant enough to ask for or expect forgiveness from either of you—only compassion. I've been alone for so very long. And my decision to return—no matter what it might mean to Vlad's life—was not an easy one to come by. So please, if you would, give me time, and I will explain everything that you ask of me."

Vlad looked at Otis, half begging him to listen, half understanding why he wouldn't. Otis avoided his gaze entirely, but Vlad wasn't sure why.

"When you're really ready, ready to be totally honest, Tomas, you know how to find me. Until then, my compassion waits in reserve." The back door slammed, signifying Otis's abrupt exit.

9
Brothers in Arms

IT WAS THREE DAYS before Otis and Tomas spoke again.

Vlad had spent many hours at his old house, keeping his dad company, even though Tomas had been eerily quiet, disturbingly reserved. Tomas had been keeping vigil inside his home, his eyes rarely straying from the windows. Vlad would have bet anything that he was waiting for Otis, waiting for his brother to come to his senses and talk to him.

But Otis, as Tomas had said, was a very stubborn man.

Not that Vlad could blame him.

Vlad had just rinsed out their mugs after a fine meal of A positive topped off with mini-marshmallows—a vampire's answer to hot cocoa—when his dad stood, with a determined look in his eye, and walked out the back door. When he looked to Vikas for answers, the Russian merely shrugged and said, "Perhaps the silence is about to be broken. You should go with him, Mahlyenki Dyavol. In case . . ."

But he didn't finish his sentence, leaving Vlad to wonder in case what.

Regardless, Vlad followed. When he caught up to his dad, he said nothing, only kept him company, secretly pleased that Tomas was clearly heading for Nelly's house.

When they got there, Tomas paused on the porch steps, as if doubting his earlier determination. Vlad frowned and strode forward, opening the door and calling out for his aunt. "Nelly, do we have any cookies? I'm feeling snacky."

Taking a deep breath, Tomas walked up the steps and through the door, closing it quietly behind him.

"I just baked some. Chocolate chip." Nelly walked into the room, drying her hands on a kitchen towel. When she spied Tomas standing there, her face paled. For a moment, Vlad thought she might order him out of her house. But then she said, "Would you like a cookie, Tomas? They're still warm."

Relief flooded Tomas's eyes. "Thank you. I'd love one."

Then, as if it were the most natural thing in the world, Nelly moved forward and hugged him tightly, wordlessly.

Vlad wasn't sure how long Otis had been in the room, but he saw him now, watching Tomas with a wary gaze.

Tomas wrapped his arms gently around Nelly and whispered words of comfort. He and Otis exchanged glances, but Vlad wasn't sure what those glances meant.

Finally, Tomas released Nelly from the embrace, meeting

her eyes with a kind smile. Otis stepped forward and put an arm around her, almost protectively. Nelly dabbed at her eyes with the towel and released a shaking breath. Her eyes hadn't left Tomas even once since he'd entered the room. "I'm glad you came over. It's time things got back to normal around here."

Tomas nodded, his smile slipping into a sorrowful purse of the lips. "Nelly, can you ever find it in your heart to forgive me?"

For the first time, Nelly looked over at Otis. When Otis lowered his eyes and said nothing, the anger still boiling off of him, she set her jaw stubbornly and forced a smile. "There's nothing to forgive. You must have been terrified, so you ran. Anyone who would claim that they'd have done otherwise is likely kidding themselves."

Vlad couldn't be certain, but that sounded like a jab at Otis.

Tomas looked relieved.

Nelly clapped her hands together. "It's getting late and I'm tired. I'm sure Vladimir is exhausted too. Why don't I get you two boys some AB negative to go with your cookies and leave you to celebrate your reunion?"

Vlad looked from Nelly to his dad and uncle. He wasn't tired in the least and Nelly looked about as perky as one can get. Otis's eyes began to slant in a glare at her suggestion, but then he caught himself, as if he just realized he was about to flash a dirty look at the woman he loved. Nelly met his eyes, her tone serious, but gentle. "For me, Otis. Please. And for your nephew."

As if remembering that Vlad was in the room, Otis glanced at him, his shoulders relaxing some, almost in defeat.

He couldn't fight Nelly. He'd lose. Vlad had learned that years ago. The woman had an arsenal of guilt-inducing tools and was adept at every one of them.

"Vladimir? You're tired, right?" Nelly looked at him expectantly.

The clock on the wall said it was just a few minutes after seven. The sun was still shining outside. But Nelly wanted him to go upstairs, to leave Otis and Tomas alone to hash out details that she thought might harm him in some way. But Vlad wasn't about to leave. He had a right to the answers that Tomas would give. He shook his head at his guardian, defiant. "I'm not going anywhere, Nelly. I have every right to hear this."

Nelly looked pained and caught, but eventually she nodded and headed up the stairs alone. When her bedroom door clicked shut, Vlad turned to face his father and uncle. "Fix this. Because it's killing me to see the two people I care most about in this world hating one another. Fix it. For me."

Otis and Tomas exchanged looks—long, silent, lingering looks that spoke volumes. Finally, Otis nodded. He would do anything for his nephew. "I need answers, Tomas."

Tomas looked relieved. "I need questions to answer. Ask them. Let's be done with this."

Otis met his gaze. The defiance and anger had completely

left his tone. All that was left behind was curiosity and under-standing. "Where have you been all this time?"

"Everywhere. Hiding out like a dog. Occasionally spying on Elysia."

"On me? On Vlad?"

"Yes."

Vlad chewed his bottom lip for a moment. It was unset-tling to think that his dad had been watching him and Otis. He couldn't help but wonder what his dad might have seen.

Otis shook his head. It was apparent he was wondering the same thing. "Why not confide in us that you were afraid for your life?"

Vlad sat forward, nodding. "We could've helped hide you with glyphs and stuff. You wouldn't have been so alone. And we could've been together."

Tomas's eyes went wide with horror at the thought. "I couldn't endanger either of you that way."

"That's stupid." Vlad shook his head, holding his dad's gaze. "If you can't count on your family, who can you count on?"

After a moment, his dad sighed heavily. "You're right. I was being stupid. I see that now."

"Why did you wait so long to come back?"

On the heels of Otis's question, Vlad added, "And why come back now?"

Tomas ran a trembling hand through his hair. "I had planned never to return. Ever. To let you both believe that I had perished. To disappear into the night, the sole carrier of my horrific burden. But I recently overheard a conversation between Em and another vampire that suggested your life may be in danger, Vlad. I knew I had to come back, to help you if I could. I had no idea that it was something as serious as a trial."

"And Mellina? Is she truly . . ." Otis voice was firm, guarded, but something else lurked beneath the surface. Pain.

Tomas's voice cracked. He sounded like he was crying, but no tears fell. "Dead. I don't know who the other person in that bed was. I can only assume the worst."

Vlad looked away. He didn't want to hear about his mom. He didn't want to hear that she'd been with someone else the day she died, or that she was dead after all. He blocked it out from his emotions and pretended not to have heard a single word about it.

Even though every syllable had been etched into his heart with a razor.

Otis's voice was caring, kind, full of empathy. He was the uncle that Vlad had come to know and love once again. He leaned across the table and grasped Tomas's hand in his. "From all that Nelly's told me, Tomas, Mellina loved you deeply. Don't think such things of her. There has to be another explanation."

There was a long pause. Then Tomas spoke again, his voice hushed, his eyes red with the threat of tears. "Will you forgive me, Otis? Can you possibly, even remotely, see yourself forgiving me one day? Or is my one hope a lost cause?"

"Nelly forgives you. Vladimir has forgiven you."

Vlad glanced at his uncle. Otis knew. Otis knew that Vlad had forgiven his father, when Vlad hadn't said a word. But he didn't need telepathy for that. It was obvious to anyone with a brain. Vlad loved his dad. And had completely, totally forgiven him for any pain his actions might have caused. It was over. It was done. It was past tense now.

Otis sighed. "What choice do I have?"

Vlad stood. He placed a hand on his dad's shoulder, and a hand on Otis's, then squeezed. "It's about time. Can I get you guys something to drink?"

Otis nodded. "Bloodwine, please, Vladimir."

Tomas nodded as well.

Vlad headed into the kitchen, eavesdropping as he reached for a bottle of bloodwine and struggled with the cork.

Tomas said, "What can I do to prove myself to you, my brother?"

"You're forgetting something, aren't you?" Otis's tone was suddenly clipped, somewhat angry.

Tomas sighed, his tone full of regret. "Otis, when I called you my half brother that day, the day I left Elysia behind for the love of Mellina, when I implied that you were less to me than a true brother, that you were only partly my family, partly of my blood . . . please know that it was out of anger and frustration. I'd wanted to make a clean break with you before running off with Mellina. I was so terrified that if I did not, you would turn on me, as you did on Vikas. I was terrified that your love of Elysia would overshadow your love of our brotherhood."

Otis's voice hushed then to almost a whisper. "Nothing means more to me, Tomas. How could you think such a thing?"

"You loved Vikas as well. But look at Nadya, the human who Vikas so deeply loved, and how quickly you sabotaged his life with her." His tone wasn't angry, wasn't accusing in the least. Just matter of fact.

Vlad remembered his conversation with Vikas about Otis's betrayal. Vikas had loved a human, and Otis had notified the council of his lawbreaking. It made perfect sense that Tomas had feared a repeat. He sat the cork on the counter and retrieved three goblets. As he poured them full to the brim with the spicy blood, he heard Otis admit something that he wondered if he had ever admitted to Vikas.

Otis's voice grew gruff, like he was on the verge of tears. "I was wrong. Misguided."

"And now?"

"Now . . . now I have Nelly." He grew quiet for a moment, and when he continued, Vlad could almost hear the smile on his lips, see the slight blush in his cheeks. "We're to be married in the spring."

Tomas chuckled some. "My brother? Marry a human?"

"Nelly isn't just any human. She's special."

"Of that I'm well aware."

Otis sighed, dropping his voice to a near-whisper, perhaps so that Vlad would not overhear. "The Council of Elders expects Vladimir to deliver you by the end of the year. What do you propose we do?"

Vlad picked up the glasses, sloshing bloodwine as he moved slowly back to the dining room.

Vlad's dad was quiet for a moment, as if mulling his situation over before speaking. "We'll do just that. But for now, let's keep my presence quiet. Give me some time with my son before I die."

"Tomas." Otis paused, as if the subject were a sensitive one. It was. "You know how Em is. I'm certain she plans to kill him too, no matter if you turn yourself over or not."

Tomas's voice shook slightly. "I know. But I will do anything within my power to stop that from happening."

"And I will help you." There was a pause then, and when Otis spoke again—even though he spoke just two simple words—Vlad knew that all was well between his father and uncle. He knew that somehow, Tomas had earned Otis's trust back, and that everything would be okay between then from now on.

Otis's voice cracked slightly as he spoke again. "My brother."

10
A Friend in Need

VLAD'S HEAD WAS SPINNING in a million different directions, kind of like his feet had been duct taped to the side of the Gravitron ride at the carnival. He'd lain in bed for four hours straight, but sleep refused to come. Mostly because that little voice in his head refused to shut up.

It spoke of his dad's miraculous return and Otis's strange reaction. But mostly, it spoke of Snow.

In fact, it wouldn't shut up about her.

Every time he rolled over, closed his eyes, or breathed, an image would cross his mind. Piecing them together, he could see her as he'd left her the last time he saw her. He'd given her a rose, bitten her forcibly, and pushed her out of his life. At the time it had felt right to release Snow as his drudge, but ever since then, Vlad was weighed down by regret. And worse yet, he couldn't think of the right way to apologize, the right way to plead for forgiveness and tell her how he felt. Mostly because he didn't know how he felt. And that, coupled with thoughts about his dad, was keeping him awake. So he slipped quietly, unnoticed, from the house, and walked. And thought.

His thoughts were jumbled.

Vlad sighed and whipped his head around, looking for a street sign. He'd been walking so long that he'd forgotten which direction he'd been walking in.

It was only then that he realized where he'd ended up.

He stood there for a long, silent, uncertain moment, staring at the house, questioning whether or not he should knock. With a deep breath, he forced himself up the porch steps and, before he could stop himself, he raised his fist and knocked.

No one would answer. After all, it was almost midnight now. And even if someone did answer, Vlad would have bet his life, that someone would be very large and very angry to see him.

When the sound of movement inside reached his ears, he almost bolted, but held fast, despite his fear of having his limbs ripped from his body.

He could do this. After all, he was in need of a friend.

The door opened to reveal pink fuzzy slippers—they reminded Vlad of cotton candy—and an equally pink robe. Glittery pink lip gloss covered her lips still, as if she'd just begun getting ready for bed and hadn't quite removed her makeup just yet.

Surprise lit up Meredith's eyes. She wasn't smiling, but to Vlad's relief, she wasn't frowning or glaring either. "Hey . . . Vlad. You're out late. What's up?"

Vlad shoved his thumbs in his front pockets, dropping his eyes back down to her cotton candy slippers. "I . . . was wondering if we could talk. I mean, I could really use someone to talk to. Is that . . . is that okay?"

It took him several seconds, but when he looked up, he saw Meredith was smiling. "Of course. Is the porch swing okay? More privacy out here."

A bit taken aback by surprise, Vlad nodded. Meredith moved past him and sat on the wooden porch swing, patting the seat next to her. Vlad followed and sat down, the wood creaking beneath his body, the chains squeaking some as the swing moved. He sat there for a long time, unsure of how to begin. Meredith remained silent.

Finally, Vlad cleared his throat. "Something strange and kinda awesome has happened and I'm a little messed up about it."

He waited to see what Meredith had to say. When her only response was silence, he figured he should probably give her a little bit more information. He also figured he should talk about his dad and not Snow. "It turns out my dad survived the house fire a few years back. He's . . . he's back home now."

He looked at Meredith, at her hand finding her mouth open in shock. Then he nodded. "That's pretty much how I reacted too. The thing is . . . I thought I'd be happy to see him again. But mostly, I'm angry. And I feel really, really guilty for being so mad. I mean, he's had it rough, what with losing my mom and then being so far away from me for so long. And then he comes back and his son is mad at him for being gone."

Meredith's shock had eased some. She reached over and took Vlad's hand in hers, her voice soft and caring, like he knew it would be. Some things you could just count on. "It's okay to be angry, y'know. I mean, he disappeared for years. You thought he was dead, and then he shows up alive? I'd be angry too, I bet, if my dad did that."

Her hand was soft and warm, and Vlad really liked the way it felt in his.

Maybe too much.

She eyed him for a moment, a bit of sadness creeping into her eyes, as if she were thinking the same thing. Then she released his hand. "I can only imagine how you must be feeling right now. You must be freaking out. Has he said where he's been all this time?"

Vlad shook his head slowly, relieved that Meredith seemed to understand, relieved that it was okay that he was mad at his father for abandoning him. "He says he's been all over the world, kind of on the run. But he says he only stayed away to protect me from something. Something awful."

"He must love you a lot."

"Maybe that's why I feel so guilty about being angry with him."

"I'm not the smartest girl in the world, Vlad, but if I've

learned one thing, it's this: forgiveness is crucial. If you can't forgive someone you're mad at, that anger will poison you. You have to learn to let it go." Her hand was in his once again. Soft, warm, and caring. Familiar. Right, even though it was wrong. "People have reasons for doing the things that they do, especially when they care about you. You may not always understand what they are, but if you can try to understand the person then you might see that they really care, despite what happened."

Vlad met her eyes then. With his peripheral vision, he could see fireflies glowing softly all around the porch. A slight breeze brushed a stray hair from her eyes, and the streetlight made her lip gloss shine slightly. When Vlad spoke, his voice was hushed, and he already knew the answer to his question, but had to ask it anyway. "Are we still talking about my dad?"

The air between them warmed and before Vlad knew it, the space between them shrank. He wasn't sure who moved first or if they moved in at the same time. He only knew that their lips met in a tender kiss, and that neither pulled away for several seconds.

When they did part, however, a flash of guilt crossed Meredith's eyes.

Guilt because she had a thing for Joss, the way Joss had a thing for her.

Guilt because she and Vlad were over.

Something struck Vlad that hadn't before. The kiss, while perfectly nice, hadn't made his toes curl, hadn't sent his heart into that fluttery rhythm, hadn't made him dizzy with happiness the way it had before.

Because Vlad had known better kisses. Kisses from a girl called Snow.

Amazing, endearing, heartfelt kisses. Kisses that he had been missing not just with his lips, but with his very soul.

Mulling this over, Vlad wiped her lip gloss from his lips with the back of his hand. Vampires, after all, didn't sparkle.

Meredith stayed quiet for a long time. Vlad wasn't sure what to say to break the tension between them. Finally, as if pretending that the kiss hadn't happened—which was probably for the best—she said, "Vlad . . . I'm really glad you came here tonight. We're friends, right? We can talk about stuff. Stuff that's on our minds. Stuff that bothers us. Can't we?"

Vlad shrugged, his thoughts still on Snow. Snow's lips. Snow's porcelain skin. Snow's undeniably wonderful everything. "Of course."

Meredith took a deep breath and furrowed her brow, her fingers curling over the edge of the wooden swing. "Okay, so look . . . I know that you probably don't like Joss very much . . ."

Vlad snapped his eyes to her in a warning—a warning that this subject was definitely off-limits—but she persisted. "But he's really concerned about you. He sent me this e-mail, mentioned that you'd gotten in a fight—"

Vlad stood and moved across the porch, throwing his goodbyes over his shoulder. "It was nice talking with you, Meredith. I've gotta go, but . . . I'll see you around, okay?"

Meredith stood and followed him to the edge of the porch.

As Vlad moved down the steps to the sidewalk, she spoke again. "Just so you know, I'm not mad anymore. Not about how you broke up with me."

Vlad's steps slowed. This he hadn't expected at all. He raised his eyebrows in surprise, turning back to face her. "You're not?"

Meredith shook her head, a soft brown curl falling to her cheek. Her eyes were full of reason and sensibility—two qualities Vlad truly believed he didn't possess. "I'm sure you had your reasons, and whatever they were, they must've been pretty important."

Vlad swallowed hard, not exactly anxious to discuss what his reasons were. After all, he'd tried that once at the Snow Ball, and it backfired big-time. There would be no telling Meredith the truth. Not again. She'd proven that she couldn't handle hearing it. He dropped his gaze to his shoes for a moment. "They were."

She grew quiet for a moment, and when she spoke, her lips trembled slightly. "Are you still going out with that girl . . . the one you brought to the Snow Ball?"

A hot pain flashed across Vlad's chest. One of immense loss. Snow. Oh, how he missed her. He shook his head, wondering where this conversation was going, but hoping for a drastic change in subject. "Not really. We don't talk much anymore."

He didn't mention that they didn't talk much because Vlad was avoiding her at all costs out of fear he might hurt her . . . or worse, love her so completely that he couldn't stay away

from her. Not to mention that he didn't know how to apologize for the way he'd left her.

Some things, he figured, were best left unsaid.

"Vlad . . ." She tilted her head to the side, her eyes large
and sad. ". . . about what you said to me that night. You
were . . . you were just kidding around, right? About being
a . . . a vampire?"

Vlad's heart sank. It was here—his moment, the perfect
time to admit his deepest secret to Meredith once again, to
let her know who and what he really was. She'd asked him.
All he had to do was confirm it.

But he couldn't. It would shatter her. Even now, he could
see the pleading in her eyes, pleading with him to take it all
away, make it not so, give her back the world she thought she
lived in.

Vlad sighed, and shook his head, slipping his hands inside
his pockets and dropping his gaze to the ground. His voice
was barely a whisper in the night. "Yeah. It was nothing. Just a
joke."

The night shrank in around him, making him feel small,
insignificant, stupid. All he wanted was to tell her the truth.
He couldn't even get that right.

Meredith's voice was quiet, soft, tinged with a hint of surprise, as if she'd expected him to tell her the opposite of what
he had. "Oh."

He looked at her then, and not for the first time wondered
what Joss had told her about his nighttime activities, and
about Vlad. He took a deep breath and pushed all of his ques-

tions deep down inside of him. Some things he could not bring himself to tell, and some things he could not bring himself to ask.

With a heavy sigh, he met her gaze. "Good night, Meredith."

She nodded, as if he'd answered her question with his less than forthcoming reply. "Good night, Vlad."

11
FAMILY

THE TEMPERATURE HAD DROPPED SOME, hinting that summer was on its way out already, and autumn was just around the corner. Which meant that school was also just around the bend. School. Full of tests and books and teachers and the dull doldrums of Vlad's senior year.

On the upside, there were also dances, lunchtime goofery, and the general bliss of knowing that, assuming he passed all of his classes, it was his last year at Bathory High. His final moments. Which meant saying goodbye—something that Vlad was experienced at. Something he had been preparing for, for many years.

After all, he'd known better than many of the kids he went to school with what it meant to say goodbye. To Vlad, saying goodbye was a painful, sometimes impossible thing to do.

But for now, he pushed thoughts of school away and looked at his dad, who was standing at his side, staring down at all that was left of Mellina's memory. The tombstone's inscription lied about who was buried there, including his father's name only because he and Nelly had made an assumption. But the truth, the truth of her name, stood out like a deep, dark shadow on the pale gray of the headstone. MELLINA TOD: BELOVED MOTHER AND WIFE, GONE FOREVER. Sure, the inscription didn't read that. But it might as well have.

Beside him, his father stared sorrowfully at Mellina's grave. No tears fell, but Vlad could tell he'd shed more than a few already over the loss of his wife.

Clearing his throat, Vlad said, "Do you think she'd be proud of me?"

Tomas didn't miss a beat. "Immensely proud. Without a doubt."

Vlad sighed, brushing the bangs from his eyes. "I barely squeak by my math classes. I can't keep a girlfriend. I'm not exactly Mr. Popularity. Do you think she'd care about any of that?"

His dad shook his head, his eyes still on Mellina's head-stone. "Not even for a second. Your mother would be very proud of the man you're becoming, Vlad."

Vlad swallowed hard, hesitating for a moment before he spoke. "Are you?"

The hint of a smile touched his lips as he met Vlad's eyes. "Absolutely."

Vlad felt a huge weight lift from his shoulders, from his soul.

His dad was proud of him. Despite everything. Despite all of his flaws. Despite his initial anger at Tomas's return.

The world swirled before Vlad's eyes. Instantly, he was transported into a waking movie, the same way he had been right after he'd drank from Dorian. He saw himself at Nelly's house, standing behind his father, behind Otis, who all looked intensely angry. Nelly was off to the side, her eyes wide, terrified. Standing in front of them were two vampires, their fangs exposed. The tall, thin vampire growled, ". . . come with us now, or we will kill your human."

His eyes moved to Nelly and the vision went away just as quickly as it had come, swirling down the imaginary drain it had slithered up. Vlad's heart rammed against his chest.

When he came back to the cemetery, back to reality, he was lying on the ground. His father was looking at him with frightened eyes, as if Vlad had simply crumpled to the ground without warning. Vlad jumped to his feet and took off toward Nelly's house, dragging his dad by the sleeve. "We have to get to Nelly! There are vampires there. Nelly's in danger!"

They both broke into a run, but not before Tomas said, "How do you know, Vlad? How do you know that's true?"

An image passed through Vlad's mind—Dorian, wise, dangerous Dorian, lying bleeding, dying at the hand of Joss. Vlad had drunk his blood because Dorian insisted, and it had changed him forever. It had given him visions—two now—of the future.

But he said none of this. Instead, he said, "I just know, okay? Now let's move."

Vlad raced ahead, the wind whipping through his hair as he ran. He didn't think about any of his fellow Bathory residents or what they might think if they saw him moving with such incredible, inhuman speed. He only thought of Nelly, and how he was going to protect her from the vampires in his vision.

When they arrived at the house, Vlad moved up the steps and through the front door in one fluid motion. Two men, two vampire men, were sitting on the sofa, looking expectantly at the door as Vlad stepped inside. Otis was standing in the living room, looking paler than usual. Nelly stood in the archway near the stairs, a confused and frightened look in her eyes. The secret of Vlad's trial and sentencing wasn't secret from her anymore. His dad stepped in behind him and when he saw the vampires Vlad had predicted, he cast his son a nervous glance.

Vlad glared at the newcomers. "What do you want?"

The taller, thinner vampire stood, his jaw set. "Em sent us to ask about your progress in locating your father."

The shorter vampire, who was kind of stocky, slowly stood, his eyes on Tomas. "Tomas Tod? You're ... alive? This ... this cannot be."

Vlad's heart sank. If they knew his dad was alive, and that Vlad had found him, there was no reason to wait any longer. It was time to carry out Tomas's trial and his subsequent punishment. Without delay.

And they wouldn't have known about Tomas if Vlad hadn't rushed his dad back in a panic.

Tomas stepped forward, his shoulders straight and proud, his jaw set. He placed a supportive, comforting hand on Vlad's right shoulder and stared the vampires down. "Neither I nor my son will be accompanying you to our demise. Not now. Not ever, gentlemen."

The shorter vampire sounded aghast. "Your trial is imminent, Tomas, and will be presided over by Em herself. Your— and your son's, I'd wager—sentence awaits. There's no denying it. And you, what, you plan to interfere? To refuse to come face the Council of Elders?"

"We do." Otis moved forward then as well, placing his hand on Vlad's left shoulder and glaring. "As my brother said, gentlemen. You can't have him. Ever."

The tall, thin vampire growled, "Tomas will come with us now, or we will kill your human."

His eyes moved to Nelly and Vlad's heart shot into his throat.

He'd seen this. He'd lived this. It was the future, and Vlad had known it was coming about in just this way. Clearly, drinking Dorian's blood wouldn't just reveal the prophecy to him. It would also reveal the future. And who knows what else?

Vlad stepped in front of his aunt and shook his head, growling, "If you lay as much as one finger on her, I'll tear you limb from limb."

With his peripheral vision, Vlad saw Otis move quietly to

the bookcase, the one containing Nelly's cookbooks. He saw Otis's hand stretch out and close over a large glass paperweight. What did Otis think he was going to do, knock them out with a paperweight? Highly unlikely. Besides, they were powerful vampires, built for speed and out for blood. It didn't exactly seem like the smartest plan.

Ignoring his uncle, he focused on the vampires in front of him, who'd both bared their fangs and were eyeing Nelly like she was their next meal.

Tomas growled, "I'm giving you both fair warning. Leave now, before someone gets hurt."

Em's cronies turned their attention to Tomas then, and the three began arguing in Elysian code. Vlad turned to check on Nelly, and as he did, he saw what Otis was up to.

Otis had bitten his finger and was dragging it hastily across the paperweight in the shape of his Mark.

A glyph. Otis was making a glyph. But what for?

Then Vlad had his answer.

The glyph glowed red. Hot, bright, noticeably red. And Vlad recalled a conversation they'd had about glyphs, and how Otis had warned him never to touch a red glyph, not ever.

Otis shouted, "Tomas!"

Immediately, Vlad's dad stepped out of the way, as if he'd known full well what Otis had been planning, had been doing. Otis tossed the paperweight toward the vampires. Instinctively, the taller one caught it.

He had time enough to blink questioningly before his entire body crumbled to dust.

The room fell completely, utterly, painfully silent.

Nelly broke the silence with a gasp. With barely a breath, Otis whisked her from the room. From the kitchen, Vlad heard Otis's voice rising and falling in comforting tones. Nelly's voice followed, shaking slightly. He was protecting her, and explaining away what had just happened. Vlad wondered if any other human on the planet knew as much about Elysia as Nelly did now. He doubted it.

Tomas moved toward the shorter vampire, whose bottom lip was quivering, and began to speak, his voice eerily calm. So calm, in fact, that it sent a strange shiver up Vlad's spine. "You are being allowed to live, but only because my brother and I have deemed it necessary to our cause that you do so. We feel no pity for you. Nor do we feel any measure of trust. Do you understand?"

The vampire nodded, his terrified eyes on the paperweight, which lay in the pile of ash on the carpet.

"Good." Tomas stepped closer, until Vlad was certain his hot breath was brushing the man's forehead. "You will go back to Em, and you will deliver her this message. Failing to do so will bring hell on your heels. A hell you cannot possibly understand and do not want. Do you understand?"

The vampire whimpered and nodded again.

Vlad stood fascinated. His dad seemed so powerful, so strong, so cunning. It was no wonder to him how Tomas had survived all those years on his own. He was strong. Like Vlad only wished he could be.

"You will tell Em that there has been no sign of Tomas Tod, but his son continues to search. You will tell her that on your way out of town, you and your friend were attacked by a small group of Slayers, and after they dispatched your friend, you fought them off valiantly, but not before overhearing that they were headed to Italy. Promise her with your life that she will find the Slayers there. Tell her this, and mean it as you've never meant anything before. I want you to believe it so that she will believe it. And so help you if she doesn't." Tomas's tone was still very calm as he spoke, and Vlad would have bet that he was feeding his mind control into the vampire's thoughts. The sound of his tone gave Vlad a frightened chill. He could only imagine how the other vampire was feeling.

Otis returned to the room, exchanging nods with Tomas, who growled at the vampire. "Now go."

12
UNEXPECTED WORDS

VLAD WATCHED THE SKY as Henry drove them back from the Stokerton Mall. During the drive, he'd explained to Henry all about his vision, Em, and her cronies. After he'd explained, Henry had asked why he'd agreed to go to the mall after all of that. The answer was simple: because sometimes even half-vampires just want to act like normal teenagers. The sky was big and blue and beautiful, but he couldn't help but focus on how empty it was, how empty the entire experience was, without Snow.

He missed her. And he was trying not to think about her. Only he was failing miserably.

He closed his eyes for a minute and pretended that the cool breeze brushing his hair back from his eyes was Snow's hand. It was enough to bring a smile to his face. One that burst like a bubble when he opened his eyes and she wasn't there.

Henry turned down the street, then pulled up in front of Nelly's house and let the car idle. Vlad started to open the door to get out, then closed it again and looked at his friend.

Henry met his eyes and shrugged. "What? Something wrong?"

Vlad chose his words carefully. "Dude, my dad's been back for like a week now and you still haven't been over to see him. What's up with that? He'd really like to see you."

Henry flinched, as if he'd been hoping he could skate by for a few more weeks on lame excuses. He put the car in park and cut the engine, then turned to Vlad with a sigh. "Your dad was always the coolest guy on the block, Vlad. I liked him, actually liked him better than my dad. It seriously bummed me out when he died."

Henry flicked him a glance, one full of uncertainty. "Well, you know what I mean. When he . . . when he disappeared."

"I know it's weird that he's back, that he's still alive and all that, but Henry . . . he needs us. All of us." Frustrated, Vlad ran a hand through his hair. "It's just . . . lonely, y'know? I feel bad for him. All he tried to do was the right thing and now when he comes back, trying once again to do the right thing, he gets punished for it. Everybody was mad at him, and even though that's changed now, even though Otis and Nelly are being nicer to him and have forgiven him and all, I can tell it still bothers him that we were all so upset. Not to mention that he walks into a huge mess—my mess—and feels the need to come to my rescue. So please, for me, for my dad . . . just come inside and say hi."

The street was quiet, as usual. No kids playing, no dogs barking. It was just as it had always been, but for Vlad, it felt different now. His dad's return had changed everything. He only hoped that it hadn't changed the one thing in this world that he could count on for sure—that Henry would have his back and support him in this too.

Henry stared out the windshield for a moment, and then sighed. It wasn't a sigh of frustration or regret. It was one of resolve. "Where's he been this whole time?"

Vlad shrugged slightly. "Everywhere. Nowhere. It doesn't matter. All that matters is that my dad's not dead."

Henry pulled his keys from the ignition and opened the driver's side door. Hesitantly hopeful, Vlad said, "Where are you going?"

"To see your dad. He sounds like he could use some company."

A small smile touched Vlad's lips. He didn't know why he ever doubted his best friend. Henry always had his back, no matter what. "Thanks, Henry."

"You're welcome, but I'm not doing it for you, Vlad. I'm doing it for him . . . and for me." Henry slid from his seat, stepped out the door and closed it in one fluid motion. Vlad followed him into Nelly's house, still smiling.

Otis had mentioned the idea that Tomas might want to move into his house permanently—it was, after all, Tomas's home—but Vlad's dad wasn't comfortable with the changes that Otis had made. He needed time to adjust, time to mourn Mellina, time to ready himself. So Tomas was staying with Nelly for now.

Vlad understood completely.

Henry walked through the gate and up the front steps, and moved into the house, shouting, "Hey, Mr. Tod! You home?"

Vlad stepped inside, now grinning at the surprised, befuddled expression on his father's face. "Henry McMillan?"

Tomas looked from Henry to Vlad and back, his own lips curling into a smile that barely mimicked theirs. "It's been years. How are you, Henry?"

"Starving. But I know there are cookies around here somewhere. Nelly bakes like a fiend and is a sucker for every big-eyed girl scout in town. So cough up the goods."

Tomas chuckled and Vlad followed suit. His dad pointed to the freezer. "Thin Mints are up there. They're better frozen."

Ten minutes later, as they were munching on chocolate cookies and catching up on current events, Henry shoved three cookies into his mouth and said, "Y'know what would go great with these? Carnage. Is your Xbox 360 still hooked up?"

Vlad nodded toward the living room, his mouth too full of sugary sweetness to speak.

Henry grabbed the box and led the way. "C'mon, Mr. Tod. You can be the red android."

"I . . . don't play video games, Henry." Both boys snapped

their eyes to Tomas, who looked admittedly ashamed. "That is, I . . . I never have. Played them. Before."

Vlad shook his head in a chastising manner. "Well, that's something we have to correct immediately. Wouldn't you say, Dr. McMillan?"

Henry folded his hands in front of him, straightening his shoulders and rocking back and forth on his feet. "Yes, Dr. Tod. I'd say the patient is suffering from lack of exposure to kick-butt graphics and gore galore. What do you prescribe?"

Vlad nodded knowingly. "Immediate and intense *Race to Armageddon* activity. It's the only cure."

Henry raised an eyebrow, a smirk on his lips. "Stat?"

Vlad grinned. "Stat!"

Dragging Tomas into the living room—Henry pulling from the front and Vlad pushing from the back—they ignored his pleas and sat him on the couch. Vlad dropped a controller into his hand and gave him the best advice he could. "Don't die."

Three hours later, Tomas had died more than Vlad ever had during an afternoon of play.

Henry shook his head, chuckling. "No offense, sir, but you suck even worse than Vlad does at this game."

Tomas laughed, warm and real. The sound of it warmed Vlad's heart.

Vlad emptied the glass of O positive he'd been sipping from and his stomach rumbled its protest. It wanted more, and refused to be satisfied.

Especially with bagged blood.

His dad smiled at him, a curious gleam in his eye. "You look thin, Vlad. Are you getting all the nutrients you need?"

Vlad nodded, but he wasn't honestly certain he was telling the truth. After all, what did he know about the differences between nutrients in bagged blood versus fresh? "Yeah. I think so."

Tomas leaned closer, and in a bemused tone, said, "But are you getting all that you'd like?"

Suddenly, Vlad's stomach rumbled with need. Before Vlad could answer his dad, Henry glanced at the clock and muttered, "Oh crap, I'm late. Mom will kill me."

"Late for what?"

"You don't want to know. Let's just say it involves ten neighborhood women, tea, quilting, and me being charming and fetching cookies." Henry shuddered visibly. "Otherwise known as the worst night of hell a guy my age could possibly experience."

"And I thought Nelly was bad." Vlad chuckled. "See ya, man."

"See ya."

Henry hesitated in the doorway for a moment before speaking. "Hey, Mr. Tod?"

"Please, Henry. Call me Tomas. We're both men, and grown men refer to one another by first name."

"Tomas." Henry seemed to mull the name over on his tongue, getting comfortable with it. Then he broke into his trademark grin and on his way out the door, said, "I'm glad you're not dead, dude."

Tomas smiled, his eyes dancing with a bemused light. "As am I, Henry. As am I."

Hours later, after dinner, and once his dad and Otis were well into a bottle of bloodwine and reminiscent tales of their youth, Vlad slipped out the door and down the street to the belfry. With barely a thought, he floated upward and stepped gingerly through the stone arch. He didn't light any candles—he knew exactly what he was going to find and where it was. As he retrieved his journal from the small table next to his dad's chair, Vlad smiled, pressing the book to his chest. He could hardly wait to share it with his dad, and hoped that Tomas would feel a stronger connection with him by reading what awaited him on the pages within.

With his journal in hand, he dropped from the belfry and headed back to Nelly's as fast as he was able, despite the nagging reminder in his thoughts that he needed to find Tomas's journal, and find it fast. Tomorrow, he told himself. He'd look for it some more tomorrow. Tonight belonged to the only semblance of normalcy Vlad's life had ever really had.

A cool breeze floated through the air, brushing Vlad's hair from his eyes as he made his way from the belfry back to Nelly's house. He was feeling oddly light, strangely hopeful, as he navigated his way through the darkness. A brief flash of memory flitted through his thoughts like a hummingbird—Ignatius, his grandfather, the maker of both his dad and his uncle, had once attacked him on this stretch, and had almost killed him. He wondered if his dad would have killed Ignatius the way that Otis did, without regret. Something told him Tomas would have.

He rounded the corner then, thinking back briefly to Jasik, and how Jasik had stolen his blood. He wondered if the money had been worth the theft and all that would come to pass, but wagered it had not. The memory of the pain, the utter emptiness that had enveloped Vlad left a dark, shallow hole at the center of his being.

It was weird how the past kept sneaking up on him. Just when he thought he was over something, there it was again.

A shadowy figure sat on Nelly's porch swing. Vlad froze with his foot on the bottom step.

The figure lifted its head, meeting Vlad's eyes.

Vlad's world came to a screeching halt, an utter stop.

He didn't even breathe. The journal in his hand was completely forgotten.

Joss nodded, as if acknowledging the strangeness that was hanging in the air between them.

Vlad parted his lips to speak, but then realized that he had nothing to say. He wanted to apologize, but somehow it felt as if they were past that, as if it were too late for words. He wanted to ask if Joss was okay after how badly Vlad had beaten him, and where he'd gone to heal from his wounds, but he closed his mouth and pursed his lips instead. Because the truth of it all remained: they were even. Each had nearly taken the other's life. They were in a dead heat in the race to kill one another. Once friends, they were now something completely different. They were vampire and Slayer. Mortal enemies.

Vlad braced himself for what he knew was coming, readying himself for a fight.

Joss shook his head. Apparently, he didn't need telepathy to read Vlad's thoughts. "I'm not here as a Slayer. I'm here as your friend. My last act as your friend, you might say."

Vlad relaxed some, but only slightly. He had to be vigilant, to remain on guard. Slayers, after all, couldn't be trusted. Otis had been right all along, something which pained Vlad terribly. He'd wanted to believe in their friendship, to believe that despite their differences, he and Joss were really friends. But what if he was wrong?

He met Joss's gaze. "Is this about revenge? Because I won't let you trick me again, Joss."

He knew it couldn't be so simple. Joss wanted what he'd wanted all along: blood. Strangely, the same thing that Vlad wanted, but in another way. For another reason. Just another one of the vast differences between them.

Joss shook his head in response. "This is about something else entirely. I've been trying to call you all summer, but . . . my mom isn't exactly keen on the idea of you and me talking."

Vlad swallowed hard, remembering her reaction to him the night he'd put Joss in the hospital. "So what do you want?"

Joss dropped his voice to a hushed tone, one that Vlad nearly had to strain to hear. It sounded like he'd been crying.

Joss. Who never cried.

"Peace, Vlad. I want peace. But no peace can exist between us. Not now." He shook his head again, this time as if to summon the strength that he would need to say whatever it was he'd come here to say. He looked at Vlad again, his eyes hidden by the night's shadows. "I was originally sent to Bathory to locate and extinguish you. I was sent back to gather information and then kill you, Otis, and Vikas. After I failed on both counts, the Slayer Society convened and it was decided that they would cleanse Bathory."

Vlad looked at him then, a question poised on his tongue. Something that in his head sounded like *"What the hell are you talking about?"*

Joss sighed heavily, as if a huge weight were on his shoulders. "A cleansing removes all life within an area that does not belong to a Slayer."

Vlad's eyes grew huge. His heart picked up its rhythm in shock. "They plan to kill everyone?"

Joss nodded gravely. "That was the plan. But I struck a deal. To save everyone—even some vampires—I have to kill one vampire, Vlad. Just one. One specific vampire."

The air left Vlad's lungs in complete understanding.

Him. Joss had to kill him. In order to save everyone, Vlad had to die.

"They agree that if I take your life, everyone else will be allowed to continue living. But if I don't . . ." Joss swallowed hard, as if the subject were a difficult one for him. ". . . or if I try to help people run and hide from the cleansing, they'll hunt everyone down and kill them all, me included. I don't care about that part, but Meredith, my mom, my dad, everyone . . ."

Vlad shook his head. It wasn't possible. Couldn't be possible. "Can they really do that?"

Joss nodded then, without hesitation. "It's what they do, Vlad. Slayers are naturally skilled. Enough to take down vampires, and you know what skills vampires possess. Now imagine unsuspecting humans. It's possible. Believe me."

Vlad sank down until he was sitting on the porch step.

It had to be him. Him or everyone he'd ever loved.

His insides felt as if they'd been painted black.

There was a soft squeak as Joss left the porch swing and came to sit beside him on the steps. After a long, silent moment, Joss slipped his wooden stake from the leather holster on his hip and placed it between them.

Vlad could think of no better fitting metaphor.

When Joss spoke again, his voice was soft. Soft and strangely kind. "The thing is . . . we both know that you're stronger than I am, Vlad. We both know I can't beat you. But I have to try. And the only way I can succeed . . . the only way that everyone we care about can possibly survive this . . . is if you let me."

"Let you?" Vlad's eyes snapped to those of his former friend. "You mean, let you kill me?"

Joss nodded slowly. "The Slayer Society is giving me until the end of the year. By December thirty-first, either you'll be dead or the cleansing will begin."

Vlad's shoulders sank in defeat. No matter what Vlad did,

it seemed, he was going to have a terrible New Year's Eve.

Joss was leaving the decision up to him, and trusting he'd make the right choice. And there was no question what that choice was.

Joss's voice was a whisper. "Just so you know, I'm working on a plan. There has to be some way we can stop the Society from doing this without killing you."

"What's your plan?"

Joss swallowed hard, his eyes straight ahead.

Vlad gauged him for several minutes before a horrified whisper escaped him. "You don't have a plan. Do you, Joss?"

Joss shifted uncomfortably. "No. But I'll come up with something."

"We." Vlad patted Joss on the back firmly, holding his gaze. "We'll come up with something."

They sat there, silent, for a long time as Vlad took the enormity of his situation in, wrapping his head around it. Live and everyone would die. Die and everyone would live.

It seemed like such a simple choice.

But nothing is ever as simple as it seems.

13
SCHOOL SUCKS

VLAD YAWNED so hard that his jaw ached slightly once he was finished. He hadn't exactly been sleeping great since . . . well, ever. But staying up late with Dad and Otis had proven ill-advised when it came to the first day of Vlad's senior year. Vlad hadn't even set foot on the grounds of Bathory High yet, and already, he was suffering from an acute case of Senioritis. How was he supposed to care about what grade he'd get in World History when everyone in the world was out to kill him? He was mulling over the ethical obligation of not skipping his first day when a familiar car pulled up.

Henry rolled down his window and grunted at Vlad to grab his backpack. Neither was looking forward to World History first thing in the morning, especially not after a summer of things that had kept them from hanging out very much.

Vlad had been totally immersed in his search for his father, and then once he'd finally found him, he'd been all about making up for lost time. So, apart from teaching Tomas how to vanquish two-dimensional evil foes, time with Henry had fallen by the wayside. Movies went unseen, concerts went unattended, or at least these things weren't done with his best friend. Vlad cast Henry a guilty glance. "So you never told me how *Return of Psycho Slasher Chainsaw Guy from Hell* was. Did you find someone to go with?"

Return of Psycho Slasher Chainsaw Guy from Hell was probably the most anticipated sequel of all time, and rumor had it, there was a scene featuring death by toothpicks that was not to be missed. Henry, in his McMillan way, had called earlier in the summer with advanced screening tickets. But Vlad had declined. It was bad timing, but that didn't mean that Vlad didn't care.

In fact, he absolutely cared. But he couldn't leave his search for his dad. And once he'd found him, he couldn't leave his side.

It might be the only time they had left together.

Henry scratched his head and yawned. To Vlad's great disgust, his hair remained flawless. As he stretched, he said, "Yeah, October and I went together."

Vlad blinked. "October? *My* October?"

Not that she was in any way, shape or form *his* October. Not like that. But still. She was more Vlad's October than Henry's. That much Vlad was willing to bet on.

Henry shrugged. "I mentioned I had tickets and she

jumped at the chance to see it. It was a great movie, dude. I've never seen so much blood and gore. And don't get me started on the garden hose scene."

Vlad's shoulders slumped a little. On some level, he was hoping the movie was mediocre at best.

Still, he was glad Henry had a good time. Even if he went with October. Which was weird.

Vlad started to wonder something about his two very different friends—something impossible and strange—then shook it from his thoughts. Nope. Never. October and Henry were about as different as night and day. It would never happen.

They moved up the steps and through the door, and once they had their locker numbers and schedules in hand, Vlad and Henry parted ways. Henry's locker was at the opposite end of the hall from Vlad's, but they'd meet up again later in World History. Vlad had just reached his when the light from the windows caught his attention.

It was the beginnings of a beautiful morning. The sun had already warmed the grass. The crystalline blue sky was only marred by puffy cotton clouds, adding to its beauty. The air smelled sweet, like roses, like lilacs. It was, in short, the perfect morning.

Apart from the dark cloud which hung over Vlad's every thought.

Thoughts of Joss. Thoughts of Em. Thoughts filled with pain and loss and death.

His life was changing—had changed—forever. And it was going nowhere good, fast.

Not to mention that his hunger was deepening, worsening. That word summed it up better than any other, he thought. Worsening.

Lately, every person who crossed his path looked more and more like a cheeseburger. More and more like all they were lacking were a side of fries.

It was troubling, to say the least.

Grabbing the lock on his locker, he flipped the center circle around, trying to get the combination to work.

And that's when he sensed . . . something.

Some*one*.

Someone familiar. Someone he would know anywhere, anytime. Someone he hadn't seen or spoken to at all since the day he'd released her as his drudge.

Straightening, he closed his eyes and inhaled, taking in the scent of roses and raspberries and all that was good about being alive. A smile threatened to touch his lips, but he fought it, knowing what it meant that she was here, knowing what he would have to do, and not knowing at all if he had the strength to do it, to push her away again.

Opening his eyes, he sensed her behind him, her delectable blood calling out to him, beckoning him. With a sigh, and without turning to face her, he said, "Snow."

She waited, perhaps wondering how he knew it was her. Finally, unable to resist any longer, Vlad turned slowly.

She was dressed in gothic finery: a long, black, flowing skirt, a black blouse, and a black pin-striped waist cincher. Her eyes were lined with thick black and her lips—her sad, pouting lips—were colored a rich burgundy, a color that instantly reminded him of blood.

Vlad looked her over and fought the longing within him. The longing, he was surprised, wasn't to feed on her—well, not *just* to feed on her, anyway. It was to reach out, to make physical contact, to hold her close. It made him ache to feel such things, to yearn for a girl he couldn't have, wouldn't have. She deserved better. She deserved much better than him.

Her eyes darted to his wrist and then back to his face. She smiled, but it didn't come through honestly enough. She was happy to see him, but miserable at the same time. "Hi."

Vlad swallowed hard. His mouth felt parched. So much so that he was amazed that dust didn't puff out when he spoke. "Hi."

She drew a deep breath. A nervous one. "Listen, Vlad. Before I say anything else to you I have to tell you something. I . . . I told Eddie Poe some things. I didn't mean to. It just . . . kind of happened. And I'm sorry. So sorry. He caught me at a really bad time, and . . . I'm sorry."

A single curse word ripped through his thoughts, but he steadied himself. It wasn't Snow's fault. Eddie was a conniving little worm. And Snow had likely been in an emotionally vulnerable state.

Maybe it was because of him. Because of how he'd left her. Bleeding and broken and confused and alone. In an alley. Near a Dumpster. Like she was trash that he'd just gotten rid of. He was a monster. And he deserved whatever happened to him.

But her dad . . . he was a monster too. Just a different kind of monster.

Vlad dropped his eyes, but just for a moment. His voice quieted to a hush. "It's okay. It's okay, Snow. I know you'd never hurt me on purpose."

At the moment, he didn't care what Eddie Poe knew or how he knew it. He only cared that Snow was here, here in Bathory, and still talking to him after the way he'd treated her. He knew a miracle when he saw one. "What are you doing here, anyway? At Bathory High, I mean."

"I'm living with a foster family here in Bathory now. My dad. He . . . well, it got pretty bad." For the first time, Vlad noticed the bruises on her face and arms, covered with a thin layer of makeup. Makeup that could not hide her pain.

He'd abandoned her to her father, that thing, that beast. He'd walked away and left her alone with someone who hurt her. Vlad's heart raced in anger—anger at her father, anger at himself. "If he hurt you—"

"It doesn't matter. He took a swing and I got sick of his abuse, so I fought back. And I won. I just . . . wanted to let you know I'm here now. In case . . . in case you ever want to talk or something. I should have called before. I should have told you. I just . . . couldn't." Sadness flitted across her face. Her eyes glistened and she turned away.

She was leaving. She was walking away without another word, and Vlad couldn't help but think that she'd been dealing with all of this on her own, that he hadn't been strong enough, man enough to just pick up the phone and call her, to see how she was doing. Sudden worry that she'd never speak to him again filled his heart with dread—terror that this was, somehow, the last moment he'd ever have this chance. His heart raced with panic at the very thought.

She'd taken no more than two steps before Vlad moved forward, catching her gently by the arm, and whispering in her ear. "Do you still feel it, Snow? That connection? Even though you're not my drudge anymore?"

Snow kept her eyes away from his, but Vlad knew she was very aware of his presence, just as he was of hers. A crackle of electricity ran between his fingers and her arm. It was subtle, gentle, but sweet. Finally, she cleared her throat and whispered. "I know I feel something. And I know that nothing you could ever do to me could make me stop feeling it. Not even releasing me as your drudge."

Vlad let go of her arm and ran a hand through his hair, sweeping his thick black bangs from his eyes. "I can't change what happened. Not even if I wanted to. Once a vampire releases a drudge, that's it. It's over."

"That's not what I'm talking about and you know it. Besides, it's not over, Vlad. I can feel it in my blood. I could sense that you were near. We're not even connected anymore and we're . . . connected. You can feel it too. Your eyes give you away."

Her eyes were on him, peering into his with a yearning, a yearning that both enticed and frightened Vlad. He couldn't be with Snow. He was dangerous. He'd hurt her. He knew that much. And maybe, just maybe, he'd hurt her worse than her father ever did.

After a long silence, she moved down the hall. Over her shoulder, she said, "See you around, Vlad."

Your eyes give you away. The words echoed in his mind, bringing him back to Dorian, back to what Dorian had said about the four who were chosen to keep the prophecy. Their eyes all flashed, for some reason. They all flashed odd colors at moments of extreme power. But why?

Great. Just what he needed. As if being completely, totally baffled about his feelings for his former drudge wasn't enough. Let's throw a batch of confusion into the mix.

His locker opened at last. Taped securely to the inside of the door was a digital voice recorder, and a note which read, "Play me."

It was an ominous thing that made Vlad's blood run cold. His stomach flip-flopped for several seconds before he pulled the recorder from the door. After a moment of hesitation, he plugged his earbuds into it and hit play.

At first, he heard static. Then Eddie's voice, eager and falsely kind. "It's okay. Just tell me again what you told me before. For the record."

Then Snow's voice, muffled, cracking, like she'd been crying a lot. "Vladimir Tod. He's a vampire. He feeds on me. I mean, he used to."

The recording stopped and a new one began. This time it was just Eddie's voice, and he was speaking directly to Vlad.

"Like what you hear, Vlad? Yeah, I bet not. There's more. So much more. Meet me tonight at EAT. Ten o'clock. Don't be late. We have to talk. And come alone."

The recording ended and Vlad slipped the buds from his ears with trembling fingers.

Eddie was becoming a problem that needed rectifying once and for all.

14

EATING WITH EDDIE
—OR—
VLAD'S WORST NIGHTMARE

VLAD PASSED THE DOOR OF EAT for the seventh time, muttering his immense displeasure under his breath in a string of obscenities. He had to go in, had no choice but to walk through that door and join Eddie for a late dinner, but he didn't have to like it.

For a brief moment, Vlad wished that someone, some vampire other than himself, some person without a conscience and good morals—someone like D'Ablo, for example—would come along and drain Eddie dry. But deep down, he knew that killing Eddie wouldn't solve his problem. There would always be someone wanting something from him. There would always be an Eddie Poe in his life, in some manner.

After one more pass, Vlad reached for the door handle

and pulled, the smells of delicious human food mixed with the scent of delectable human blood wafting out the door, overwhelming his senses.

It was crazy how hungry he was. Suddenly, he missed Snow—the closeness, the feeding, the kisses—but he pushed it back down, away from his immediate attention. Later, when he was away from Eddie, away from the troubles of his day, he could think about Snow and determine exactly what to do with these feelings he had for her. But for now, he had to focus on Eddie Poe, the boy who could very easily ruin his entire life.

He stepped inside, his heart heavy.

Eddie was sitting in a booth by the window, mulling over a plastic-coated menu, as if this were any other night, as if he weren't a vile, evil little weasel, as if he weren't completely selfish and utterly drunk with power, power which he held over Vlad's every choice. He was dressed in a blue-and-white-striped polo and jeans, his wire-framed glasses slightly crooked, a dimple in one cheek. Vlad had never noticed the dimple before. Nor had he noticed that Eddie was both cruel and calculating, not back in kindergarten, not when they'd started middle school together, not ever . . . at least, not until today. Sure, Eddie had become a bit obsessed with exposing Vlad in recent years, but Vlad never really, not deep down anyway, thought that Eddie was really, truly capable of ruining his life.

Okay, maybe he had, but something about Eddie including

Snow in his sordid plan had seriously upset Vlad. He had no business including her, he had no right to use her pain—pain that Vlad feared he had partly caused—in his twisted plans to hurt Vlad and lift himself into fame's arms.

Vlad approached slowly, deliberately, so as not to startle Eddie. He wanted the little weasel to be calm, to feel like he was in complete control. Midstep Vlad came up with a plan. It was so simple, he didn't know why he hadn't thought of it before. After dinner, he'd follow Eddie home and bite him, making Eddie his drudge. Then he'd order Eddie to stop all of this nonsense. It was brilliant in its simplicity. It couldn't fail.

Feeling a bit more confident about their encounter, Vlad slid into the booth, opposite his nemesis.

Eddie didn't even take his eyes off the menu, a smirk touching his lips. "I think I'll have the meat loaf. What about you?"

Vlad's jaw tensed. It was all he could do not to bite Eddie here and now, and be done with this nightmare. "I'm not hungry."

It was a lie. And the look Eddie flashed him not only said that it was a lie, it also said that Eddie knew he wasn't hungry for anything but blood.

The waitress came by and Eddie ordered the meat loaf with a side of French fries, then took the liberty of ordering Vlad a burger—extra rare—with fries, and two sodas. The two sat quietly waiting for their food. When it arrived after several tense, silent minutes, Vlad pushed the plate away and eyed his stalker down. "Let's get this over with, Eddie. What exactly do you want from me?"

Eddie squirted some ketchup on his fries and popped a really gooey one into his mouth. As he chewed, he smiled and spoke matter-of-factly. "We'll get to that. But we'll start with what I initially wanted, which is, of course, fame. I want to be a somebody Vlad. And you're my road to being somebody. I can expose you, y'know. I have enough evidence to expose you right and proper."

From the leather satchel on the seat beside him, Eddie withdrew a thick manila envelope. He spilled the contents on the table: photographs of Vlad in various vampire poses, small Ziplocs with things like hair and fingernail clippings, Vlad's birth record, and on and on and on. The photographs were the most damning evidence, as were the physical samples—Vlad was pretty certain his DNA wouldn't show up as entirely human. It was troubling to look at. But Eddie was forgetting one important thing. "No one is going to believe you, Eddie. Except maybe one of those rag magazines that people buy at the grocery store just to laugh at."

But Eddie wasn't fazed.

That strange smile remained on his lips.

"You don't listen very well, Vlad. That's what I *wanted*. Past tense. My demands have changed. I want more now. And you're going to give it to me, or else I'll expose you to the world." He reached back into his satchel and pulled out a stack of letters—some from well-respected television producers, some from important, notable university professors—all of which stated that they were very, very interested in seeing any evidence that Eddie might have that another species of mammal exists on earth, one that could lay to rest the story behind the "vampire myth." It was different than his usual threat. This time Eddie had what amounted to evidence, and important people lined up ready to believe him.

He was good. Too good.

Vlad inhaled sharply. Eddie's blood was AB negative. The temptation to forego the whole drudge plan and drain Eddie dry was immediate and intense. But Vlad took a deep breath, released it, and focused on his plan of action. "So what do you want *now*?"

Eddie chewed a bite of meat loaf and swallowed, then washed it down with a drink of his soda. He gathered up his evidence and letters, placing them neatly inside his satchel once again. Then he leaned forward, smiling like they shared a special secret. "I want you to make me a vampire."

Vlad blinked. His chest felt heavy and tight and not at all like it was supposed to. "You . . . what?"

Eddie's smile was confident and calm. He knew he'd surprised Vlad. Eddie, it seemed, knew too much about him these days. "A vampire, Vlad. And if you don't make me a vampire, I'm going to expose you."

A vampire. Vlad had never seen it coming. After everything that Eddie had done to expose him, after all of the evidence he had, he was willing to forego his chance at popularity for the act of transforming into a bloodthirsty creature of the night. Vlad shook his head in utter disbelief. "Why would you want to be a vampire, Eddie? Trust me, it won't make your life any easier. Now, do me—do *both* of us—a favor and forget about all of this. And stay away from Snow."

Eddie shook his head. "Not on your life, sport. Snow is my key to becoming a vampire. After all, I know how to get to her. So you'll do as I say, or Snow will have an unfortunate accident."

Who did this guy think he was—the Godfather?

Vlad growled, "What makes you think I won't just kill you?"

A smirk touched Eddie's lips. He met Vlad's gaze and said, "Frankly . . . I don't think you have it in you."

Anger and indignation welled up in Vlad. Here he sat—a vampire, for crying out loud—and even a little weasel like Eddie couldn't respect that, couldn't fear the possibility that Vlad was capable of killing him.

Carefully looking around to make sure no one was watching, Vlad let his fangs elongate. He snapped at Eddie, "I could kill you right now."

Eddie leaned forward, a serious, dark dare in his eyes. "So do it."

A long silence passed, and slowly, Vlad's fangs shrank back inside his gums. Because the truth of it all was something that Eddie had no way of really knowing: Vlad couldn't kill Eddie, because he knew it was wrong.

Eddie popped a fry into his mouth and chewed. He didn't bother to swallow before he started talking again. "I'll give you five months. That gives me time to put my affairs in order, say goodbye to this life, and it gives you time to decide.

Come Valentine's Day, you're going to decide what you want least—to create a fellow creature of the night, or to expose yourself and all of Elysia."

Elysia? Vlad started. Eddie really did know what he was talking about. But how?

"Besides," Eddie continued, "I've never had a good Valentine's Day. Not once. It's about time I did, and this one will totally take the cake."

Vlad sat in silence as Eddie finished his meal, so relieved that all of this wasn't an issue, that he had the solution right there in his mouth, hiding inside his gums. One bite. That's all it would take.

The bill came and Eddie slapped some money down on the table. As they stood, Eddie threw Vlad another smile. "Oh, and if you're thinking of making me your human slave—like Henry—you can forget it. I've been taking garlic supplements every day for over a year now. I'm willing to bet my blood would make you pretty sick, maybe even kill you. So I wouldn't try it if I were you. But don't worry . . . by Valentine's Day, I'll be all sorts of tasty again. And don't even think about making me your drudge then, either. I have a friend on the lookout for any signs that you made me your slave, and I've instructed him to move forward with the exposure plan if that should happen."

Vlad doubted very much that Eddie had any friends at all, but it did give him pause.

Eddie walked out the door and Vlad swore loudly, attracting the eyes of everyone in the small diner. He slid quickly from the booth and followed Eddie out the door, stopping him on the sidewalk with his words, words that left his mouth in angry tones. "Eddie, you don't want this. I know it sounds glamorous and amazing, but being a vampire isn't anything like Hollywood paints it. It's gruesome and lonely and at times, pretty horrible. It's like being a regular teenager, only worse. It's the last thing I'd wish on anybody."

Eddie sighed, turning back to face him. "You can float, Vlad. And you can move inhumanly fast. You're incredibly strong and can outlive any human. Why wouldn't I want it? Drinking blood I can deal with, and being alone I'm used to. Besides, I won't be alone. I'll have my maker to keep me company."

Vlad's fangs slid from his gums, as if coaxing him to take the risk, to bite Eddie and drain him dry, and deal with the possible consequences of ingesting garlic. His heart thumped steadily against his ribs in anticipation.

But Vlad remained still.

He had five months to either change Eddie's mind or come up with a plan. Five months.

Of course, if the Slayers or Em had their way, none of this would even matter.

"Eddie," he growled.

Eddie raised his eyebrows expectantly.

Vlad nodded at him. "Watch yourself. I'd hate for anything bad to happen to you."

Eddie chuckled before turning to leave. "You're full of crap, Vlad. I like that about you."

As Vlad watched him disappear down the sidewalk, the center of his chest ached, like it was full of poison. In a way, it was. It was filled to the brim with hatred.

Hatred for a boy that Vlad had once felt sorry for.

15
KRISTOFF'S REVENGE

VLAD WAS HALFWAY ACROSS THE PARKING LOT when Henry said something that made Vlad's eyes roll back in his head.

"You're acting so bizarre lately."

Vlad turned back to his friend with disbelieving eyes. "Are you serious? You're the one acting weird. You're actually willingly walking into The Crypt with me. Not to mention that this whole thing was your idea. So what's up with that?"

Henry shrugged. "I just meant that you've been oddly mellow lately. I expected more from you, what with your dad still being alive, your life being threatened at every turn, Eddie getting more aggressive, and Snow now going to Bathory High."

Vlad shook his head, determined not to let Henry change

the subject. "Why did you bring me here, Henry? Why are we at The Crypt?"

Henry grew quiet, then shrugged again. "It's nothing. I just wanted to bring this CD I burned to October. I forgot to give it to her at lunch."

As Henry moved forward, toward the club's front door, Vlad's footfalls slowed, his jaw dropping open just as slowly as his feet were moving. Then, as Henry opened the door, Vlad picked up the pace again. "A mix tape?! You made her a mix tape?!"

The door closed and Vlad shook his head in utter shock. Something told him there was more to Henry and October now than he'd realized.

He wasn't sure how he felt about the idea that maybe his very different friends were into one another. On one hand, he cared deeply about both of them and wanted them to be happy. On the other hand, Henry McMillan didn't exactly have a great history with girls. This was the guy who used to make it his goal to kiss a different girl every week. Then he started dating Melissa and went completely the opposite way, becoming totally and completely, almost scarily, devoted to one girl. If Henry had any kind of balance at all, he'd wish them luck. But he worried about Henry. And he worried about October. He'd never known her to have a boyfriend, and he couldn't imagine her hanging out with a guy who shopped at stores in the mall that she sneered at as she walked by.

The whole thing was very, very weird.

But . . . it was only a CD. Maybe it meant nothing.

Or maybe it meant everything.

Either way, there was really nothing he could do about it.

Vlad released a deep breath and pulled open the door.

He descended the sloped ramp into the club, and was greeted by the familiar thump of music that made him feel alive and a crowd of people he felt truly at home with. The lights were low, as usual, and the place was packed. On the dance floor, Henry was handing October her new CD. She threw her arms around his neck and hugged him. Vlad sighed and leaned back against the wall, thumping his head against the drywall in frustration and closing his eyes, waiting for a solution to present itself.

It didn't.

But something else did.

Immense and immediate pain ripped through Vlad's face. His nose made a crunching sound as someone's fist pounded into it—one hit, but hard enough to count as four. Blood sprayed from his nose and hot white pain shot through his entire skull. He ducked, crouching, shaken and worried that his attacker would punch again. Daring a glance up at whoever had hit him, Vlad was actually surprised to see a very furious Kristoff standing over him, Vlad's blood in his hair, Vlad's blood on his fist. Kristoff's eyes were cold and calculating, and Vlad bet that if he didn't get out of this fast, Kristoff was going to do his best to hospitalize him.

And without exposing himself as a vampire, Vlad was definitely in danger of that.

Of course, he'd heal fast. But getting beaten up didn't feel good in the least.

Kristoff's bloody fist was held at the ready as he growled at Vlad, who'd slid to the floor, his head and face pounding, his nose feeling like a big balloon. "You hurt Snow, so I hurt you. She doesn't come here anymore, all because of you. And now October is hanging out with Henry McMillan. Henry McMillan, of all people! And you brought him here. You've ruined everything about The Crypt. You've ruined everything I love."

He raised his fist again, murderous intent in his eyes. "And now I'm gonna ruin you."

Behind closed lips, Vlad's fangs shot from his gums. He wasn't sure if it was in reaction to the smell of blood—his own blood, even—or a defensive maneuver. He only knew that the smell was too much for him to bear. He was hungry, so hungry, and surrounded by the very thing his body had been screaming for.

Sustenance.

Humans.

Vlad's world spun, swirling before him like water down a drain. Then he was captured by a vision. A vision of Kristoff running across the football field of Bathory High.

It was insane. Kristoff—once David—running on a football field? Vlad had never known him to enjoy sports before, but yet there he was, his silver hair blowing in the wind, his eyes wide and alive. His feet falling solidly in a sprint.

Right on his heels was Eddie Poe. Little Eddie Poe.

Eddie was grinning, and Vlad gasped at what he saw in that grin.

Fangs.

Vampire fangs.

Vlad pulled from the vision with a shocked gasp to see Henry grabbing Kristoff's arm, his voice a low growl. "You do, you die."

The two eyeballed one another for a moment, before Kristoff finally yanked his arm away and crossed the room to the velvet couches there. The crowd that had gathered to witness the exchange dispersed and Henry helped Vlad to his feet.

Vlad's eyes were locked on Kristoff. He grabbed Henry by the sleeve, his breaths coming quick and shallow. "We have to help him, Henry. We have to protect him."

"Who?" Henry looked around, completely lost.

Vlad nodded toward the velvet couches, where Kristoff was being pampered by several goth girls. "Kristoff. We have to save him."

Henry narrowed his eyes. He didn't seem the least bit concerned about the guy who had just punched his best friend in the face. He did, however, seem a little surprised at Vlad's concern. "From who? Or what?"

Vlad's headache subsided as his nose healed, but it was

replaced by another pain—the pain of knowing what was to come. "From Eddie Poe. Eddie's going to become a vampire and go after Kristoff."

Henry's eyes grew wide. He darted glances between Vlad and Kristoff. "How can you know that?"

"Because . . ." Vlad's voice dropped to a horrified whisper. The knowledge of what he was about to say was crushing him from the inside. "I'm going to make him one."

16
STRENGTH

VLAD SLUNG HIS BACKPACK OVER HIS SHOULDER and had just opened the door when his dad stopped him. "Vladimir . . . a word, if you will."

He already knew what his dad was going to ask. It was the same thing he'd asked every day since he'd been home, and recently, his tone had changed to one of desperation. Vlad got how important it was that they find the journal. He'd been looking everywhere, short of shaking it from Joss's person.

"I haven't found it yet, Dad. Any luck?"

Tomas shook his head. "I fear we may have to search the Slayer's home."

Vlad winced, the idea not sitting right with him at all. He hadn't asked Joss for the journal yet. Mostly because he still wasn't certain he could trust Joss a hundred percent. Plus, he was hoping he'd find it elsewhere, hoping like hell that he'd imagined it sticking out of Joss's backpack that night in the clearing. He'd even asked Henry to poke around a bit, to see if he could find it at Joss's house. But Henry's search had turned up nothing.

"You do realize how important it is that we find my journal, yes? It could save us both, Vlad."

Vlad sighed. "I know. Just . . . just let me try a few more spots before we go raiding Joss's bedroom, okay?"

After a long moment, Tomas nodded, and Vlad headed toward the door. When his fingers brushed the knob, Vlad turned back to his father. "I'm still not entirely sure why we're looking for the journal. Exactly how will it help us stop Em and the trial?"

His dad lowered his voice, as if he was sharing a great secret with Vlad. "The journal was written on pages of very old text—text that can only be revealed by being exposed to blood or fire."

Vlad thought back to Diablo and his ritual. He'd smeared the backs of some pages with blood and words had been revealed.

"I believe the details of a special ritual are contained within the pages. If we apply fire to those pages, I believe we will uncover exactly how to stop Em and all who might oppose us." Tomas folded his arms in front of him, raising a stark eyebrow. "But first we must find the journal."

Vlad nodded and made his way out the door. If what his dad said was right, it could mean the end to all of their problems. He and his dad could live out their days a happy family once more. They could stop Em, even stop the Slayer Society, and all would be well. They just needed that journal.

The entire walk to school was a fog, his thoughts focused on the journal and where it might be. He knew it was likely in Joss's possession. After all, the last he'd seen of it, it had been in his backpack. But Vlad still didn't feel right about breaking into Joss's home. It felt dirty. It felt wrong.

As Vlad reached the school, his eyes were drawn to the sight of two very familiar girls, arguing at the top of the steps of Bathory High.

One in pink. The other in black.

Meredith and Snow.

Meredith had her nose scrunched, as if something didn't smell very good. Behind her stood Melissa Hart and a handful of other semipopular girls whose names had slipped Vlad's memory. "Oh please. Just look at what you're wearing!"

Snow shook her head, calm, cool, collected. "I refuse to accept fashion advice from someone whose closet looks like Pepto-Bismol."

"I'm just saying that Vlad's behavior is pretty unpredictable. Maybe you should leave him alone. I mean, you don't even know him."

"I know him better than anyone at this school." Snow glanced across the parking lot at Henry's car, which was just pulling in. Vlad was suddenly glad he hadn't bothered to wait for his best friend. This exchange was far more entertaining than anything on the radio. "Except for Henry, I mean."

Neither girl had noticed Vlad. And Vlad liked it that way.

Meredith tossed her chocolate curls over her shoulder, her tone superior. "Face it. He'll never go out with you, Snow."

Snow stepped toward her then, and Meredith stepped back. Snow's words were a hiss. "You face it, princess. I don't need a boy crushing on me in order to feel good about myself. If Vlad doesn't date me, that's fine. If he does, great. But I'm not going to base my entire sense of self-esteem on whether or not I have a date to the prom."

Meredith snorted. "I honestly don't know what he sees in you."

"Maybe it's my charming sense of humor and ability to put up with crap from his ex-girlfriend." With that, Snow opened the door and slipped inside.

And Vlad was left with something he'd never realized before.

Meredith didn't know him at all. If she couldn't see why he liked Snow, she had no idea who he even was.

Slowly, he made his way up the steps, toward her. When he stopped in front of Meredith, Melissa and the other girls flashed her knowing smiles before disappearing inside. Meredith brightened at the sight of him. "Morning, Vlad. How are you?"

"Strength."

She blinked, the smile slipping from her face. "What?"

"Strength, Meredith. That's what I see in Snow. Her amazing strength." He held her gaze, his lips pursed.

Meredith shook her head. "I just want you to be happy."

Vlad turned and opened the door. As he looked back at Meredith—at the girl he thought he loved before he knew what love was, he shook his head. "I am happy . . . with Snow."

17
The Hunger

VLAD ROLLED OVER IN BED, trying to ignore his aching stomach and failing miserably. He'd already downed three blood bags on his way up to his room, and then later snuck downstairs and downed three more. But his appetite wasn't satiated by the donated blood. It tasted still, stagnant, lifeless on his tongue. He wanted more.

Needed more.

He slipped from his bed and down the stairs, still dressed, as if he knew he'd be taking a walk later, and put his shoes on in the dark. As he descended the stairs, he heard his dad snoring quietly on the couch.

He moved down the steps and out the front door without making a sound, then headed up the street toward the park. What Vlad needed was a good, long walk, and then, once he'd exhausted himself, he'd fall back in bed, too tired to even think about how hungry he was.

A scent was on the air—one of adrenaline and spirit and blood. Vlad followed that scent into the park and, standing in the shadows, watched a woman making her laps around the track.

She was running at a steady clip, though Vlad had no idea why she thought it was a good idea to exercise in the middle of the night—even in this town. Her footfalls slapped the pavement in a rhythm that matched closely the rhythm of her heart. Vlad watched her as she rounded the bend, heading straight for him now. He stepped backward, deeper into the shadows.

He didn't know what he planned to do. He only knew that she wouldn't see it coming, that she would be the end to a means, that his terrible thirst, his unbearable hunger would be satiated at last.

He licked his lips as she approached, and just as she stepped within a few feet of him, Vlad looked at her, really looked at her.

She was a person.

A real, live person. With a family. With friends.

What was he thinking?

Her steps slowed as she caught sight of him. Her eyes widened in surprised fear. Alarm shot through her veins, both shaking Vlad and filling him with disgust. Disgust with himself for what he'd been about to do.

He forced a smile and said, "You should be careful out here. Bathory's not as safe as you might think. Have a good night."

Then he did what had seemed impossible only seconds before.

He turned around and walked away, his stomach rumbling in protest.

"Vladimir Tod?"

A word, four letters, shocked and foul, crossed his lips as he turned back to face the woman.

He wasn't at all surprised to see her pulling a silver-tipped stake from the holster on her thigh. But he was surprised to see her whip into action and run straight for him without so much as a blink.

She raised the stake, and Vlad looked up at it, hating that stupid piece of wood, that thing that had caused him so much stress. It was a symbol, the stake. And to Vlad it was a symbol of hatred, of absolute refusal of peace.

It was also a distraction technique, because as Vlad was watching the stake, thinking quickly of a plan of defense, the Slayer woman whipped around, sweeping Vlad's legs with a kick. Vlad fell backward, but caught his balance just before he fell. As he stumbled, she brought the stake forward. Vlad reached up in a blink, gripping her wrist, eyeing her down.

He could snap it. Snap the bone and cause her real pain. He knew it and, more importantly, she knew it too. But she still wouldn't stop, and her eyes slanted into a defying glare.

Vlad weighed his options—fight or flight—and in the end, he pushed her backward several yards, releasing her without harm, and turned to leave. It was over. Vlad didn't want to fight. There would, if he and Joss didn't come up with a solid plan of action, come a time when he would have to face the Slayer Society. But not now. Not if he had anything to say about it.

His stomach rumbled its protests. The woman's veins were full of a delectable B negative, and it was calling out to him, taunting his thirst.

Behind him, he heard the woman's feet running softly over the ground. She was coming at him again. She would not stop, would never stop. And as she got closer, the monster inside of him screamed with hungry delight. Fresh blood, enough to satiate his immense hunger, and it was being delivered to him by someone who probably deserved to be bitten.

A sudden jolt went through Vlad. The realization of what he was thinking, of what he was about to allow himself to do.

Pushing the monster back deep down inside, and without putting a conscious effort into his actions at all, Vlad moved. Fast. In blinding speed, he turned and approached the Slayer, spinning around, lifting his leg chest high. He kicked the Slayer back, sending her flying from him. He had time enough to notice that she was still gripping the stake when she hit the large oak across the park with full force.

She crumpled to the ground, unconscious and unbitten.

Another four letter word—a different one this time—

crossed Vlad's lips, but for a different reason. Because not only was Joss right about Slayers heading to Bathory ...

... they looked like regular people, which would make them impossible to pick out of a crowd. They could hide out in the open. And there would be a lot of them.

18
Echoes from the Past

VLAD WAS SITTING ON NELLY'S BACK STEP, listening to the sounds of night around him, punishing himself for having even considered feeding from the source. Forcibly. Without consent.

There was something wrong with him.

Yeah, said that other voice—the one that only spoke when he was feeling ravenous—*something* was *wrong, and that something was that he was hungry. He was a hungry vampire. What else did he expect?*

A little self-control. That's for sure.

But he wasn't just beating himself up over considering drinking from that Slayer woman in the park—or even over attacking her and knocking her unconscious. He was also waiting. Waiting for answers.

After he'd left the park, he'd returned to Nelly's house. And as he'd placed his shoes inside the coat closet, he couldn't help but notice something wrapped up in a plastic bag and tucked in the very back of the closet. Curiosity had gotten the better of him, and he'd peered inside the bag. What he found had shaken his world and brought a flood of questions to the tip of his tongue. Questions that only Otis could answer.

He'd paced the kitchen for almost an hour, his thoughts flitting from one strange equation to another, with nothing adding up in Otis's favor. At last, with a deep breath, he walked out the back door, sat down on the step, and reached out with telepathy to his uncle. *"Otis, are you sleeping?"*

Moments later, Otis creaked open the back door and poked his head out. "What's the matter, Vladimir, couldn't sleep?"

He patted the step beside him. "Have a seat, Uncle Otis. There are some things I need to talk to you about."

Otis nodded, the smile slipping from his face, as if he knew this were coming. He took a seat beside Vlad and they watched the night for a while. The stars were bright and shining, and the sky was so full of them that it almost seemed like there were too many stars in the sky, too much brightness in the world when Vlad's thoughts were so dark and shadowed. Vlad glanced at his uncle and said, "I was attacked by a Slayer tonight."

He could see Otis visibly tense, but his uncle's tone remained as calm as could be. "Are you all right?"

Vlad nodded. He decided not to mention how close he'd come to draining the woman dry. There were, of course, far more important things to discuss. Things that had been plaguing Vlad ever since he'd opened the bag at the back of the coat closet. "Uncle Otis . . . I've been doing a lot of thinking. And some things you've told me over the years don't quite add up."

His uncle didn't respond, merely folded his hands together and kept his eyes on the ground in front of him. It seemed to Vlad an act of contrition, like he were guilty of just about anything Vlad would accuse him of, and was a little bit relieved that he'd been found out.

Taking a deep breath, Vlad continued. "A few years ago, you told me that my dad had been a vampire for a hundred years before you made the change. Then a couple years later, you gave me a letter describing the day you were turned. You made it sound like you were both turned into vampires that day."

Otis was very still, as if waiting for Vlad to force him to speak.

Vlad raised an eyebrow at his uncle. "So which story's true?"

At first, Otis said nothing. But then he spoke—his voice hushed and raspy—and Vlad knew that Otis felt badly. About what, he had no idea. "Both, Vladimir. Both stories are true. But that doesn't mean I should have shared either with you."

"How can they both be true?"

"Tomas was made a vampire one hundred years before I was taken to the Bastille. At the time, I thought he was also human—I didn't believe in such things as vampires back then. Like most humans, I was blissfully unaware of what lurks in the shadows of the night. Like most humans, I was a fool." He swallowed hard then and, gathering his thoughts, said, "Your grandfather, Ignatius, was a cunning man, but he was also cruel. He'd made Tomas a vampire and used him as his slave, you see. Tomas was miserable, and so alone. He's suffered, Vladimir. Your father has suffered more than anyone I've ever known."

Vlad took it all in, but was still left with a question poised on the tip of his tongue. "What happened? What happened exactly that day in the Bastille?"

"There is a law in Elysia. We can only change willing humans into vampires. It was a law created to limit the vampire population. A strange law, considering a vampire would have to reveal himself in order to gain permission." He shook his head, as did Vlad, both marveling over the many inconsistencies in Elysian law. "Ignatius had arranged for my and Tomas's imprisonment. I lived what I thought were my final days in that cell, with only the company of the man who would become your father. I thought I was doomed, Vladimir, and in the end I made a choice."

A sinking feeling entered Vlad's chest. His dad had lied. His dad had tricked Otis into becoming a vampire.

Otis shook his head. "Don't think poorly of him. It was my choice to make and I don't regret it at all. Ignatius—your grandfather—was a horrible man, and though Tomas had initially resisted his devious plan to gain my permission, he soon realized that while he might not have been strong enough to escape Ignatius alone, he might be strong enough with a brother there to back him up. He would be free, finally, of a tyrannical father, of the man who planned to enslave us both."

"The way it's been told to me, after I turned, Tomas attacked Ignatius, calling to me to assist and I did. Even then we were inseparable, you see. We fought, but I have no memory of it. Ignatius had wounded me—a fledgling, just a babe, not at all capable of facing a vampire as old or as strong as Ignatius—so terribly that I almost perished. But Tomas fended our father off and took me to Siberia, where Vikas tended to my wounds."

Otis's eyes were wide and sad. A tiny muscle in his jaw twitched as he turned to face Vlad. "So yes, both stories are correct. But if you hold any ill will at all against your father, I shall never forgive myself for telling these tales to you. He is a good man. I owe him my life."

Vlad opened his mouth. He was about to say that he couldn't possibly be angry at his dad for having followed the whims of his insane creator. His dad had been afraid, and besides, the entire act had given Vlad Otis. And that wasn't anything he regretted at all.

But then the sound of raised voices edged its way around the corner of the house. Vlad and Otis exchanged glances, then moved wordlessly around to the front of the house to see what was going on.

What they saw had Vlad's jaw on the floor.

Enrico was standing in the street, merely feet from Tomas—his eyes wide with lunacy, a sword in his hand. His fangs were bared, despite the fact that they were in public, where any human might see them.

They were arguing in Elysian code. Unable to understand the language in its spoken form, Vlad glanced at Otis, hoping he'd translate. But Otis had set his jaw and stepped forward, interrupting. "Gentleman, this conversation was unavoidable, but must it take place where any human can peer out their window and witness? Yes, Enrico, your beloved son has perished. But it was at the hand of a Slayer, and due to his own actions. You cannot blame Tomas for that."

"I don't, Otis. I don't blame him." Enrico shook his head, and then cast a cold glance on Vlad. "I blame his son."

Then something happened that made Vlad realize that he was probably the only vampire there that hadn't been aware of what was really going on, what Otis and Tomas were really trying to prevent.

Enrico moved behind Vlad with lightning fast speed, pressing the sharp blade to his throat. One small move and he would be beheaded.

The blade was cold and the cold was only warmed by the slight trickle of blood down Vlad's neck as Enrico pressed the sword into him in a warning to Tomas and Otis. "One move and I'll decapitate him. You both know I will."

Enrico was crying. Vlad could hear it in his voice, feel it against his cheek. Then he whispered, "I have to do this, Vlad·

imir. I am sorry, but my son . . . my son was everything to me. Without him, I cannot go on."

Raising his voice he cried out into the night, "I want justice!"

Then he whispered it again into Vlad's hair, all sense of reason gone. "I want justice."

Tomas didn't step forward—in fact, both he and Otis seemed frozen to the spot—but he did raise a sharp eyebrow at Enrico. "If it's justice that you want, I suggest you seek it in the blood of the Slayer Society."

Vlad swallowed hard, then winced as the blade sank into his skin a bit deeper. He hoped like hell his dad had some idea of what he was doing. Turning his head slightly, he looked at Enrico. "Please, Enrico. It wasn't me. I . . . I loved Dorian. He was a good friend to me. I cried when he was killed."

Enrico's crazy, metallic laughter filled the air. Vlad could hear the madness on its edges. Apparently, he really had lost his mind. Vlad's fingers trembled, giving his whole body a cue to shake in fear as well.

Crazy vampires were terrifying, and more dangerous than he ever wanted to witness.

Enrico's laughter died down at last. "You cried. You cried when my Dorian was taken from me. But did you tell me when I came to see you that day with Em? Or did I have to learn of my son's demise—his *murder*—" Enrico gripped a handful of Vlad's hair, "—through a casual conversation with Cratus?"

Otis took a bold step forward. In response, Enrico tightened his hold on Vlad's hair and yanked it back, exposing his bleeding neck. It was a wordless warning: stay back, or I'll kill him faster. Then Enrico loosened his grip some and said, "My pain is immeasurable, and without you, Vladimir, this pain would not be."

Vlad swooned. His world became a blending of colors and sound. Just when he thought he might black out, everything came into focus again.

He was seeing clearly. He knew what he had to do.

Vlad reached up with his right hand and gripped Enrico's wrist. The moment his thumb brushed Enrico's Mark, a surge of power shot through Vlad, the power of the Pravus. After all, a Mark was merely a glyph by another name, and glyphs had a tendency to heighten and unleash Vlad's Pravus gifts.

At least, that was a theory. Every time he touched a glyph, his eyes glowed. Every time he touched a glyph, he felt more powerful than he had before. So, it was a theory. But one he was willing to bet on.

Vlad focused on his hand, willing it to become hot—hotter than ever before. The glow from the Mark traveled down Enrico's arm, until it enveloped the blade with a heat that even Enrico could not withstand. He cried out, dropping the sword.

And Vlad was free.

The sword was no longer pressed against his throat. Enrico was no longer standing behind him, holding him prisoner.

Enrico was no longer standing, period. The moment his weapon had fallen, Tomas and Otis were on him, pinning him to the ground. Once Enrico was under control, Tomas stood again and moved toward Vlad, but cautiously, as if Vlad might cause him harm if he moved too quickly. He plucked Enrico's sword from the ground and turned it over in his hands, then met Otis's eyes. "It seems there may be something to this Pravus prophecy after all."

19
THE TRUTH HURTS

VLAD WAS SITTING ON THE COUCH, staring at the floor
between his feet, wondering if his family, the closest vampires to him, were ever going to shut up and explain to him
exactly what had just happened.

Because Vlad knew but couldn't understand. And it scared
the hell out of him.

His hands were shaking.

Once Tomas had collected the sword, Otis tapped into Enrico's mind, calming him, soothing his tortured thoughts with
mind control, putting him to sleep for the time being. Vlad's
dad then placed a call to Enrico's brother, who promised to
come collect him immediately. Then he and Otis had ushered
Vlad silently across town, not wanting to wake Nelly, wanting
to be alone to discuss whatever it was that had occurred. And
that meant going to the house on Lugosi Trail, where Vikas

was waiting. Where Vlad was now sitting, waiting for answers.

He only wished they would stop arguing already and get on with their explanation.

"What other explanation is there for the things that Vlad is capable of, Otis?" His dad sounded completely aggravated, frustrated with Otis's stubbornness.

"What is he capable of? No more than any other vampire, Tomas. Vladimir is as normal as they come." Otis was trying his absolute hardest to remain calm, to keep any twinge of tension from his voice, but his tone was slipping.

Tomas looked as if his brother had just slapped him. "You can't be serious. What about his speed? What about his unconscious control? His vampire detection? His mind control? From what Vikas tells me, Vlad is skilled beyond any of us."

Otis shook his head. He looked frazzled, desperate. "You'd like to think that, Tomas, but I assure you, Vlad is an ordinary creature of the night. He is nothing at all like the so-called prophecy describes."

"What about his eyes, Otis?" Tomas had leaned forward, meeting his brother's gaze. Otis winced, as if not wanting to be reminded. Tomas's voice was calm, collected, kind, but insistent. "They flash iridescent purple at the oddest times. Much like Dorian's eyes used to flash iridescent blue."

Vlad's voice came out scratchy and rough. "What happened to me?"

As if noticing him for the first time, all eyes fell on Vlad.

"What happened to me just now? And what happened to Enrico? Did I actually burn him just by thinking about it?"

His heart had sank into his stomach. He had a horrible feeling that he'd injured Enrico somehow.

Tomas and Otis exchanged glances, but it was Vikas who decided to reply. "You don't know how you burned Enrico, Mahlyenki Dyavol?"

Vlad swallowed hard, shaking his head. "Not . . . not really. I wanted to stop him. And then the sword grew hot. It was like I willed it to happen, and then it happened."

Otis took a seat beside him, and sat quietly for a moment before he spoke, his voice soft and full of shock. "It was amazing. You forced him to drop the weapon without seriously injuring or killing him. But what stunned me most were your eyes. So bright purple, but that was almost drowned out by the shimmer overlaying it. An iridescent glow that reeked of power."

Tomas had been eyeing Otis the entire time that he was speaking. At last, he said, "My son is the Pravus, Otis. You cannot deny what you have seen."

Otis flung an arm up in aggravation. "Preposterous! There is no such thing. It's drivel. All of it! There's a sound explanation for his eyes changing and for what he did to Enrico. There has to be!"

Vikas shook his head. "My friend, even I am at a loss to explain what I have seen this boy accomplish. Perhaps there is more to this so-called prophecy than we realize. Perhaps Vladimir is this Pravus of which the stories speak."

The color drained from Otis's face. "It's just a story. And if it were true, Vladimir would be evil incarnate. I refuse to believe such things about my own nephew. I cannot. I will not."

Tomas's voice grew softer. "Nothing says the Pravus will be evil, Otis."

"It is said that the Pravus will come to rule over vampire-kind and enslave the human race. How can that be interpreted as anything but evil?" Otis's entire body seemed tense. Every muscle was tight, every nerve on alert. He was deep in denial and ready to defend his cause.

"Dorian said that I will enslave the human race out of charity." Everyone grew silent for a moment as Vlad spoke. He stood and moved in front of Otis, meeting his gaze and refusing to stand down. He kept his voice calm, subdued, but certain. "I am the Pravus, Otis. Even I can't deny it anymore. You have to believe me, though, I'm not evil. But I am the Pravus."

Otis's face went from white to bright red in a manner of seconds. He flicked his eyes from his nephew to his brother to his friend and back to Vlad again. As Otis opened the door, he paused, his face returning to that same ghostly pale. He shook his head and looked back at Vlad. "Good night, nephew."

Something about the tone in his voice created a knot in Vlad's stomach. As did the fact that Vlad hadn't gotten a chance to ask Otis about what he'd found in the closet.

20
LIFE'S LITTLE SURPRISES

VLAD ROLLED OUT OF BED, scratching his head and yawn-
ing as he made his way downstairs. The sun was just
barely peeking in through the windows, and the house was
eerily quiet. As he hit the bottom step, the front door opened
to reveal Otis. His shirt was covered in dried blood, his eyes
wide and surprised to see Vlad. He seemed to gauge Vlad for
a moment before speaking. "You're up early. I thought you'd
still be sleeping."

Vlad shrugged. "Nightmares. Had a hard time sleeping.
Were you out feeding all night?"

"Feeding?" Otis raised an eyebrow, then a look of realization crossed his face. "Ah yes . . . of course. I was . . . famished.
Stress does that to me."

Otis unbuttoned his blood-soaked shirt and tossed it in
the bathroom hamper, then grabbed a black T-shirt from a

nearby clothes basket and slipped it on. He didn't speak.

He was wearing a T-shirt, which Vlad had never seen him do before.

Once Otis was dressed again, he moved to the kitchen and filled a coffee mug with blood. He moved as if his mind were completely somewhere else, focused on things that were more important than his day-to-day tasks. After he set the mug inside the microwave, Vlad said, "I thought you were out feeding all night."

Otis nodded. "I was."

Vlad looked from his uncle to the microwave with a perplexed glance. "Then what's with the mug of blood?"

Otis furrowed his brow and snapped, "Not everything I do must meet with your approval, Vladimir."

The room grew very quiet, only filling with sound as the microwave beeped. Otis collected it and sat at the table, sipping quietly and reading the morning paper. Vlad watched him for a moment, wondering exactly what Otis had been up to. His uncle had only snapped at him on rare occasions, but something about this time was different. Otis seemed distant, lost in thought.

It bothered Vlad.

Vlad turned without another word and headed for the living room, content to waste the morning away with a game of *Race to Armageddon: The Final Ascent*. His dad was lying on the couch, eyes closed, sleeping soundly.

His hair was the same black as Vlad's. His mouth was the same shape.

Ten years flash through Vlad's mind. Years with his parents, years with his dad.

In his wildest dreams, he never imagined it was possible that his father was still alive. And even if he had, he never would have imagined their reunion to be filled with so much tension, so much uncertainty.

Deciding that video games could wait, he moved back to the kitchen and took a seat opposite Otis at the long plank table. Maybe Otis didn't want to talk, but Vlad did. "It's strange, isn't it? Having my dad back, I mean. Just when I think I'm used to it, I get weirded out again."

Otis's hands on the paper tensed, his fingers curled. He picked up his mug and sipped, his eyes on the paper. Not reading, just pointedly not looking at Vlad. "Yes. It's very strange."

"You seem to be getting along pretty okay now."

Otis grunted in response.

Vlad chewed his bottom lip for a moment before speaking. "Do you believe his excuse for not being around? That he was trying to protect me?"

"I told you years before and I reiterate, Vladimir. Trust no one." A dark shadow crossed Otis's eyes. His voice quieted until it was just above a whisper. "Not even me."

Vlad looked at him and said aloud what he'd been wondering since he saw Otis's bloody shirt. Otis, who wasn't a sloppy eater at all. Covered in blood. "Where exactly were you last night, Otis? What exactly were you doing?"

Vlad's questions hung in the air between them, and Vlad

couldn't recall a time before when he had ever felt such a distance between his uncle and himself. Otis felt far away, almost unreachable, and he wasn't sure why.

"I was taking care of some things." Otis drained his mug and set it on the table, licking his lips absently. "By the way, I have news. News you should be told. Enrico is dead."

Vlad's jaw dropped. His heart slammed against his chest once, then went still. "What?"

The phone rang. Once. Twice. Vlad barely heard it.

Dead? Enrico was dead? The vampire that had been a warm friend, and Dorian's maker, Otis's friend, owner of V Bar . . . was *dead*? It wasn't possible. He just saw Enrico last night.

Three rings. Four.

Otis's voice was gravelly. "You'd better answer that. It's your drudge."

Reluctantly, Vlad stood and picked up the receiver. "Hey, can I call you back? I'm—"

"Real quick. *The Mopey Teenage Bears* are doing a surprise concert in Stokerton tonight. I've heard at one point they light the edge of the stage on fire, and the lead singer dives into the crowd. It's gonna be epic, dude. And did I mention the backstage meet and greet? Greg hooked me up with two tickets. You in?" Henry's voice was full of joy—in exact contrast to the vibe in Vlad's kitchen at the moment.

Vlad blinked, his world tipping. Dead. Enrico was dead. "What? I—no. I can't. Something's come up. I kinda need to talk to you about it. But later, okay?"

Henry's tone immediately shifted to one of loyal concern. "What happened, man? You okay?"

Sighing, Vlad said, "Yeah. I guess. I'll fill you in later. Have fun at the concert."

"You sure?"

"Totally. But come over after and I'll catch you up on the utter hell that is my life."

"Okay. Hey . . . maybe I'll ask October . . ."

Shaking his head, Vlad hung the phone up as quickly as he could and turned back to his uncle. "What happened to Enrico?"

But Otis was gone.

21
A SLAYER'S DETERMINATION

PLEASE."

The word escaped Joss's lips before he had time to think about how the Society would view it. "Please" wasn't in their vocabulary. "Please" was an admission of weakness.

But it was too late now. He'd said it, and they'd heard it.

Softly, quietly, so that his parents wouldn't overhear his telephone conversation from downstairs, Joss whispered, "No one has to die. The citizens of Bathory are innocent."

"Someone must die, Slayer." He knew that voice. It was the voice of Bradford, the voice of the Slayer Society's high council. It was a kind voice, but unrelenting and full of hidden meaning. Meaning that Joss fully intended to comprehend.

"Someone." Joss scratched his forehead, mulling over the word. "Why not kill me instead? I'll make it easy, I'll come to London. You can dispatch me as you please. Leave the innocent bystanders out of it."

"We want Tod dead. Consider it a kindness that we're giving you until the end of the year."

Joss's hand was shaking on the receiver. "Why so long? Why be so patient? You never have in the past. Unless I was doing recon."

But he knew why they were giving him so much time. Because it took time to contact the members of the Society. They were scattered all over the globe—some of them in places that were unreachable by telephone or without Internet. They were giving him time not out of kindness, but because they had it to give. Even now, they were gathering up the Slayers from around the world for the cleansing.

Because it took more than a few Slayers to pull it off. It would take all of them.

And all of them *could* cleanse a town full of vampires. They'd done it before. Together, they were far more powerful than they ever were apart. There'd be no stopping them.

A hard lump formed in Joss's throat as any glimmer of hope faded away into the night. One last time, he uttered, "Please."

"You have our answer, Slayer."

The line went dead then, and Joss was left with an emptiness that he had never known before.

22

BREAKING AND ENTERING

JOSS SAT BACK ON THE SWING on Nelly's porch, his eyes wide. "Whoa."

Vlad shot him a look. "What's wrong?"

Joss shook his head. He still looked kinda shocked. They'd been talking for a few hours now, about anything but the possibility that Joss was going to have to stake him. Finally, Vlad couldn't take it anymore and had told Joss what his dad had said about the journal, in hopes that if Joss had it, he'd hand it over. "I just had no idea that vampires had access to rituals that powerful. How did your dad get it? I mean, it's in his journal—wherever it is, right?"

"I don't know, but if we find that journal, all of our problems are solved." Vlad watched him, trying to gauge whether or not Joss was hiding something. Say the journal, for instance. But his expression didn't give any hint of deception.

"I don't trust it." Joss shook his head again, this time sitting up straight, looking more confident. "It can't be that easy, Vlad. Nothing ever is."

Vlad's jaw dropped. "Easy? We have no idea even where to look!"

"Okay, so easy was the wrong word, but—"

"Joss. It's our only option short of you staking me. Are you going to help me look for it or not?" He set his jaw stubbornly. They were in this together. He needed Joss. Needed his help.

Joss sighed heavily. He looked out at the night, watched a car pass slowly by, glanced at the shadow of a cat in the bushes, and then sighed again. "Where should we start?"

Ten minutes later, they were across town, hiding in the shadows, away from prying eyes.

"Wait!" Joss called to Vlad in a whisper, but it was too late—he'd already slid through the window of Eddie's dumpy little house, right into what looked like his parent's bedroom.

Vlad peeked his head back out the window and shook his head in a question.

Joss sighed, and still whispering, but this time, more frantically, said, "I think somebody's home."

Vlad glanced to his left. A blue light was flickering in the window next to the room he was in. The living room, he was guessing, and someone was watching television. Vlad thought, but only for a moment. Then he whispered to Joss, "Wait right here. We've come this far, and I'm not leaving that little weasel's room unsearched."

Despite Joss's quiet protests, Vlad moved silently through the messy room to the door. Creaking it open slightly, he listened, but all he could hear was the Price Is Right blaring in the room next to him. With a deep breath for bravery, Vlad opened the door and slipped into the hall. After an easy decision of which way to go—toward the television noise or away from it, Vlad moved down the hall. The next door was the bathroom, but the door after that . . . that was all Eddie's.

Pasted, pinned, stapled, and taped to the wall were tons of tabloid headlines about this monster or that—mostly vampires. On the far wall was a desk piled with papers.

It took Vlad a good ten minutes to search for his dad's journal, to no avail.

He tried to open the window in Eddie's room, but it was nailed shut. Probably panicky little Eddie's idea on how to keep a vampire at bay.

He moved back to the master bedroom and looked out of the open window to a nervous-looking Joss. "So?"

Vlad shook his head. "Nothing."

Joss asked, "Where's the last place you saw this thing anyway, Vlad?"

Vlad thought for just a moment before answering. "In your backpack on the night you staked Dorian."

It was Joss's turn to stop talking. Shaking his head, his features paling, he said, "I didn't take it, Vlad. I swear. Someone must've put it there. And then that someone must've taken it out again. Because I don't have it."

Vlad gauged his honesty level for a moment.

He believed Joss. Even though everyone on the planet would tell him not to.

"I don't suppose you know where the *Compendium* is either, huh?"

"The what?"

Vlad sighed. "Nothing. Just a book I lost."

From behind him, Vlad heard someone moving down the hallway. "All right, ma! Let me put my backpack away! Geesh . . ."

Joss mouthed, "Eddie?"

Vlad nodded. He was sorely tempted to dive from the window, but instead he waited for Eddie to go to the main area of the house. Then he slunked back down the hall to Eddie's room. Eddie's backpack was on the bed in a heap. Vlad closed his eyes as he reached for it, praying to anyone and anything at all that his dad's journal would be inside.

It wasn't.

Vlad's heart sank, and hopelessness enveloped him.

23
HALLOWEEN

I T SUCKED WHEN Halloween night fell on a school night, but it sucked even worse when it fell on a school night in the middle of the week.

That being said, Vlad wasn't about to let it ruin his fun. After all, it was going to be his last Halloween ever. Nobody was going to ruin it for him. Nobody.

He and Henry had had a good, long laugh about the costumes they were going to wear this year, and not even Principal Snelgrove was going to rob them of their good time. Henry was dressed in a cheesy black nylon cape—one he'd borrowed from Vlad—and had his hair slicked back and spray painted black, complete with a widow's peak. He was every bit a stereotypical old-school Hollywood vampire, and Vlad was his companion, his slave, his drudge. But in the worst way possible. Vlad was dressed in a filthy suit, complete with fake bugs attached. He was Renfield to Henry's Dracula. And the very idea of switching places for the evening had sent them into hysterical fits.

Of course, it wasn't evening. Not yet. It was just after lunch period. But fortunately, Principal Snelgrove was feeling giving this year and had allowed the students of Bathory High to dress in costume for the day.

But no parties. And no posters or banners with the word Halloween. And no costume parades. And no jack-o'-lanterns.

We wouldn't want anyone to have any fun, now would we? After all, fun like that could lead to kids liking school. And that, Vlad thought as he smirked, just wouldn't be right, now would it, Snelgrove?

Vlad closed his locker door and as he did, the smile slipped from his face. Joss was standing there, not in costume at all, his eyes red and lined with purple bruises that indicated he hadn't been sleeping well, a somber expression on his face. He eyed Vlad for a moment before nodding. "Let me guess . . . Renfield?"

Vlad nodded back, ever aware of the slight bulge under Joss's shirt. His stake. "Henry and I thought it would be funny."

Only it didn't feel funny right now. Nothing did.

Joss sighed, leaning against the lockers. He looked like he could fall asleep standing up. Poor guy. "Have you thought any more about our . . . our situation? I mean, if we can't find the journal, what are we going to do?"

Vlad bit his lip and nodded. It was hard not to think about. Die so everyone you love can live, or live and everyone you love will die. It was a no-brainer, really. "I have thought about it."

"And?"

"And I think you're right. If we don't find the journal, I'll have to die, Joss. I can't be selfish like that." Vlad met his gaze, meaning every word he'd spoken. "And no one can know but us."

Joss nodded, a sad, dark light in his eyes. "Of course. No one but us. And I'll . . . I'll do what I can to make it quick, okay?"

"I appreciate that." It settled the sick feeling in Vlad's stomach some to know that Joss was dreading this almost as much as he was. Running a hand through his hair, he lowered his voice and said, "But it's not even a factor. Because we're going to find that journal, and everything's going to be all right."

Joss nodded, but Vlad could see doubt fill his eyes.

Sighing, Vlad said, "Look, it turns out Elysia is planning to kill me come the end of December anyway. So if we do this the morning of New Year's Eve . . . well, then at least I get one more Christmas with Nelly, Otis, and my dad, right? You know. If we *don't* find the journal."

A shadow, one of mournful regret, passed over Joss's face. His eyes filled with tears and he met Vlad's eyes, guilt flowing from him. "I'm sorry, Vlad."

Vlad squeezed Joss's shoulder and sighed. "Me too."

As Joss turned away to head to his next class, Vlad called out to him. "Joss, if you're not busy later . . . I'd like to take you somewhere."

Joss hesitated for a moment, then nodded. Suspicion crossed his eyes, followed quickly by guilt for having been suspicious of his friend's motives.

Vlad couldn't blame him. They'd been through a lot together. Not all of it good. "Henry will pick you up. Be ready at eight, okay?"

An exhausted smile lit up Joss's face. "Yeah. Yeah, no problem."

Vlad watched out the window for Henry's car to pull up that night, and when it did, he wasn't the least bit surprised that it took Henry's cousin more than a few minutes to get out of the car. The plan was simple—introduce Joss to Tomas before heading out to Matthew's annual Halloween party.

Before they could ring the doorbell, Vlad had opened the door. "Come on in. I want you to meet someone."

He walked a very nervous looking Joss through the house and into the kitchen, where Otis was carving a pumpkin with Nelly, and Tomas and Vikas were emptying a bottle of blood-wine. All eyes turned to Joss as he entered the room, and instantly, he flicked his eyes to Vlad, as if wondering if he'd been betrayed.

Nelly smiled brightly. "Joss! How are you, dear? There are fresh baked cookies on the counter, boys. Help yourselves."

Vlad nudged Joss over to where Tomas was standing and said, "Joss . . . I want you to meet my dad. He's where I get my vampire traits from."

Both Joss and Tomas looked caught, shocked, as if neither thought Vlad had any sense left in his skull.

Henry helped himself to a handful of cookies. Earlier, when Vlad had told him his idea, Henry had agreed that it was pretty brilliant.

Of course, Henry also thought that finding new things to blow up with firecrackers was pretty brilliant.

"And Dad," Vlad cleared his throat, readying himself for any kind of outburst, "Joss is a very good friend of mine. He's also Henry's cousin. And a Slayer."

Tomas tensed, but Otis and Vikas didn't. They were too busy pretending that Joss wasn't even in the room. Through clenched teeth, Tomas said, "And you brought him here to meet your vampire father."

Vlad nodded, setting his jaw. "I want the people I care about to know one another, and what's more, I want them to have a healthy respect for one another."

The room fell silent. That is, until Nelly rinsed her hands off in the sink. She was drying them on a kitchen towel when she smiled at Joss. "You and Tomas share a love of history, you know. You've read it, and well, he's lived it. An old man like Tomas has lots of wonderful stories to share."

Tomas's tension broke as he chuckled. "Old man?! Nelly, I'll have you know I am very young. Just experienced."

Henry nodded. "*Experienced* is code for *old*."

Everyone—even Otis, even Vikas—laughed.

Then Tomas turned back to Joss, who still looked a little on edge, and said, "Can I get you something to drink, Joss?"

"That would be great. Thanks." Joss smiled at Vlad then—a careful, still concerned smile.

After finishing a few sodas, the boys said their goodbyes and headed out the door to Matthew's party. Just as they were stepping up onto Matthew's porch, Henry stopped Vlad and said, "Dude. I don't get it. Why did you feel the need to introduce Joss and your dad? I mean, I'm totally happy to help. I just don't understand exactly what purpose it serves."

Vlad watched as Joss greeted Meredith and then looked back at Henry. "I live in two worlds, Henry. And in one of those worlds, I stand between mortal enemies. I needed to know, just for one moment, that peace is possible."

Henry sighed and shook his head. "But if peace isn't likely—and trust me, it's not—then why bother getting them together?"

Vlad shrugged and headed for the door. "I have to try, Henry."

The living room had been completely transformed into a foggy, misty swamp, complete with swamp monsters bursting from the fog and Spanish moss dangling from the spooky fake trees. Vlad and Henry made their way through the crowd and down the stairs to the basement, where the party was in full swing. Matthew's parents had completely outdone themselves this year, and what Vlad descended into looked nothing at all like a basement and everything like a creepy haunted castle.

Standing by the punch bowl, though, was a beautiful fairy. With black, tattered wings.

Vlad beamed at Snow and made his way across the room. "Hey. Nice wings."

Snow eyed him up and down for a moment before grinning. "Let me guess. Renfield?"

Vlad chuckled. "Of course! Y'know . . . you're one of the few people that will see the humor in my being Henry's human slave."

She took a drink of punch and set her glass on the table. Vlad couldn't help but notice that her smile was smaller when she spoke. "Well, I have some experience in that department."

Vlad cleared his throat, suddenly uncomfortable. There it was. That eternal reminder that he had hurt Snow. That he had changed their lives forever.

"I'm sorry, Snow. For leaving you the way I did. I should have explained."

Snow watched him for a moment, then nodded. "Yeah. You should have."

Music was playing, something with a heavy techno beat. But after a moment it stopped, and was replaced by something slow and melodic. After a moment, Vlad recognized it as "Broken" by Seether. After the first verse, Vlad met Snow's eyes. "Wanna dance?"

She smiled again, this time more completely, and said, "I'd love to."

He led her to the fog-covered dance floor. By the time they reached the center, the chorus had started, and Vlad's hands were shaking slightly.

He reached for her hand and she gave his a squeeze, her lips in a nervous purse. Then Vlad pulled her closer and they began to sway. His hands were on her waist and her arms looped his neck. And the warmth between them was amazing.

She smelled sweet and good and so wonderful that Vlad breathed in her scent, and he didn't once think about her blood, or how it had ever tasted on his tongue. He only thought of the way she looked at him, and the way it made him feel. He only thought of what his life had been like with Snow, and what it had been like without. It had been better with Snow, despite the guilt of using her as a food source. Better, because she listened whenever he needed to talk. Better, because she had been everything he'd ever needed her to be for him, whenever he needed her to be it. She'd understood him, accepted him, and loved him.

And in return, he'd pushed her away.

Vlad's heart was thumping strongly. It felt good to hold Snow in his arms. It felt right. But he couldn't seem to open his mouth to tell Snow what he was feeling, or how he wished that it would never end.

She looked up at him wordlessly, and her eyes said it all. She felt the same way, but something refused to let her say it aloud. Maybe they were cursed by the same thing: fear. Utter terror of knowing what it was to love someone so deeply that they became a part of you. Snow was no longer his drudge—she was his match. She was funny, intriguing, confident, and cool. She was, Vlad saw now, everything he had ever wanted in a girl. And as they swayed to the music, they grew closer and closer, until their bodies were pressed together, their foreheads touching.

Vlad pulled back, but only long enough to look into her eyes before placing a tender kiss on her lips. Snow kissed back and when their lips parted, she drew him closer, her arms wrapped tightly around him.

When the song ended and they broke apart at last, Vlad swore that he saw the glimmer of tears in her eyes.

24
SHUTTING UP

ALL VLAD WANTED to think about was how Snow felt in his arms last night. But other things—darker things—kept invading his thoughts, demanding his attention. Enrico was dead. Dead and gone, and all that Otis would say about it was that he'd heard from someone—some nameless vampire—that someone had killed him.

D'Ablo was dead too. Someone had ripped the heart from his chest and crushed it into a pulp.

Vlad was very worried that that someone just might be Otis. That Otis, maybe, had killed both vampires. For reasons he did not yet know.

Not that he could blame Otis for wanting to obliterate D'Ablo. After all, he and D'Ablo completely despised one another. Judging by the fight they engaged in during Vlad's sophomore year, they shared a dark history that Vlad didn't know the half of.

The evidence was staggering. Otis's blood-soaked shirt the morning after Enrico had been killed, and this.

Vlad turned Otis's hat over in his hands. It was what he'd found in the closet, and hadn't yet had a chance to question his uncle about. But he really needed to. The hat was splattered with blood—blood that smelled like D'Ablo's, even after an obvious dry-cleaning attempt. Was Otis trying to cover his tracks? Why? And why kill Enrico?

It bothered him that Otis would take a life, let alone vampire life. Even D'Ablo's. Vlad felt like if anyone had to do it, if anyone really had to kill D'Ablo, that it would've come down to him.

But it hadn't.

It had come down to someone else—maybe his uncle—and Vlad hadn't even gotten a chance to make D'Ablo see the error of his ways.

Stupid vampire. Stupid half-insane D'Ablo.

Vlad returned the hat to the bag in the closet. He'd have to talk to Otis soon and find out exactly what was going on. Because bloody shirts and hats and learning of the deaths of people all around Vlad didn't exactly make him want to trust Otis.

His thoughts flashed back on their beginning. Once Otis had revealed his relationship to Vlad, Vlad had been so willing to trust him, so anxious to help him and listen to him.

What if the whole thing had been an act, a trick? What if Otis was a horrible person, even worse than D'Ablo? What if Otis had been spending all this time studying him and trying to find a way to steal his Pravus powers? What if his insistence that the Pravus prophecy was just a myth was all an act?

Vlad shuddered at the idea. He made a mental note to discuss the possibility with his dad, who he knew would protect him, if needed. He hadn't found his dad's journal yet, but it had to be somewhere. And once he did locate it, his dad would fix everything.

That's what dads do.

Though the death of Enrico weighed heavily on his thoughts, it wasn't his reason for leaving Nelly's place and crossing town, and then standing outside the front doors of Bathory High, watching students as they hurried from warm cars, through the blistering early chill of autumn, into the warm building. There was no avoiding school. And there was something else there. Someone else.

Snow.

Before they'd danced at the Halloween party, Vlad had been avoiding her for weeks. Watching her closely, longing for her touch, but keeping a careful, safe distance. Because he didn't want to hurt her.

He'd been both thankful and disappointed that they shared no classes, and relieved that she stayed true to her curfew so that he wouldn't bump into her on his way to the belfry at night. But there she was, her pale cheeks flushed pink from the cold, a stocking cap with bat wings on her head, shivering her way up the steps.

He had to hand it to her. Snow certainly wasn't like other girls. She didn't call or write him notes. She didn't talk about him to his friends or wait outside his locker. She went on with her life with quiet dignity and grace.

And it was really starting to bug the crap out of Vlad.

The truth was, he'd missed her. Missed her kisses, missed her company. And last night showed him that he was tired of being without her, tired of fighting against his feelings for her. He only hoped that she felt the same way.

But how was he supposed to relate that to Snow without sounding desperate? And wasn't it cruel to confess his feelings to her only now that he was going to die? At Nelly's house—still at Nelly's; he and his dad hadn't moved back home just yet because his dad was still tormented by the memory of Mellina's death—Vlad had circled the date on the calendar that he and Joss had agreed to. The date he would die, if he didn't locate the journal in time, in order to save everyone that both of them loved. December thirty-first. His death was imminent. He'd see them all just one last time and then disappear into the blustery snow with Joss. To end it. To end it all.

Maybe it was selfish to choose to leave them all behind on a holiday. But he had no choice.

Selfish or not, that made telling Snow how he felt all the more important. And after not being able to say anything at the party to her about it, he knew he had to tell her today.

Vlad smiled as she ascended the steps, completely unaware that he was even waiting for her. She was wearing black pants with laces that went all the way up each leg, Converse shoes with tiny skulls all over them, and a T-shirt which read Come to the Dark Side: We Have Cookies. She was beautiful, with her eyes lined thickly with black, her lips in a slight, confident smirk as she passed a group of popular girls, who made quiet, snarky comments about her fashion choices. Like him, Snow was different. Like him, she stood out from the crowd. But unlike him, she totally owned it.

A shiver of nervousness crawled up his spine. She might resent him for not being in touch until she moved to Bathory. She might not have any feelings toward him at all anymore, despite what it had seemed like at the Halloween party. None of these responses would surprise Vlad. He was wrong to cut her out of his life. He was wrong to push her away in some insane pursuit of protecting her.

But he was really just trying to protect himself. Snow was his match, his perfect match. She was understanding, open, honest, and so very beautiful that it made Vlad's chest ache.

A good ache. One that hinted that his heart would explode if he didn't hold her again soon.

"Snow . . ." Her name fell from his lips in a whisper, but it was enough to make her stop in her tracks.

She looked up at him and smiled, a sadness lurking in her eyes. Maybe it was a sadness that spoke of her longing for him. Or maybe it was something else. Maybe she'd moved on, had found another boy, and that's what the threat of tears at the end of their dancing had meant, and what her eyes were trying to tell him now.

Vlad moved down the steps, until he was standing right in front of her. He held her gaze for a long time, searching for the right words. None of the ones he'd practiced with on his way to school seemed right. Finally, with a deep breath for bravery, he spoke. "Sometimes, I do incredibly stupid things. Like challenging Henry to a Mountain Dew chug-off. Like giving Amenti extra catnip when Nelly isn't looking. Like breaking off all contact with my perfect match. Can you forgive me? Can you ever forgive me? Because . . . I love you, Snow. And if you can't forgive me, I—"

"Vlad." She shook her head. "Shut up."

At first, his heart sank. Then she moved forward, pressing her lips tightly to his in a dizzying, wonderful kiss—one so much better than even the kiss they'd shared on the dance floor—and Vlad's heart soared up into the atmosphere, through clouds and sky and stars, and it never came back down.

He loved Snow. And Snow loved him.

And for the moment, that was all that mattered.

25

THE END OF ALL SECRETS

"THERE IS NO WAY this is gonna work." Henry shook his head adamantly, peering up at the open arched windows of the belfry with doubt. "No offense, Vlad, but I've seen you in gym class and I'm not about to trust my future career as a ballroom dancer to someone who can't bench press eighty pounds without using his freaky vampire powers."

Vlad raised an eyebrow. Ballroom dancing? Henry was about as graceful as a three-legged dog. He had to be joking.

Henry surveyed the distance, shaking his head once again. "You'll break our legs, for sure."

Joss's eyes grew wide, and Vlad almost slugged Henry. The last thing he needed was two panicky passengers. "It'll be fine, Henry. Now hold on."

Joss had looped his arm through Vlad's left arm, and Henry grabbed onto Vlad's shoulders. With a deep breath, Vlad concentrated and willed his body upward, floating through the air, carrying his two closest friends to his most secret of sanctuaries.

It was time to let go of all secrets.

Besides, they needed somewhere quiet and private to talk, somewhere that Henry couldn't run away from.

When Vlad reached the ledge, the three of them stepped inside the room. Henry looked around and whistled, impressed. "Whoa . . . when you said you hung out up here, I'd expected some old books and a few dust bunnies. Not this."

Vlad lit the candles and nodded to Joss, who'd been watching him expectantly since they entered the belfry. They'd planned it all out. Henry's cousin would start the explanation, and Vlad would assist. Maybe it would be easier to hear coming from family.

Maybe it wouldn't.

It didn't matter. Henry had to hear, had to know what was coming for him. For them all.

Joss cleared his throat and looked at his cousin. Nothing about his posture said that he was ready for this. "Henry . . . listen. There's something Vlad and I need to tell you.

Henry flicked his eyes between them, suspicion and concern lighting up his expression.

"Something's about to happen. Something that none of us can stop. And I need your support—*we* need your support."

"Is it something bad?" Henry whispered.

Vlad gave his shoulder a squeeze, but said nothing.

It was bad. Really bad. Worse than Henry would ever know—he and Joss had agreed on that. They'd tell Henry about the Slayer Society and about Em. They'd tell him about the journal and how important it was. But they wouldn't tell him about their last-resort plan of action, about Joss staking Vlad.

He was better off not knowing.

Or, more accurately, Joss's face was better off without Henry's fists knowing.

"You know I'm a . . . Slayer . . . right?" At Henry's nod, Joss looked a bit relieved and continued. "I belong to a group known as the Slayer Society. They exist solely for the purpose of extinguishing vampires. They believe that vampires are an abomination, an evil that has to be snuffed out before it infects mankind."

To Vlad's surprise—and great joy—he saw disgust in Joss's eyes. He didn't know if that was because Joss had changed his mind about vampires, or if it was something to do with his feelings for the Society now. He only knew that seeing it was way better than seeing the blind follower that Joss had once been.

Joss looked like he was struggling with what was coming next. But Henry had to know. "The Society is coming to Bathory. And they plan to murder everyone in this town, unless I do something they've instructed me to do."

Henry raised an eyebrow. "How many of them?"

Joss whispered, "All of them. Hundreds. Almost a thousand."

Henry seemed to relax some. "That's not so many."

Vlad leaned forward. "It's enough, Henry. Enough to cleanse this town of every human being in it."

Joss nodded his agreement. "One well-trained Slayer can take down a group of a hundred men without blinking an eye."

"Okay . . . so that's bad." Henry took a deep breath and released it. "But what makes you think they're capable of actually doing it, actually killing everyone?"

"Because they've done it before. Only no one but the Society knows they've done it. From natural disasters, like wildfires, to populations just disappearing—the Slayer Society has made an art out of making people disappear." Joss looked immensely embarrassed to be a part of that group. Maybe, Vlad thought, he wasn't anymore. Not deep down. Not in his heart.

Henry ran an exhausted hand through his hair and sighed. "So . . . what do they want you to do exactly?"

Joss swallowed hard and wet his lips before speaking. "They want me to kill a vampire."

Henry's face dropped.

Joss cleared his throat. He and Vlad stood slowly and Joss said, "Actually . . . they want me to kill one vampire in particular."

Slowly—very slowly, almost painfully so—understanding came to Henry's eyes. His face turned red. He jumped up, swinging his fist, but Vlad moved as fast as he was able to and stopped him, holding Henry in place with the use of his vampire strength. Without it, Henry probably would've broken Vlad's arm just to get to Joss. "I won't let you kill him, Joss! I won't let you hurt Vlad!"

Joss held up his hands and stepped back. It was Vlad's turn.

Vlad kept his voice as calm as he was able. "Come on, Henry. Calm down. Please don't make me order you to sit and listen, okay? Please?"

At first, Henry wasn't budging. He fought back as hard as he could, but McMillan or not, he was no match for Vlad. Finally, he sighed, his shoulders slumping, his eyes red and moist with frustration and upset.

With a nod from Vlad, Joss continued. "They want Vlad to die, Henry. And if he doesn't die, everyone else—including you—will."

Henry glared at Joss, and Vlad knew every foul word that was going through his best friend's head. He hated his cousin for what he was saying, and hated that his vampire master wouldn't let him just beat the snot out of him for saying it.

Vlad said, "Everyone, Henry. Nelly, Otis, Snow, your parents. Everyone."

"He's lying." The bitter words left Henry's tongue in a sizzle. But as soon as he said them, he doubted them. "He could be lying."

Vlad shook his head. Joss was telling the truth. They both knew that. "Joss came to me and told me about what the Society's plans were, and it turns out, there's this ritual in my dad's journal that could stop the Slayers, and could even stop Em."

Henry's eyes lit up with surprise. "So where is it?"

Vlad and Joss exchanged looks. It was Vlad who answered. "We don't know. But we're looking for it."

A whisper escaped Henry. "And if you don't find it?"

The room went silent for several minutes. Then Vlad squeezed Henry's shoulder. "Let's not worry about that just yet, okay? First we have to focus on finding that journal."

"I'm all for finding the journal, but why not kill some other vampire and tell them it was Vlad? Or tell them he stepped into the sunlight and burst into flames?"

Joss shook his head and sighed, as if he'd gone over every scenario a billion times, trying to find a way for Vlad to live. "They'd know, Henry. Vlad is . . . well . . ."

"The Pravus?" Something in Henry's tone sounded almost annoyed.

Joss nodded slowly.

For the first time since hearing the news of Vlad's impending death, Henry tore his gaze from his cousin and looked at Vlad, one eyebrow cocked. "What about bringing in more vampires—like the vampires who were gathered last year at your old house in support against your trial?"

Vlad shook his head. "Anyone who stands against Em publicly will die, Henry. I can't risk their lives just to save my own."

Henry threw his arms up and growled, his face flushing red as his temper flew. "Well, use mind control and convince everyone you moved to Tahiti then!"

"Henry . . ." Vlad met his best friend's gaze, trying like hell to get Henry to understand that he and Joss had thought of every possible avenue. "Don't you think we've tried to come up with other ideas? Because we have! This is it, okay? This is the only way. We find the journal. That's it."

Joss ran a hand through his hair and sighed. "I wish there was something more we could do."

Vlad shot him a warning glance. He couldn't let it slip that the only other option and their fall-back plan was for Joss to stake Vlad. They had to keep that secret from Henry at all costs. Or else Henry would end up doing something really stupid.

Henry leaned closer to Vlad, his voice dropping to a conspiring whisper. "Have you considered that Joss may be lying?"

Vlad had considered it. But he knew that deep down, in his gut, he felt like Joss was telling him the truth.

And that was good enough for Vlad.

Vlad looked from Joss back to Henry. "I trust him, Henry. And I need you to trust him too."

Henry shook his head gravely, defiantly. "I can't."

"Then trust me, the way you always have."

Henry was quiet for a long time. Finally, he sighed heavily, defeated. "I guess I don't have a choice."

Vlad patted him roughly on the shoulder. His words were a whisper. "That makes three of us."

26
GOING HOME

WHAT ABOUT some sort of disguise?"

Vlad rolled his eyes as he and Henry made their way down the sidewalk from the Stop & Shop. On their way back from searching the park for his dad's journal, they'd each bought a two-liter of Vault and several bags of candy, because nothing says weekday afternoon like a massive, head-exploding sugar rush. "A disguise? Seriously, Henry? I can't hide from vampires, because they can find me by reaching out for my blood. And I can't hide from Slayers in a costume of some sort because it's stupid. A fake mustache isn't the answer."

Henry shrugged. "Well . . . change your name then."

Vlad slowed his steps to a stop. Henry stopped too. "They can't find Vladimir Tod if Egbert Hargrove is sleeping in his bed."

With that, Vlad smacked Henry upside the head.

Henry shouted, "Dude!" and rubbed at the offended area.

Vlad shook his head. "You really are a genius, Henry. I'll see ya later, okay?"

As Vlad turned toward Nelly's gate, Henry called out, "See ya later, Egbert."

Shaking his head, Vlad moved through the gate, up the steps, and into the house. What he saw inside left him confused and wondering.

"I just don't understand what the rush is, Tomas. It's . . . it's so soon. Can't you wait another month?" Nelly's voice was shaking slightly in upset. Vlad could tell that she was doing everything in her power not to start crying, but that dam could break at any moment. "Just one month. What's the harm?"

Tomas sighed and gathered Nelly's hands in his, meeting her eyes with calm understanding. "Nelly, you've been a wonderful mother figure to Vlad, but it's time. It's time for us to move home again and continue with the life we left behind. It's time for us to move back to Lugosi Trail."

Otis was standing in the background, not speaking. Vlad hadn't been able to read his expression since his dad had begun telling them about moving back home, but if he had to wager a guess, he'd say that Otis was worried.

About what, he had no idea.

Nelly squeezed Tomas's hands, her fingers shaking. "I just don't understand the rush."

"Nelly . . ." Tomas took on a parental tone, chastising her.

"What rush? I've been here for months and Vlad has been in your care for years. It's time we went home. And nothing you say can change my mind."

He held her gaze for a moment and as he let go of her hands, Nelly's eyes dropped to the floor in defeat. Vlad glanced at Otis, who still hadn't moved, who still hadn't shown so much as a crack in his blank expression.

Tomas squeezed Vlad's shoulder. "Pack your belongings tonight. We move in the morning."

Vlad blinked. That *was* fast. "What about Otis? Will he stay with us?"

Tomas shook his head. Otis, at last, spoke, though Vlad still couldn't tell what he was thinking. "I'll move in here, with Nelly. It's only appropriate, as we'll be a married couple soon."

"What about Vikas?" Vlad's bottom lip trembled as he spoke. It surprised him how nervous he was about moving back into his old house, but he was. Nervous and apprehensive and completely weirded out by the idea.

Much like he'd been weirded out that his dad was still alive after all.

His dad nodded. Judging by the look in his eye, he was in no mood to entertain arguments from his son. "Vikas will remain in the guest room until the end of the year, when he'll return to Siberia."

Vlad swallowed hard. It was a cold reminder that he and his dad wouldn't see the new year. If he didn't find that journal, he'd die at the hand of Joss, at the hand of his friend the Slayer, to save everyone in town from a horrible demise. Otis and his dad would be none the wiser. Not until it was too late.

No one would know until then. Except for Henry, Joss, and Snow.

Snow, who he hadn't even told yet.

And the only reason he'd told Henry and was planning to tell Snow was so Joss had people to back him up, to defend that it had been Vlad's choice, that Joss wasn't really a bad guy after all.

But he had no idea how to even broach the subject with Snow.

Snow, who walked him home every day after school now. Snow, who snuck quick kisses in the hall before lunch. Snow, who had quickly become his reason for going to school every day, despite knowing that he'd never live to see graduation.

As if summoned by thought—something that was totally impossible now that she was no longer his drudge—the doorbell rang. Vlad opened it to reveal Snow, dressed in knee-high moto boots, black trench coat, black skinny jeans, and a black T-shirt that read I KISSED A VAMPIRE AND ALL I GOT WAS THIS LOUSY T-SHIRT. Her hair was brushed behind one ear, revealing a pewter ear cuff that clung to her lobe. Seeing him, her smile broadened and she threw herself at him in a squealy hug. Vlad squeezed her tight and sat her down gently, blushing slightly that his dad, uncle, and Nelly were still in the room.

As if collecting herself from the trauma of hearing that

Vlad was finally moving out of her house, Nelly took a deep breath and smiled at Snow. "Come on in, Snow dear, the cookies are just waiting to be frosted."

Something that Vlad had noticed about Nelly since he'd started dating Snow: she kept finding reasons for Snow to come over for a visit, which probably meant she liked Snow. This time they were frosting sugar cookies for a bake sale that Nelly had organized at the hospital. Something else he'd noticed: Nelly was very careful not to leave them alone together. Maybe she worried that Vlad would lose control of his hunger and hurt Snow. Maybe she worried about hickeys. Vlad had no idea. It was sweet, in its own way.

Sweet, and only mildly annoying.

Snow walked into the kitchen and Vlad followed, smiling. It was always good to see her, and amazing that she was his girlfriend. His actual girlfriend. His real, live, in the flesh, happy to hold his hand and frost stupid cookies with him girlfriend.

Otis and his dad retired to the living room, and Nelly directed Vlad and Snow to the table in the kitchen, where Tupperware containers of unfrosted cookies were sitting. There had to be at least thirty large containers, and at least three hundred cookies. Vlad raised his eyebrows at Nelly. "I hope you're not expecting perfection."

Snow nodded. "I hope you're not expecting all of them to get frosted. They look delicious, Nelly."

Nelly smiled. "You can eat any cookies you break."

Vlad grinned and snapped a cookie in two, handing one half to Snow, who munched on it happily. Nelly clucked her tongue. "Vladimir!"

Over the next two hours, Vlad and Snow frosted each cookie with white or red or green frosting, then sprinkled some with silver candy sprinkles and drew various pictures on the others with extra frosting in a tube. After a while, Vlad's hand was cramping. Snow held up a cookie for him, one she'd decorated. The smirk on her face said it all, but what she'd written on the cookie sent Vlad into hysterics.

The cookie was frosted white and written on it in red frosting were two words: Bite Me.

Vlad wiped the tears from his eyes and, fighting another fit of hysterical giggles, said, "I'm not sure that sentiment would go over well at a charitable bake sale."

Snow shoved the cookie into Vlad's mouth, frosting squishing out all over his lips. "I made it for you! I made it special!"

Vlad chewed the cookie and swallowed it in a gulp, then reached for the green frosting and smeared a lump on Snow's nose.

Snow blinked at him, sitting there with a big glob of green on the end of her nose, looking like some mutated zombie form of Rudolph, and growled. "You. Are. Dead!"

Snatching up a tube of red frosting, she squeezed it hard, pointing it right at him. Frosting squirted out and landed on his head. Vlad barely had time to react before Snow was rubbing it into his scalp.

They were laughing so hard, and throwing so much frosting around, that they barely heard Nelly walk back into the room with a horrified gasp. "What have you done to my kitchen?"

Vlad and Snow exchanged grins and tried hard to contain their laughter. Vlad said, "We're sorry, Nelly. We'll clean it up."

Before Nelly could ground him, Otis entered the room. With a glance at Vlad, who was covered in frosting from head to toe, he distracted Nelly with a kiss. "Darling, let's go out to dinner. I'm sure Vladimir has everything under control and your kitchen will be good as new when we return."

Nelly threw up her hands in disgust. "Did you see—"

"I did, and I'm certain Vladimir will scrub every inch before we get home." Otis led Nelly from the room. With his thoughts, he said to Vlad, *If you don't, she'll murder you. You know that, right?*

I know. And I will. Promise. Vlad smiled. But his smile was tinged with his ongoing suspicion of his uncle. He hadn't confronted Otis yet. He'd wanted to . . . but couldn't summon up the bravery required.

Not yet, anyway.

Nelly paused, as if remembering she was about to leave Vlad alone with his girlfriend. "What about—"

"Tomas will be here. It's fine. Let's go." After a brief pause, Nelly finally let him lead her out the front door.

An hour later, the kitchen was almost completely restored. Snow was scrubbing the table with a moist sponge. Vlad was wiping down the counters, his thoughts drifting to a place he'd hoped to avoid.

There would be no more of this.

No more frosting fights. No more Nelly's wrath. No more hearing Snow's laughter. No more silent conversations with Otis.

No more anything, if he, Joss, and Henry didn't find the journal fast.

"Vlad?" Snow was watching him, her eyes full of concern. "Are you okay?"

He wasn't. And wouldn't ever be again.

When he didn't answer, she dropped the sponge on the table, put a caring hand on his shoulder and asked, "Is everything all right?"

Vlad cupped her hand and shook his head. "No, Snow. Everything isn't all right. Everything is about as far from all right as it can get."

He reached out with his blood, but couldn't detect his dad anywhere in the house. It took him a minute to remember that he couldn't track his dad the way he could other vampires. But still, it seemed they were alone, for the moment. And it was time to tell Snow about Joss. Time to tell her that these were their final days together.

He sat her down at the table, and after explaining everything—the Slayer Society, Joss, Henry, his trial, everything—he waited for her to respond. Unlike the conversation with Henry, Vlad felt compelled to tell her everything.

Large, round tears spilled silently from her eyes. Then she hugged him tightly and whispered, "I'm glad you told me. I understand, I do. I wish it didn't have to be this way. I wish we had longer to be together. But . . . I understand. Thanks for trusting me."

He hugged her tightly and held her for a long time, wishing that he was living some other life, in some other place, that he wasn't causing Snow any pain.

Somewhere where he was a normal teenager, with normal problems, and answers to the questions that were plaguing his every thought.

27
INVITATIONS

V LAD CLOSED HIS LOCKER at the end of the school day. He was about to throw his backpack over his shoulder and head for Snow's locker, when he spied a familiar, weasel-like face passing by. "Eddie, come here a sec, would ya?"

Eddie Poe paused midstep, then approached Vlad, an eager glint in his eye. He knew that he had Vlad where he wanted him. He knew there was nothing Vlad could do but accept his fate and turn him into a vampire. Because he'd threatened Snow, and Vlad wasn't exactly certain he could protect her from Eddie. Because Vlad wasn't really capable of killing him. Because Vlad had been given no choice in this matter.

But Vlad didn't care about Eddie's threats anymore.

"I'm not making you a vampire, Eddie."

Eddie's eyes clouded with anger. "Yes, you are."

"No, Eddie. I'm not." Vlad kept his words clipped, his tone matter-of-fact.

The fact of the matter was that Eddie Poe was a terrible, evil, vindictive human being. Vlad could only imagine what Eddie would turn into once he was a vampire. He'd be powerful, violent, and hateful to the core. He take revenge on humans who'd wronged him, and would show no mercy or understanding to the victims he'd feed on. And Vlad would be to blame.

No. No, he wouldn't make Eddie into a vampire. Eddie was already a monster. Besides, he'd decided that once he was dead, Eddie would be viewed as a terrible person for spreading such insane rumors about a dead boy—a boy who died in a terrible accident. So why should he give in to Eddie's ridiculous demands? If Eddie Poe wanted fame and fortune, Vlad wasn't about to hand it to him. He was going to have to find another way to get it.

Vlad supposed he could have just let it go. After all, his deadline wasn't going to come along until after Vlad would be dead and gone. But it was the principle of the matter, and very much something that Vlad needed to make clear.

He stared Eddie down, determined.

The muscles in Eddie's jaw began to twitch. "I'll expose you. You have no idea the hell that I can bring down on you."

Vlad's words were a low growl. "Save it, Eddie. I've made up my mind and nothing you can do will change it. Expose me. Do your worst. I don't really give a damn anymore."

Then an image filled Vlad's mind. The same image that Vlad had glimpsed at The Crypt. Kristoff, running across the high school football field, utterly terrified, with a vampiric, hungry Eddie Poe on his tail. The picture in his mind was so clear that Vlad wasn't certain if it were a vision or the memory of his vision. But it was clear.

His stomach flipped, and Vlad ran a tense hand through his hair.

What did it all mean?

Henry snatched Eddie's folder from his grasp and tossed it down the hallway Frisbee-style. He got better distance this time. With a glare at Eddie, Henry said, "Fetch, loser."

Eddie's face turned purple and he wandered down the hall, in search of his lost folder.

Henry leaned up against Vlad's closed locker door. He played it casual, but Vlad could tell he was deep in mourning for his best friend. Vlad said, "Do you wanna catch a movie or something tonight?"

"Not really."

"Come on. I was thinking we'd see *Zombie Pirates from Outer Space.*" The corner of Vlad's mouth tugged up in a smirk.

Henry shook his head. "It doesn't come out till Friday."

Vlad shrugged. "Nelly snagged some tickets to an advanced screening. We can invite Joss too and just hang out. Give up the Great Journal Search for a night and just chill."

"Invite me to what?" Joss had moved down the hall and joined them. The circles under his eyes were looking a little less dark since they told Henry what was going on come December thirty-first. But only a little.

Vlad smiled at him. "To see *Zombie Pirates from Outer Space*."

"It's out?"

"Not till Friday, but I have advanced tickets. You in?"

Joss visibly deflated. "I'm supposed to go see *Cotton Candy Kisses* with Meredith tonight."

Vlad and Henry exchanged horrified glances. Not only was Meredith dragging Joss to a romantic comedy. But she was dragging him to a romantic comedy . . . with bunnies.

Henry squeezed his cousin's shoulder. "So . . . this gives you a great excuse not to?"

Joss beamed, as if he could see the zombie light at the end of the outer space tunnel. "Exactly. See you at eight."

Remembering Nelly's nagging instructions, Vlad said, "Oh hey, I'm supposed to invite you guys to Thanksgiving dinner at Nelly's next week."

Joss brightened some. "Is it okay if Meredith comes along?"

Something heavy settled at the pit of Vlad's stomach. "Sure."

But Vlad wasn't sure. He wasn't sure at all.

Because that meant that Meredith and Snow were going to both be there. And he would have nowhere to hide from the uncomfortable combination of his ex and his girlfriend.

Except maybe in the mashed potatoes.

"Crap," Henry muttered. "I forgot my binder in Ms. Lippman's class."

Joss said, "I'm outta here. See you guys later."

Henry and Vlad nodded to Joss and Henry closed his locker. "Be right back, man. Don't leave without me."

Vlad grabbed his backpack and shut his locker. Of course he'd wait for Henry. That's what friends do. As he waited, the hall population thinned drastically. Nobody hung around school any longer than they had to. Nobody normal, anyway.

"Hey, loser."

Vlad tensed, but he didn't turn around.

A meaty hand gave his shoulder a shove. "I said hey, loser."

Vlad turned his head toward the voice, but already knew what he'd see. Bill and Tom. Still thick-headed, still stupid, and still very much anxious to smack Vlad around. "Not today, guys. I'm not in the mood."

Bill snorted. "We're not trying to make out with you, queer. We just want to show you something."

Vlad sighed and scanned the hall for any sign of Henry. Unsuccessful in his search, he sighed again. "Show me what?"

Tom stepped closer, a cruel grin spreading across his face. His breath smelled oddly like kitty litter. "What it feels like to get your butt kicked."

Vlad's eyes went wide and locked on Tom's fist as he swung toward Vlad's right eye. Then Vlad ducked and started to run, but Bill blocked his escape.

Tom swung again, and this time, he connected. Vlad's cheek exploded with pain and he fell to the floor on all fours. Behind him, Bill and Tom were laughing.

But Vlad found none of this funny.

Not the way they'd intimidated him since kindergarten. Not the way they called him names and knocked his books from his hands. Not the way they'd shoved his head inside his locker or wrote vile insults on his notebook when he wasn't looking. Not the way they teased him about the house fire. None of it.

And he was awfully sick of listening to them laugh.

Vlad pushed back, using all of his vampire might, not giving a damn if the bullies realized what he was, sick and tired and ticked off at being treated less like a human being and more like a piñata for most of his life, and did a windmill kick, catching Bill in the knee. Bill went down hard on his left arm, and Vlad heard a snap. But before the crack of bone even registered in his mind, Vlad had flipped himself up to standing with vampiric speed and grabbed Tom by the shirt. He pulled back his fist and Tom's eyes went wide. "Oh my God, your eyes! What . . . what the hell are you?!"

Vlad set his jaw and threw his arm forward in a punch. Tom's blood splattered onto his fist and he threw the bully back, into the lockers. As Tom slid down, landing in a heap with Bill, Vlad turned and walked away.

As he did so, he replied, "I'm the Pravus. And don't you forget it."

28
Thanksgiving

T HE SMELL OF PUMPKIN PIE was killing Vlad. There weren't many smells that really got his drool going outside of human blood, but pumpkin pie—that was a killer. And Nelly had warned him to stay away from the succulent dessert until after Thanksgiving dinner was over.

He liked pumpkin pie so much, in fact, that about a week ago Nelly had baked him one in place of a birthday cake. Turning eighteen had never tasted so sweet.

But he wanted more. Now.

He contented himself with sitting in the kitchen, sniffing the sweet, spice-laden scent of freshly baked pumpkin pie, and contemplated what it might taste like with a side of steaming A positive.

He was betting it would be delectable.

Licking his lips, he warmed up a mug of blood in the microwave and tried to keep his eyes off the pie.

Dinner was about to begin. He could hold out another hour or two.

But so help Henry if he hogged it all.

The doorbell rang and the relative peace of Nelly's house—which Vlad greatly missed calling home, as he and his dad had been living in their house once more for almost a week now—was devoured by the sounds of friends and family. Everyone was there: Matilda, Big Mike, Henry, Greg, Joss's parents, Joss, Vlad's dad, Otis, Nelly, Meredith, and Snow.

Vlad greeted everyone, offering an awkward smile to Meredith—remembering the awkward kiss she'd given him just a few short months ago—and helped Snow with her coat. This, of course, inspired Nelly that Vlad should take care of all of the coats. So Vlad wandered blindly up the stairs, a pile of coats in his arms, unable to see where he was stepping. He finally, miraculously, made it upstairs to the library unharmed and set the coats in a neat pile on Amenti's favorite chair. Amenti mewed up at him from the floor, as if to ask him just what he thought he was doing. Vlad bent at the knees and scratched her chin, inciting a purr. "Sorry, girl. But you'll have to find somewhere else for your millionth nap of the day."

As if in response, Amenti walked straight into Vlad's old room and jumped on the bed, curling up in a ball.

Vlad sighed.

"Hey."

The whispered voice made him jump, but he turned to see that Joss had snuck away from the chaos downstairs. After settling his heart rate, Vlad said, "Hey, Joss."

Joss flicked his eyes about nervously and then, stepping closer, said, "I just wanted to let you know that I spotted a Slayer earlier today, lurking around town, scoping things out. So I don't think the Society is going to hold out much longer. I searched the south end of town for the journal, but some of those houses were really hard to get into."

Vlad nodded. "I got chased out by old man Stevens last night. Good thing he has that prosthetic leg or I'd be in jail right now."

Joss frowned. "We've almost searched the entire town, Vlad. What if it's not in Bathory?"

Vlad patted Joss on the arm. "It has to be. It just has to be. Because if it's not . . ."

He didn't have to finish his sentence. They both knew what would happen if they didn't find the journal.

Joss nodded, but he still looked tense. Vlad raised an eyebrow at him. "What's going on, Joss? Everything okay?"

Joss sighed, looked down at his feet, shuffled them. "It's just that . . ."

"Just what?"

When Joss met his eyes, Vlad could see just what. Joss was having doubts. "I don't know if I can do it. Stake you, I mean. You're . . . you're my friend. Truth be told, you're my best friend. I don't know if I can kill you, Vlad. I mean, first there's the question of whether your Pravus powers will prevent me from doing so at all . . . but there's also the fact that you're my friend. What if I can't even try?"

Vlad bit his bottom lip, shaking his head. After all this, after all the planning and heartache and doubt he'd experienced, he was finally ready . . . and Joss wasn't. "There's no other way to protect everyone, Joss. Unless we can locate that ritual and stop all of this, you have to try. I know it's hard, but you have to. Neither one of us has a choice in this. So just do it, okay?"

Tomas's voice echoed up the stairs. "Vlad? Joss? Dinnertime."

After a reassuring glance at Joss, Vlad moved down the stairs. A moment later, Joss followed.

Earlier in the day, Nelly had Vlad and Henry move the spare table from the basement to the kitchen and place it at the end of the long plank table. She'd covered them both with burgundy damask tablecloths and decorated them in autumn finery. There would be, Nelly insisted, no kids' table at her house. Nelly viewed teenagers as people, not babies.

Nelly rocked.

When Vlad entered the dining room, he found Nelly going over tiny details, like how the napkins were folded. "Nelly," he said, putting an arm around her shoulder, "it looks perfect."

Nelly smiled, her tension easing some. "You always know just what to say, Vladimir."

He gave her a hug and thought about every holiday he'd

spent with Nelly. She'd always made everything so perfect for him, for everyone but herself. It was part of what made Nelly so great.

The table was set with tons of candles, beautiful dishes, earth and jewel-tone decorations, and, of course, the finest food that Vlad had ever laid eyes on.

Which meant that Matilda had done the majority of the cooking.

Joss took a seat by Meredith, which just happened to be directly across from Vlad. Snow sat to Vlad's right. The air felt awkward, strange. But he wasn't sure if it felt that way for anyone else but him.

Under the table, Snow laced her fingers through his and squeezed. Her hand was cold. Vlad guessed that she was nervous too.

After all, sitting across from him was the girl he'd been crushing on since the third grade, the girl he'd compared all girls to until recently. And she was pretty. Meredith was beautiful and funny and sweet. She looked nothing at all like Snow, and Vlad was sure that scared Snow. After all, Snow didn't think she was all that beautiful—even though she was. She didn't think she was sweet or nice or worthy of dating any boy, let alone Vlad—even though she was that too. Vlad didn't have to read her mind to know these things. He just knew them. Snow had been hurt growing up, and it was going to take her a long time to realize what a wonderful, pretty, insanely cool person she was. She was different than Meredith. But different didn't mean she wasn't just as amazing.

Or even more so.

He squeezed her hand back and offered her a smile.

Tomas took his seat next to Meredith, whose eyes brightened at the sight of his pocket watch. "What a pretty watch, Mr. Tod."

"Thank you, Meredith. The most beautiful part is on the inside." Tomas smiled and flipped the watch open, revealing a picture of Vlad's mom. Joss glanced over at the picture and asked, "Who is she?"

"My wife, Mellina." Tomas looked somewhat on edge and snapped the pocket watch closed.

The strangest sensation spread through Vlad's insides. Tingling and pulling and very, very odd. Vlad felt himself slide through time and space, back to a moment that he thought he knew. All at once, he wasn't sitting at Thanksgiving dinner with his friends and family. He was standing on the corner somewhere in downtown Stokerton.

Snow was falling and the streetlights were lit. Vlad crossed the street, not knowing how he'd gotten here, but somehow instinctively knowing where he was supposed to go.

When he reached the corner, he stopped. Just a few yards down the sidewalk, he spotted something that told him what was really going on.

His mother—or rather, the woman who would one day become his mother—was talking to a handsome stranger, a man that Vlad knew as Tomas, a man who was a vampire. But Mellina didn't know yet. After all, this was their initial meeting— Vlad had read about it in his father's journal a hundred times.

She smiled brightly at him and said, "Walk me home?"

Part of Vlad feared for her safety. Part of him wanted to warn her that she shouldn't walk home with strange men. Strange men were dangerous. Especially strange men with fangs.

But this was the past, and Vlad was merely reliving it through Tomas's memories.

He wondered briefly if this was how Dorian seemed to know so much about everything, if he'd spent much of his time being sucked into the past, into people's memories, people's thoughts.

Vlad tailed them down the street, not always keeping his distance, and then, at a particularly shadow-filled corner, he stopped dead in his tracks.

Tomas looked up and down the street. Seeing that they were alone, he grabbed Mellina by the arm, his fangs exposed, and bit into her wrist.

She cried out, yanking her hand back. Tomas released her. "You are my drudge now. Come with me."

Mellina followed, sniffling, unable to resist her vampire master's direct command. "What do you want?"

Tomas nodded matter-of-factly. "I want a child."

Just as quickly as Vlad had been ripped from the dinner table, he was returned, his fork halfway to his mouth with a bite of marshmallow-covered sweet potatoes. He sat the fork down, no longer hungry, and looked at his father.

Tomas laughed and smiled warmly at something Otis had

just said. His eyes were bright with joy—joy at being returned to his family.

Vlad sat in stony silence, playing the scene over and over again in his mind.

He snapped his eyes to Otis, but Otis was busy chatting with Big Mike. He glanced at his dad again, but Tomas was scooping mashed potatoes onto his plate.

Drudge. Mellina had been Tomas's drudge.

Which meant he'd been feeding from her, not from blood bags. Which meant he'd lied to Vlad, about so many things.

His drudge.

Anger burned within his chest. Anger that required answers. And soon.

Snow squeezed his hand again, this time to get his attention. Vlad squeezed back, but said nothing.

Vlad's mom had been his dad's drudge. And for some reason, Tomas had kept it a secret.

Vlad just had to figure out why.

What's more, Vlad wasn't conceived in some dizzying sense of romance. He was conceived for a purpose by a driven man and a woman who was under someone else's control.

But why?

29

A QUESTION OF HONESTY

VLAD WALKED THROUGH THE KITCHEN DOOR of his house and slammed it behind him. His dad, who had left Nelly's about a half hour before Vlad, was already inside and looked up expectantly at Vlad's rather loud entrance. Vikas looked up too, then excused himself from the room. Tomas said, "You were rather quiet all through dinner. Something on your mind, son?"

Vlad set his jaw. "I want to know exactly what happened the day Mom died, and I want to know now."

Tomas dropped his gaze to the floor. His voice lowered as well. "Then let's go upstairs, and I'll explain all that I can recall."

Their walk through the house was silent as the grave. Tomas lead. Vlad followed. By the time they got to the master bedroom, which had been recently thoroughly renovated,

Vlad was pretty sure he could actually feel the tension in the air between them. His dad was probably feeling guilty about not telling Vlad that Mellina had been his drudge, and rightfully so. That wasn't the sort of thing you left out of conversations with your half-vampire son.

He'd trusted his dad. He'd not questioned his motives even once. But this . . . this was too much.

And if this had been kept a secret all these years, what else was Tomas capable of hiding?

His dad paused in front of the bedroom door, then reached out and opened it with a flick of his wrist. When he spoke, his voice was gruff, as if he were on the verge of exhaustion. "What do you want to know?"

"Everything." Vlad walked past him into the room, blocking out the horrible memory of finding his mother—and someone he thought was his father—on that terrible day. He moved closer to the window, not turning on the lights, letting the moonlight light the way. "That morning, I turned off your alarms, but you got up before the fire started. Where were you going?"

Tomas released a tense breath before speaking. "As I mentioned before, I was going to spy on Elysia. More specifically, to steal books from their library in Stokerton."

Vlad's defenses rose even further. "Books about the Pravus?"

After a brief pause, Tomas answered, "Yes."

"And when you got back?"

"It was too late. Your mother was gone."

"Who was in bed next to her?"

"I don't know."

"If you had to wager a guess . . ."

His dad's voice rose in terrible upset. "This was possibly the worst moment in my entire life and you want me to relive that pain. Why?"

Vlad looked at him for a long time before speaking. He was trying to decide if this man, his father, had been lying to him for years, and if he could tell that just by looking at him.

He couldn't.

"I just want to understand. I want to know what happened to her and why."

"So do I, Vlad. But those answers are never going to come." Tomas shook his head adamantly.

Vlad released a sigh. He'd hoped it wouldn't come to this, hoped that his dad would come clean without needing to be pushed. "How did you not feed on Mom, being so close to her? Otis says he just loves Nelly too much to feed from her. Was it that way for you?"

"Yes." His dad flicked his eyes nervously about the room. "Of course."

Vlad shook his head. He was tired of this, tired of the lies. He wanted the truth. Even a shred of it. "Did you really subsist on bagged blood, Dad? Or were you feeding on someone?"

Tomas dropped his eyes to the floor. He knew he'd been caught. It was right there in his expression. Vlad almost felt sorry for him. "I used the bagged blood the majority of the time, but supplemented with blood from the homeless in Stokerton."

Vlad tightened his jaw and boldly asked, "Was Mom your drudge, Dad? Did you feed from her?"

The silence was stunning.

Tomas's voice dropped to a whisper. "Would it matter if she was?"

"Yes."

"Why?"

"Because it changes things. Because it means that you weren't exactly forthcoming with me. It means you lied." Vlad's voice caught in his throat. "Did you lie to me?"

"What brought all of this on all of a sudd—" Understanding lit up his eyes. "Ahh . . . Otis. I should have known. What did he tell you, that I'm not to be trusted?"

Vlad shook his head again. "This isn't about Otis. It's about what I saw during dinner. It's about the night you and Mom met. You bit her. Against her will, you made her your drudge."

"The blood. Dorian's blood. It's given you gifts that I had not imagined. Wonderful!" Tomas smiled. His voice had taken on an eerily casual tone, like they were talking about their plans for later rather than whether or not Vlad's dad had ever fed on Vlad's mom, whether or not he could control her with a thought. "She was my drudge. But I loved her, Vlad. From the moment I saw her, I loved her. She gave me you, after all. My son. The Pravus."

Disgust filled him. "And if I wasn't the Pravus? If I were just some normal vampire kid . . . would you be so proud of me then?"

"Of course. But you are the Pravus. There's no doubting that now." Tomas smiled and a strange fog glazed his eyes, as if he were miles away, lost in whatever make-believe world made him the happiest. "Everything I have done, I have done for you, Vlad. Everything I've done, I've done because I love you. You are the Pravus. And you will embrace your future. You will manifest destiny."

30
CONFRONTING OTIS

VLAD WAS ABOUT TO ASK his dad just what the hell he was talking about, when he was interrupted by a familiar voice.

"Vlad," Joss sounded out of breath as he flung himself into the room. His skin was also disturbingly pale and small beads of sweat clung to his brow. "I have to talk to you. Now. Alone."

Tomas raised a sharp eyebrow, but moved silently from the room. Vlad couldn't help but wonder where the conversation might have turned if Joss hadn't interrupted. When Tomas was gone, Vlad turned to Joss. "What's going on?"

Joss closed the door and began pacing, his tone hurried, tense. He sounded angry. "What did you do?"

Vlad blinked. "Can you be more specific?"

Joss threw his arms in the air, his eyes lighting up with hot fury and betrayal. "That Slayer I told you about is dead! You

(233)

didn't have to kill him. Do you have any idea what this will mean? There are already another four hundred Slayers coming to Bathory because of this! It's only a matter of time before the cleansing begins."

Vlad shook his head, holding his hands up in front of him like a prisoner begging for forgiveness for his crimes. Even though he hadn't committed any. "Joss, slow down. I didn't kill anyone."

Joss looked stunned. "You didn't?"

Vlad shook his head, curtly, once.

"Then who did you tell? Your uncle? Your father? Vikas?" The anger was still there, lurking under the surface, ready to explode at any second.

It scared Vlad to see it.

"No one, okay? I didn't tell anyone there was another Slayer in town. What makes you so certain it was a vampire who killed him?"

Joss ran a hand through his hair, sighing. "No human could have killed him that way. He was found with his heart ripped from inside his chest and crushed to a pulp."

Vlad's heart shot into his throat. His eyes went wide. "I have to go."

"Vlad, what about the Slayers? We have to—"

"Not now, Joss." He had to get to Otis. He had to ask Otis if he'd killed the Slayer.

Joss sounded frustrated. "But we have to—"

"Not now!" Vlad yelled, and whipped out the door and

across town as fast as he could move. He found Otis in Nelly's kitchen. Breathlessly, he said, "Otis."

"Vladimir." Otis met his eyes and his smile wilted. "Something on your mind?"

There was. And that something was the death of everyone in Bathory.

Vlad wet his lips, suddenly nervous. Nervous to know whether or not Otis had just single-handedly started a war between the Slayer Society and everyone Vlad ever loved. "There's something I need to ask you, and I need for you to be completely honest with me, at all costs. Okay?"

Otis closed his eyes briefly. When he opened them again and spoke, his tone was soft, gentle. He also sounded like he'd been expecting this conversation, which was in and of itself an admission of guilt. "Complete honesty? No matter how you may react?"

"Yes."

"Okay."

"Did you kill D'Ablo?"

Otis's eyes grew wide with alarm. The surprise in his tone completely threw Vlad. "What? No."

"And the Slayer that's been wandering around Bathory— did you kill him?"

"I have no idea what you're talking about."

Vlad furrowed his brow. He searched Otis's face for any sign that he was lying, but found none. "And Enrico?"

Insult and pain crossed Otis's expression then, but he

didn't give voice to it. He merely replied, "I swear on my love for Nelly, Vlad. I am not responsible for any of these deaths."

Confusion enveloped Vlad. His uncle seemed completely innocent. But if Otis didn't do these things, who did? "You didn't rip their hearts out and mash them to a pulp?"

It was Otis's turn to furrow his brow. "No, but I have to admit, your line of questioning has piqued my interest. What brought this about?"

This didn't make any sense at all. It had to be Otis. There was no one else.

Vlad shook his head. "Your shirt was drenched in blood the day after Enrico was murdered. Your hat has D'Ablo's blood on it."

"It wasn't me, Vladimir. I swear on Nelly's life and all that she means to me. It wasn't me. I confess that I don't mourn D'Ablo's passing, and I have no idea how his blood came to stain my hat. I haven't even seen that hat in ages. My shirt was bloody because I went on a bit of a feeding frenzy. And I hadn't even been aware that there was another Slayer besides your friend Joss in town. But I killed neither man. And Enrico . . . I mourn Enrico's loss. You're free to search my memories, if you wish." Otis met his eyes then, and Vlad saw the truth within them.

His uncle hadn't done any of these things.

Vlad shook his head, almost guiltily. "I don't need to search your memories, Otis. I trust you."

His uncle held his gaze, as if daring him to read his mind. *"Perhaps you should search them. There are things locked away that you should learn. Things that I cannot bring myself to tell you. Things about your father.*"

Vlad raised a sharp eyebrow. "*Like how my mom was his drudge?*"

Otis looked surprised that Vlad knew about the true nature of his parents' relationship. He nodded, as if there were more to know. "That's one of the things, yes."

"What else is there?"

Otis sighed. "I love your father, Vladimir, but he has always had a taste for the forbidden."

Vlad paused, uncertain if he wanted to hear whatever it was that Otis had to tell him. But at the same time, he had to hear it. He had to know. Knowing something, after all, was far better than being ignorant about it. Even if it was a bad something. "Forbidden? What's forbidden? What do you know that you're not telling me, Otis? Remember, you promised me total honesty. I'm holding you to your word as a vampire."

Otis nodded. That lost-in-thought look returned to his eyes for a moment before he spoke again. It was unsettling.

"Tomas was always reading. From the time I knew him, he always had his nose in a book." Otis ran his fingertips along the length of the kitchen table as he moved around it. "But not just any book. Books from the Elysian libraries. Special books. Forbidden books." Otis dropped his gaze to the tabletop for a moment. His voice was a whisper, light and airy. But the meaning behind his words made Vlad's heart feel heavy, though Vlad wasn't sure why exactly.

Vlad thought back to the note he'd found in his dad's office a few years ago. The one with a single word scribbled on the back. It wasn't a difficult guess to make. "Books about the Pravus."

"Yes." Pressing his palms to the tabletop, Otis met Vlad's gaze and held it. "He set out to create the Pravus, Vladimir. He chose your mother based on theories surrounding the Pravus myth, and made her his drudge so that she could not resist. He loved her, yes. But the love came later. First, he used her to bring about an impossible thing—to procreate with a human and bring a half-breed child into the world, a child that would come to rule over vampirekind and enslave the human race. He created you for that purpose. I'm just not certain why."

Hatred and fury and all sorts of evil things that Vlad had not thought he was capable of feeling toward his uncle came boiling up from within Vlad's very soul. How dare he. How dare Otis insinuate that Tomas would ever do something so despicable. "You lie!"

Otis's voice remained calm and sure. "I speak the truth. Complete honesty, no matter how you may react—remember?"

Vlad began pacing back and forth across the kitchen; running through his mind was every loyalty that Otis had ever proven to him. Why would he start lying now? There had to be a reason. He glared at his uncle. "You're saying he planned it, that he planned my birth so that he would be the father of the Pravus."

"That's precisely what I'm saying."

"And if I don't believe you?" Vlad's heart was hammering against his ribs.

The corner of Otis's mouth twitched, but only slightly. "Ask your father."

31

To Trust or Not to Trust

VLAD MOVED DOWN THE SIDEWALK in a determined stride, wishing that he could just fly across town at vampiric speed again. But Otis had lectured him on using his gifts out in the open, and how he was endangering everyone he loved—even Nelly—by doing so. But he wanted to get back home fast, to confront his father with what Otis had said, before he had too much time to think about it.

He approached his house on Lugosi Trail and slowed his steps, surprised to find Joss and Henry outside, engaged in a heated argument. As he moved closer, Joss glanced at him, his face red, his eyes strained, his voice exhausted. "He knows, Vlad. He knows what we planned to do if we don't find the journal."

Vlad's eyes went wide. He looked from Joss to Henry and back. "You told him?"

Henry shoved Joss hard. Joss barely moved. Henry's eyes were red and furious. "I read it in his stupid journal!"

Vlad looked at Henry, so confused and so wishing that his drudge had picked a better time for this. "What journal?"

Henry shoved Joss again. "You're not the only one who keeps a journal, Vlad. Now tell me, who's idea was it not to tell me Joss was going to have to kill you?"

The air was stifling, despite the cool breeze. Vlad and Joss exchanged looks that spoke volumes. They both had come to that conclusion. But they both didn't have to suffer for it. Vlad said, "It was my idea, Henry."

Before Vlad could react, Henry balled up his fist and punched him in the nose. It felt like Vlad's skull had imploded. And there was blood. Fresh blood. All over Vlad's face, his lips. He had to fight the sudden urge to tear into Henry's jugular.

Vlad's fangs shot from his gums and he turned on Henry, growling. "This is why we didn't tell you! Because we knew you'd react this way!"

"You could have told me! Should have told me! I'm your friend, and his cousin! What the hell, man? I've kept you safe for thirteen years, Vlad. What makes you think I'd stop now?" He was still upset, that much was clear, but much of Henry's fury had been released in that punch.

Just as Vlad could feel his nose swelling, it started to shrink again, healing in a way that only a vampire nose could heal. He looked at Joss, and then back at Henry. "You're right. We should have told you. But you know now. So help us."

Henry shook his head. "Dude, we've searched the entire stupid town. Your dad's journal is gone."

Vlad sighed. "Then we need another option."

The three of them stood silently for several minutes.

Then Vlad said, "But we'll discuss it later, okay? For now, I have something important to talk to my dad about."

Joss nodded and made his way down the sidewalk. After he'd gone, Henry squeezed Vlad's shoulder before turning to leave. "Sorry about the nose, dude."

Vlad tried not to look down, even though he'd climbed up into the big oak tree easily enough. It still made him nervous, and he still wondered why Henry had insisted on climbing it when they were little kids. He'd been up there for about an hour, mulling over exactly how to approach his dad. So far, he still had no idea.

So maybe it was fate that opened the back door of Vlad's house and pushed Tomas out and in the direction of the old oak tree.

His dad smiled up at him. "I thought I'd find you here."

Vlad shifted some on the branch to a more comfortable position. "Why? I never liked climbing this tree."

Tomas shrugged. "Just a feeling I had."

"Can you still detect fellow vampires, now that your Mark is gone?"

"Yes."

"But they can't detect you?"

"No."

"Can they control you?"

Tomas raised an eyebrow, looking very much like Vlad's older reflection. "Is that really what's on your mind, Vlad?"

Vlad set his jaw. "Well, can they?"

"No. I'm free of Elysia's binds." Tomas met Vlad's gaze. "What's troubling you, son? Talk to me. What's going through that head of yours? If something's going on, just tell me. I'm always here for you."

Vlad slid forward, dropping from the branch and floated effortlessly to the ground. After he landed, he met his dad's eyes. "Someone told me something about you. Something disturbing. I came here to ask you if it's true or not. But I'm not really sure I want to know."

"Maybe I'm not the one you should be asking."

"You're the only one who can answer my question."

"Then maybe you should be asking a different question, son."

Vlad sighed. It felt like his world was falling apart. "Like what?"

"Like . . . do you trust me?" His dad smiled slightly and gave his shoulder a squeeze, his eyes full of a warmth that only a father could convey. "Because if you do, then no other question need be asked. If you trust me, no one and nothing else matters."

His words hung in the air between them, and Vlad examined each one like an extremely careful surgeon, picking them apart and putting them back together again.

In the end, they made perfect sense.

Vlad nodded slowly, pushing away all of Otis's crazy theories and every bad thought that he'd had about his dad since he left Nelly's house just an hour ago.

He did trust his dad.

And that was all that mattered.

32

The Food of Genius

IT WAS LUNCHTIME at Bathory High School. Lunchtime on a Tuesday, which could only mean one thing.

It was Taco Tuesday. Henry's favorite day of the week.

Henry's lunch tray had been covered with eight tacos when they'd stepped out of line, but they'd only been at the table for about ten minutes and his supply was already running dangerously low. He was down to three, and another fresh, crunchy shell was already in his hand and lifted to his open mouth.

Vlad's tray contained four tacos. Joss's contained three. But neither was feeling very hungry at the moment.

"What about your uncle? You said he's open-minded. Can't he get together a bunch of vampires to help us? Or maybe talk some sense into this Em person?" Joss's voice was low, but Vlad could tell he was on the verge of shouting in frustration. They'd been searching for a solution, a plan, for weeks now to no avail. Every idea they'd had so far was dangerously stupid.

Vlad sighed. "Not gonna happen, Joss. Otis can't change Em's mind, and I'm betting she has more followers than he does in Elysia. She's ancient. People fear her. What about your uncle? Can't he change the minds of the Slayer Society?"

Joss threw him a glance that said that that subject was closed. Apparently, Joss was about as close to his uncle as Vlad had been to D'Ablo.

Joss pushed his tray back, folded his arms on the table in front of him, and rested his chin on them. He was silent for a long time, but when he spoke, his words touched Vlad deeply. "I don't want to kill you."

Vlad slumped his shoulders in defeat. "And I don't want to die. But we're running out of options and time."

Joss released a heavy, troubled sigh. "I don't know what to do. The Slayer Society won't stop unless you're dead."

"And Em won't stop until I'm dead." Vlad sighed too. It came from deep within him, from the center of his very being. "What are we gonna do?"

A loud crunch came from Henry as he took the last bite of his last taco. He chewed loudly, then stretched his arm across the table to Joss's tray, snagging another taco. As he brought the taco back to his own tray, he shrugged with one shoulder. "Fake your death."

Joss sat up slowly, blinking at Henry. Vlad straightened his posture, glancing from Joss to Henry and back.

Henry hadn't been doing much talking at all since the other night, when they'd told him all about the fallback plan. And the killer thing was . . . his suggestion was kind of brilliant, and way too obvious for Vlad and Joss to have missed it during their long debates about what to do.

Joss shook his head, as unwilling as Vlad to accept that Henry had just had an excellent idea. "How are we going to do that exactly? The Slayers aren't blind and the vampires can detect Vlad by reaching out with their blood."

Henry paused for a moment, midchew, as if mulling Joss's question over in his mind. Seemingly satisfied with his thought process, he swallowed another bite, looked at Vlad, and said, "That clearing just outside of town has a cliff on the north end, just beyond the trees. If the Slayers see you go over and you use your freaky Pravus powers to block the vampires' detection . . . it could work."

Vlad thought about it, and even though the idea had settled the sick feeling in the pit of his stomach at least a little— to the point where he almost reached for a taco himself, there was still that other thing to be considered. "But Henry, if I go over that cliff, I'll break my neck."

Henry shook his head and rolled his eyes before helping himself to a taco from Vlad's tray. "Dude. Have you forgotten who you are? You can hover."

Joss and Vlad exchanged looks. Tense, scrutinizing, wondering looks. This could work. This could really work. They collectively shook their heads and the corner of Vlad's mouth lifted in a small smile. "You've been holding out on us, Henry. I had no idea you were so full of great ideas."

Henry held up his taco—formerly Vlad's—and grinned. "Little-known fact, gentlemen. Tacos are the food of genius."

Vlad and Joss grinned too and the three toasted to Henry's brilliant plan with tacos, thankful that it was Tuesday, and that they finally had a small chance of fixing all of their problems in one fell swoop.

33
UNHAPPY NEW YEAR

VLAD WAS DONNING THE NEW SKULL SCARF that Nelly had knitted him and given to him on Christmas, standing outside in the cold. His fingers were starting to go numb. Beside him, Joss was twirling his stake between his fingers, waiting. Today was the day. The day that they would dupe Slayers and vampires alike, and see just how well Henry's taco-fueled plan would work.

They'd been waiting for hours now and the sun had finally begun its descent. But there was still no sign of either the Society or Elysia. Vlad was beginning to wonder if they'd ever show.

He and Joss hadn't spoken much since arriving in the clearing. Maybe because there was nothing to say. Or maybe because they were both going over the plan again and again in their minds. It had to work. It just had to.

Just as Joss had turned to Vlad and started to say something to break the silence, there was a rustle in the bushes to the right and out stepped a man. He was dressed in earth tones, slacks with boots, a button-down shirt and vest, a flowing, almost capelike trench coat. A brown leather baldric holding six small blades crossed his chest. At his hip was a leather holster, holding a wooden stake. His cheek was scarred, a four-inch-wide crescent shape. He cocked a displeased eyebrow at Joss. "You're supposed to kill it. Not speak with it."

Joss stumbled over his words, hurrying to retrieve his own stake from the ground and return it to its place on his hip. "Uncle Abraham ... you're ... here ..."

Abraham pursed his lips. "On your feet, Slayer. Dispatch this vampire. Rid the world of this evil. Do as you have been instructed to do."

By the tone in his voice, Vlad got the feeling that Joss's uncle didn't like weakness, and when Abraham looked at Joss, it was all he could see.

Joss looked from his uncle to Vlad and back again. "I was about to."

Here it was. Time to enact their get-out-of-jail-free plan. All they needed was a vampire to witness Vlad's miraculous execution.

"Abraham. It's been too long." Vlad's dad wore a peculiar smile as he entered the clearing. Vlad raised an eyebrow at the familiarity in his tone, and resisted the urge to sigh in relief. They had their vampire. Now it was Joss's turn. Vlad eyed Joss's stake, ready as he'd ever be.

Abraham's hand hesitated on his stake. His tone was full of surprise and alarm, and just a little bit of fear. He reached up and gently stroked the scar on his cheek. "Tomas."

"Oh, now isn't this a surprising reunion?" Vlad turned at the familiar voice. Otis offered him a wink and then turned to face the Slayer.

"Otis." Abraham's voice held no surprise this time, like he'd expected Otis to be along anytime since Tomas was here.

Vlad raised a sharp eyebrow. "You three know one another?"

Otis smiled, keeping his eyes on Joss's uncle the entire time. "Oh yes. Abraham and your father are well acquainted."

"Nice scar, by the way." Tomas grinned, then glanced at his son. "And Otis and Abraham are simply the best of friends."

"That's not at all how I recall it. But my memory's fading." Otis took a step closer to Abraham, but, to Vlad's surprise, Abraham didn't take a step back. He stood there defiantly. Otis smiled. "Perhaps we should reminisce about old times?"

"Over a drink?" Tomas stifled a chuckle as he too stepped closer to Abraham.

Abraham gripped his stake and glared at them both, growling, "I'll have your heads."

Otis clucked his tongue. "Like that fateful day, Abraham, there are only two Slayers here, and three vampires. You are outwitted and outmatched."

Tomas shook his head, stepping even closer. "And this time, we won't turn the other cheek."

Abraham laughed, and by the sound of it, Vlad was pretty sure it wasn't something he did often. "You actually think I'm here alone? What kind of fool do you take me for?"

A wooden stake whipped by Tomas's head. He had just barely ducked it before it slammed six inches into a tree behind him. Vlad whipped his head around to see a Slayer standing in the woods, a modified crossbow in his hands.

Otis quipped, "One with a short lifespan."

Vlad looked at Joss and nodded. Joss nodded back, then ran toward Vlad, stake held high. Vlad bolted across the clearing, but kept his movements slow enough that Joss could keep up. They wrestled for a moment, struggling for the stake and then Joss raised his eyebrows, as if to silently ask Vlad if he was ready. Vlad nodded.

That's when Joss pretended to stake him, and then tossed him over the cliff.

Vlad flew over the edge, but with a little concentration, hovering just out of sight was an easy thing to do. From above, all he heard were whispers and muttering. It had worked. They had totally faked his own death.

He owed Henry about a zillion tacos.

Strong fingers tangled in his hair and pulled him upward. Vlad almost screamed as it felt like his scalp was being torn off. Lying on the ground, once more in the clearing, Vlad looked up to find Em holding his hair, looking disgusted. "Faking your death, are we? Not a bright boy, my great-grandson. That has to be the oldest—and dumbest—trick in the book."

She looked back at Abraham and said, "If you truly believe, Slayer, that you're going to take Tomas's life before I've had the pleasure, you should think again. I've come to carry out a sentence that has been a long time coming."

She glanced at Vlad's dad. "Italy, Tomas? Really."

When she looked back at Abraham, her eyes were no longer rolling. "Don't think the threat of wood will do so much as make me hesitate. I knew your great-great-grandfather." She snapped her teeth playfully at Abraham and grinned. "He was delicious."

At her final word, a group of no less than six Slayers descended on the clearing. Em, as if expecting this, snatched Abraham close to her while elongating her fangs and hissing into his ear, "Call off your pets, Abraham. Or die."

Abraham hesitated, then waved them away.

Vlad never thought he'd ever be happy to see Em, but at the moment, he kinda was.

Live and learn.

34
THE BEGINNING
OF THE END

EVERYONE IN THE CLEARING—all but Abraham and Joss—relaxed some then.

"Not so fast, Tomas." Em's voice was an echo in the night. Both Tomas and Vlad blinked at her. "There is the slight matter of your execution to tend to."

Vlad stood, brushing the dirt from his clothes, and looked at his father. Tomas merely shrugged casually, as if her threats meant nothing to him.

"I think we might have slightly more pressing matters at hand, Madame Council." The sarcasm in Tomas's voice was evident.

"I think that the assembled mass of vampires currently in Bathory can more than take care of a small group of Slayers." An evil glint crossed her eyes. "I brought them in hungry."

With a twitch of her finger two of her cronies stepped forward from their spot in the surrounding woods. "Alert the others and take care of them."

The bigger of the two nodded. His lips spread into a smile as he let his fangs elongate, and broke into a run, followed closely by the other.

Vlad said, "That won't be enough." Em glared at him, and he met her gaze with equal intensity. Vlad shook his head, overwhelmed by the enormity of his situation. "There are more Slayers coming. Joss has to kill me or everyone will die."

Vlad moved forward, eyeing Em with certainty. "You included."

"Vlad, don't." Tomas reached out a hand to stop his son from moving toward the oldest vampire in existence, but was unable to restrain him. Two more of her cronies exited the woods and moved protectively in front of Em. Vlad stopped just short of them, his eyes locked on Em. "My life will end, just as you want it to. The only difference is that Joss will be the one to kill me."

Em said, "That eager to die, are we?" Vlad wasn't sure how, but it seemed that each time Em smiled she looked even more evil. "Your chance will come. For now my attention is on your father. Once I have dispatched him, I will take my sweet pleasures with you."

One of Em's henchmen grabbed Vlad by the shoulders and turned him around to hold him in place. Em's gaze fell on Tomas. She was going to make Vlad watch his father die.

Vlad swallowed hard. It couldn't happen. It wouldn't.

From the corner of his eye, he watched as Abraham and

Joss slinked away. Abraham practically had to force Joss from the clearing, but Vlad was glad he went.

When her bodyguards started to go after the Slayers, Em merely smiled. "Let them go. We'll hunt them later. It'll be entertaining."

"Em, aren't you forgetting something? Tomas has yet to have a trial." Otis flicked his eyes from his brother to Em, as if hoping that this loophole might buy some time for Tomas, and for him to come up with a plan.

"We're not really concerned with the formalities anymore, dear Otis. There is no question of his guilt. The proof of it is standing there." Em's head motioned to where Vlad was being held, though her eyes never left Tomas. "Now, all that is left is to watch joyously as the life drains from his eyes."

The remaining vampires in Em's entourage moved forward to restrain Tomas as Em pulled an ornate dagger from her long black coat and began to walk slowly toward him.

"Aww, to hell with this." Something told Vlad that Otis hadn't meant to speak his thoughts out loud.

Throwing his coat off his shoulders, Otis ran forward like a lightning bolt. If killing Em was the only way to stop this madness, then so be it. The speed at which he moved made him appear as a blur to all eyes around him. Vlad had never seen his uncle move so fast before.

A hand stretched out from nowhere and met Otis's face at full speed. The crunch of bone breaking made Vlad wince. Otis flipped over backward in the air, landing on the back of his neck and crumpling into a heap at the vampire bodyguard's feet. He had hit the ground before his coat had a chance to fall in the place he had left it standing.

Em leaned down to where Otis lay. "Now that wasn't very smart was it?"

She put her fingers into the blood that was dripping from his wounds and cleaned them off in her mouth, much like a child who just finished a chocolate bar on a hot day. "And I was going to let you live. Oh well, I guess you just got in line after your nephew."

She stood with a twinkle in her eye.

"But first," Em raised the dagger above her head, "Good-bye, Tomas Tod."

An arrow carved from a single piece of wood, tipped in silver embedded in Em's shoulder. The dagger fell to the ground as she screamed. Figures, cloaked in shadow, surrounded the clearing. Stepping into the light in front of Em, Abraham had a smug look on his face. "That was just a warning. But I'm glad that arrow was fired by one of our first years, Em. I was hoping I would be the one who got to kill you."

"You have no idea that you just volunteered your little group for extinction, Abraham." Em grasped the arrow and, with a yelp, pulled hard, yanking it free of its fleshy quiver. The wound began to heal almost instantly; her eyes held the ferocity of a cornered tiger. "This battle has been looming for centuries. This war has gone on for too long. Today it ends when I feast on the blood of the last Slayer."

35

THE CLEANSING

THE OPPORTUNITY THAT OTIS HAD been hoping for had presented itself, and he'd be damned if he was going to let it pass him by. The vampire who was holding Tomas had released him and gone to the aid of his puppeteer. Otis stood next to his brother, his face already healed. The only evidence of the injury stained the front of his shirt red.

Otis put a hand on Tomas's shoulder, "Come on, let's help Vlad."

"I don't think we need to." Tomas was smiling as he nodded toward his son.

Apparently Otis wasn't the only one who had heard the telltale knock of opportunity's fist. Vlad stood above the vampire who had been holding him. The vampire's wrist was twisted in Vlad's hand, his thumb sticking painfully out onto the air. Vlad's foot was on the back of the man's neck, pushing his face into the ground.

Tomas looked on with an air of pride, Otis with a gasp of amazement.

Vlad smirked. "What? Henry's brother, Greg, was also on the wrestling team. He taught me a couple of moves."

"And you learned them very well, son." Tomas leaned down to the vampire on the ground. "I'd tell you to pick on someone your own size, but I don't think it really matters in this case."

Otis shook his head in amazement. "Come on, you two. Let's get out of here."

Vlad released the vampire he was holding and started to follow his uncle out of the clearing. There was a loud thump behind them. When they turned, Tomas was picking himself up off of the ground, kicking away the hand that had tripped him. The vampire that had just been bested by a teenager didn't want to give up his quarry so easily.

"You guys go ahead, I'll handle this." Tomas's eyes darkened as his fangs shot out in anger. Vlad saw his dad deliver a kick to the face of the fallen vampire before Otis grabbed Vlad's shoulder and led him out of the clearing and into the streets of Bathory.

"Uncle Otis, where are we going?" They walked at a hurried pace, occasionally breaking into a jog.

"Back to Nelly's house. We have to get you out of here." Otis spun around to avoid being hit by the car that was barreling down the street. "What in the world is going on?"

He turned to look up the street, then down. Cars were everywhere, lights beaming down on them, horns sounding. Vlad followed his gaze. The scene reminded him of every disaster movie he'd ever seen. The people of the peaceful, midwestern town were fleeing for their lives, and they didn't care who they trampled on their way out.

"Oh no." Vlad's face fell. What color there had been in his cheeks was now gone. "They've started the cleansing."

Vlad broke into a run.

Otis called behind him, "Where are you going?"

"I have to find Joss!"

In a flash of vampiric speed, Otis was in front of him, blocking his path. "Vlad, can't you see that it's too late for that now. If the cleansing has begun the only way to stop it is to annihilate the Slayers. Your friend Joss, included. He could be compromised. He could be on their side. He may have lied."

"Joss didn't lie, Otis! And it looks like Em's cronies have already started." Vlad pointed to the intersection a block in front of them. There were at least twenty Slayers locked in full combat with an equal number of vampires. Stakes flew, fangs were bared, Vlad could smell the garlic from where he stood. It made him sick to his stomach. Bodies on both sides fell like oak leaves on an autumn day, lifeless and red.

Otis looked worried. "Come on, Vlad, we need to go."

"Yeah . . . yeah, right behind ya." Vlad turned again to follow his uncle. They backtracked and turned down a different street to avoid the battle. As they rounded the next corner on their way back to Nelly's house, they came face-to-face with another small battalion of Slayers.

There were probably twelve or thirteen of them, Vlad couldn't be sure. He and Otis stopped in their tracks as one of the Slayers began to speak.

"Well, well, well, now there's a face I recognize. Vladimir Tod, isn't it?" The man smirked as he drew a silver-tipped stake from his pocket. Vlad had no idea who this man was or how he was able to recognize him. "Yes, Joss has kept us well informed. He may not be much of a Slayer, but he is an excellent spy."

Otis and Vlad began to back away slowly, not in retreat, but enough to give them time to take in their plight.

"Boy, your skills in combat have been improving in the past couple of years, but if you do have any special powers in there, this would be a good time to figure out how to use them." Instinctively Otis and Vlad moved until they were back-to-back as the Slayers moved to encircle them.

In his mind, Vlad could hear Otis's voice, *They'll be coming from all sides, but they'll only be one deep. This is actually good for us.*

"Got it." In the heat of the moment, Vlad forgot that he could speak telepathically.

I know how hard this is for you, Vladimir, but you have to aim to kill. Otherwise, we've already lost this battle.

Vlad stopped for a moment. He knew what had to be done, but thought he could still deny that fact to himself. That is until his uncle put it into words. There was no way around it. Vlad would have to kill if he were to survive. There was a Slayer coming right at him.

There was no time to think, only time to act.

Vlad ran with incredible speed, moving from Slayer to Slayer, snapping necks as he moved. They didn't have time to react. They didn't even have time to blink. By the time he slowed his movements, he realized they were surrounded by several dead bodies. Roughly half of the Slayers that had been about to attack were lying before him, lifeless.

Vlad felt a wave of nausea almost knock him down.

And guilt. Horrible guilt.

He'd killed. He'd killed them all.

Otis squeezed his shoulder, breathless. "Vladimir, where did you learn to fight like that? I know it's not something that Vikas taught you. You moved so fast."

Vlad shook his head. He was assuming it was a Pravus thing, but it scared the hell out of him to lose himself like that. "There's no time to explain now, Otis. I have to go find Joss. He's the only one who can put a stop to this."

"Vladimir, I told you. It's too late for that. Besides, if you think I'm going to let you walk out there and volunteer to get staked, you're crazy."

"It's not like that, Uncle Otis. You're right, it's too late for that. But if I don't do something, then everyone will die." Vlad's chest felt tight, like he might start hyperventilating at any moment. "Don't worry, I can handle myself. You need to get Nelly to safety."

Otis looked at him, as if gauging his sincerity. Then he

sighed and offered Vlad a nod. "All right, but we're not leaving town without you. Do what you have to do and meet us at the high school."

Vlad nodded and took off as fast as he could.

To where, he had no idea.

36
COMING OUT OF THE COFFIN

MANEUVERING THROUGH THE STREETS of his small town, Vlad could hardly recognize where he was. It looked more like one of the battlegrounds that he saw on the news rather than the place he had grown up. Police lights and sirens blared as they sped through the streets. Fires burned in trash cans and on wrecked or abandoned cars. There were bodies lying all around, vampire, Slayer, and innocent bystander alike.

As he passed the lifeless body of Principal Snelgrove, Vlad lost his composure as well as his lunch. Sure he hadn't liked the guy, but he deserved better than this. Maybe he was right to not have liked Vlad all these years. After all, look where Vlad had led him, led the whole town for that matter.

Vlad grew angry. Angry at Joss. Angry at Abraham. Angry

at the Slayers and the vampires. But most of all, angry at himself. This was all his fault.

But he was past that now and there was no going back. Vlad had chosen this path and he had to prove, to himself more than anyone else, that he was man enough to walk it.

Turning the corner, Vlad spotted another battle raging in front of him, but there was something different about this one. Vlad didn't see any vampires fighting. The townspeople were fighting back. And what's more, they were doing a pretty good job.

Vlad smiled; maybe the people of Bathory were a little more than the Slayer Society had expected.

After two more battles blocking his path and one fight of his own, involving three Slayers who would certainly feel it when they woke up in the morning, Vlad decided to take to the top of the trees. He had to find Joss and Abraham and there was only one place in Bathory where one could survey the whole town at once. Vlad had to get to the belfry.

As Vlad rounded the corner of the school he spied a familiar sight. The goths were assembled on the steps of the school.

"Guys!" Vlad hurried over to them, almost breathless, full of panic. "Have you guys seen Joss?"

"Yeah, I did." Sprat jumped up and pointed toward the middle of town, "Some old guy was draggin' him around by the arm, over by EAT, but that was like twenty minutes ago."

"Vlad," October had a worried look in her eyes, "have you seen Henry? He's not answering his phone."

Vlad's heart ached for her. October was clearly very worried. "I'm sure he's fine. In fact I know he is. I'd have felt it if something had happened to him."

"Felt it? Boy, I guess you guys *are* really close friends, aren't you?" The sarcasm flowed in Kristoff's words.

Ignoring him, Vlad turned to the others in the group, "Look, guys, I need your help. But first I have to tell you some-thing. Something ... well ... about the truth. My truth, that is."

Vlad took a deep breath. He was about to willingly break Elysian law. If he were able to stop the Slayers then he might still be able to get out of execution if he played his cards right. They might actually give him a fair trial. After all, he hadn't known about the law when he broke it before. If he broke the law now, he would condemn himself to death. That is, if he survived the day.

But he had to tell them. He had to tell the goths about who and what he was. Because he needed them. Now more than ever. And the only way for him to know they were on his side was if he was completely honest with them.

"What is it, Vlad?" October had moved closer to him, putting her hand on his shoulder in concern.

He took a deep breath. Then another one, this time deeper.

He was nervous.

Strike that. He was downright terrified.

"I'm . . . a vampire." He braced himself for the laughter and ridicule that was about to come. It would. After all, none of them really believed in vampires. And even if they did, that would make him a freak. A bigger freak than they'd thought he was before his admission.

October, Sprat, Andrew, and Kristoff exchanged glances, then looked at Vlad like they were still waiting for him to reveal his big secret.

October smiled. "Yeah . . . we kinda know that already. Is there . . . something else you wanna clue us in on?"

"You told us sophomore year, remember?" Sprat shrugged like it was no big deal.

Andrew merely nodded.

Kristoff said nothing.

Vlad blinked in utter confusion. "Wait . . . you already know? How do you already know? It's my deepest, darkest secret."

October shrugged. "You told us a few years ago at The Crypt, remember?"

Vlad did remember. They had been playacting. Or so he'd thought. And for fun, because he knew they'd assume he was pretending, Vlad had told them his inner truth—that he was a vampire. Running a hand through his hair in confusion, Vlad blinked again. "But I thought you thought I was joking."

She raised a sharp eyebrow at him. "Vlad, no offense, but look at you. If you're not a vampire, you're clearly the most anemic goth I've ever seen."

Sprat nodded enthusiastically. He seemed to have a hard time standing in one spot. Vlad wagered it had something to do with his pixie stick obsession. "Yeah, you're way pale. Plus, your fangs are cooler than Kristoff's . . . and he had his custom made."

Kristoff's face flushed red as he whipped around to glare at his hyper friend.

October gave Vlad's shoulder a squeeze. "We believed you. Because that's what friends do."

"Big whoop. So you're a real vampire, who cares." Kristoff stormed off around the school, his shoulders slumped, the edges of his very being sizzling.

Vlad watched after him, somewhat taken aback. He and Kristoff had never really been what you'd call friends, but it still bugged him that Kristoff was acting so upset. "What's his problem anyway?"

"He wants what you have, Vlad." October peeked around the end of the school building and watched Kristoff walk away. "That's why he never liked you."

"Oh, I didn't know. I mean . . . wait a minute . . ." Realizing what she was saying, that Kristoff had always been jealous of him for actually being a vampire, Vlad gaped openly. "You mean, you all believed me back then? Every word I said about being a vampire? I thought it came off as a joke."

"I'm sure that's how you meant it, but c'mon, Vlad. If you can be honest with anyone, you know it's us, right?" October smiled at him. "So, what do you need our help with?"

Vlad found himself smiling, even amidst all the chaos. "I need to find Joss."

"Done." Andrew led the way, and the rest of the goths followed. Sans Kristoff.

And Vlad was left knowing that his true friends didn't care that he was such a freak after all.

37
Time Heals All Wounds

THEY'D JUST REACHED EAT, when Vlad spied a familiar sight. Eddie Poe, vampire, chasing Kristoff down an alley. Kristoff, who looked absolutely terrified.

Just like in Vlad's vision.

Vlad shouted to October, and then took off after them. He didn't catch up until Eddie and Kristoff were crossing the football field. Vlad moved with vampiric speed, until he was standing right in front of Eddie Poe.

Eddie, who now had fangs.

Eddie, who had somehow gotten himself in too deep.

Vlad looked him over, his pale skin, his elongated fangs, and shook his head slowly, both in disappointment and disbelief. "How, Eddie? Exactly how did you become a vampire?"

Eddie clucked his tongue, shaking his head in bemusement and running the tip of his tongue over the points of his fangs. "Vlad, you know how. Why ask a question when you already know the answer?"

Terror filled Vlad's insides. What was Eddie insinuating? That Vlad had turned him into a vampire and then somehow forgotten? That was insane ... wasn't it?

"I mean ... how did you become a vampire without my help?"

"You're not the only vampire on the planet, as you well know." A sly grin spread across Eddie's face. It was all Vlad could do to refrain from slapping it off of him. "After you refused to become my creator, I was furious. I was on my way to the post office, ready to ship off a package that would expose you and, eventually, the rest of Elysia."

Elysia. Eddie knew all about Elysia now. Intimately. In a way that only vampires did.

This couldn't be possible. It couldn't be happening. Eddie was a vampire. A real, live, bloodthirsty vampire.

It was like a bad dream.

But it was real.

"But then I ran into Em." A smile danced on Eddie's lips, one that made Vlad cringe. Em. Of course. If anyone was maniacal and insane enough to think that making Eddie Poe into a vampire was a good idea, it was her. "She told me she admired my strengths and would give me the gift of eternity. All I'd have to do is rid the world of you when the time came."

Vlad shook his head and spoke as if he were talking to a

child. "Hasn't Em told you about the prophecy, Eddie? I'm the Pravus. And the Pravus can't be killed."

"You can now. Ever since D'Ablo removed your invincibility a few years ago with that ritual." Eddie's tone was bitter. Each word that left his lips hit Vlad hard in the gut, like punches. Then Eddie smiled pleasantly, a cruel glint in his eyes. "I'm not stupid. You really shouldn't underestimate me."

Eddie knew. He knew everything. Em had made him into a vampire, armed him with knowledge, and set his sights on Vlad.

Eddie's eyes grew disturbed as he looked over Vlad's shoulder. "You also shouldn't underestimate your Slayer friend."

Vlad whipped around to find Joss approaching, his stake held firmly in one hand. A moment of doubt shadowed his thoughts, and he wondered if Joss was there to make another attempt on his life.

Then a familiar feeling swept over him. The feeling of being punched in the back. That same sensation he'd experienced his freshman year, when Joss had staked him.

Vlad looked down as he dropped to his knees. His world swirled before him, then sharpened once again.

Wood. There was wood sticking out of his chest. He'd been staked. For the second time.

Only this time . . . it was by Eddie.

Shock took him over. His heart beat strongly, defiantly, against the splintered wood of the crude instrument that Eddie had constructed.

Vlad wondered briefly if Eddie had created it in wood shop.

If so, he probably got points off for not sanding it smooth enough.

Vlad hoped so, anyway.

Joss's eyes grew wide in horror as he rushed to Vlad's aid. He dropped to his knees, his hand shaking over the end of the stake. "Vlad! Vlad, are you okay? What do I do? What do I do?!"

Vlad coughed, sending a small trickle of blood from the corner of his mouth.

There was nothing Joss could do. Nothing at all.

And strangely, Vlad wasn't scared. Just surprised. Surprised that it had been Eddie to stake him. Surprised that it hadn't been Joss.

He also wasn't in a whole lot of pain, which meant one of two things. Either he'd begun to go numb from shock, or something was different this time around.

And with every blood-drinking fiber of his being . . . Vlad was betting on option B.

He reached up with a steady hand and grasped the tip of the stake between his fingers. With all his might, he pulled on the wood until it slipped painfully from his chest, leaving tiny splinters behind in his lungs, his heart.

There was no gush of blood, no dizzying pain.

It was easy.

Far easier than Vlad had ever imagined.

Once the stake was out, he stood, aware of a tickling

sensation in his chest. Eddie and Joss were staring, dumb-founded, as the hole that Eddie's stake had made, healed closed before their eyes.

It sounded a bit like spiders . . . just like when his blood had healed the hole in D'Ablo a few years ago.

Vlad moved closer to Eddie and growled. "I told you I can't die."

Eddie's eyes grew enormous in fright. He turned and ran as fast as his vampire legs could carry him. Vlad was amazed not to see a stream of urine trailing after him.

He thought about chasing after Eddie, about finishing him off and putting him out of his misery. But in the end, he let Eddie go.

After a moment, Joss placed a still-shaking hand on Vlad's shoulder. "You did the right thing, letting him go like that."

Vlad shook his head. "I'm not entirely sure it was the right thing to do."

He ran his fingertips lightly over his chest, where the skin was now smooth through the hole in his shirt.

One thing was for sure. D'Ablo's ritual hadn't removed his invincibility after all.

38
Fallen Snow

VLAD TURNED FROM JOSS when he spied a familiar sight. Snow, looking lovely and rather kick butt in her stompy military boots, moving down the steps of Bathory High, her eyes reflecting the determination in her soul. He hadn't worried about her, not even once, during the war that had broken out all over Bathory. There was no need for him to worry about Snow. She knew how to take care of herself. She was strong.

But he was incredibly grateful to see that she was okay, that she hadn't been harmed by a flying stake or a biting fang.

She had just used a pretty fierce roundhouse kick on a Slayer, disarming him like a pro. Vlad didn't even know she could fight. But it was cool to watch.

Despite what was going on all around them, Vlad found himself smiling at the sight of her. And when her eyes found his, she smiled too—in that same impossible way. Impossible because thre was no reason for them to smile now. But just seeing one another was proving reason enough.

Suddenly, Snow's eyes went wide, so wide that Vlad thought she might be in physical pain. She ran toward him, down the steps, and lurched forward. Vlad moved to catch her, but she knocked him to the side. Twisting his body around, he caught her as he fell and they tumbled down the steps in a heap.

It was almost comical.

That is . . . until Vlad saw the blood.

Snow's blood. Flowing from her chest.

A broad-shouldered Slayer with a long, thin scar drawing a line from his left eye to the corner of his mouth approached with a heavy step and ripped the stake from Snow's chest. She cried out and Vlad covered the wound, his hands shaking in shock.

He knew that Slayer. That was the Slayer from the alley, one of the four who'd been posing as policemen, from earlier in the year after he'd put Joss in the hospital.

But more importantly . . .

Snow had been staked. Snow had been horribly injured. The Slayer must have mistaken her gothic beauty for the traits of a vampire.

The Slayer eyed Vlad for a second, and then lifted his wooden weapon in the air.

Inside Vlad's veins, he felt a surge of immense power. He

locked eyes with his would-be killer and uttered a single command, not knowing if it would work. "Drop it."

The stake hit the steps and clattered down several more steps until it was yards away. The Slayer's lips shook in fear. "Your eyes . . ."

Vlad gripped Snow—too pale now—to his chest and screamed at the Slayer with every bit of his anger and hatred and overwhelming frustration. "DIE!"

The Slayer's eyes bugged and his jaw went slack.

Vlad's heart beat twice before the man fell to the ground, dead.

A deep, critical horror enveloped Vlad as he stared at the man's corpse.

He'd just killed the Slayer with a word.

He took one breath, released it slowly. Then another.

This power. It was too much to wield. Too much for anyone to even taste.

Struggling with his emotions—which were filled with all kinds of self-loathing, even though he'd only said it because of what the man had done to Snow—he turned back to the matter at hand.

Blood bloomed from Snow's wound. Vlad had never seen so much red.

He opened his mouth to scream, to shout for someone, anyone, to save her, help her.

But no one could hear him over the sounds of war.

Snow's pulse grew weak. Her eyes began to flutter closed,

but before they did, she parted bloodstained lips and whispered, "I saved you. I had . . . a vision. You were killed . . . in my dream. But then I saw the Slayer . . . and I stopped him. I saved you."

His world swirled around him, but he forced the vision to remain at bay. He didn't want to know what the future would bring. Not now. Not when he was on the verge of losing Snow.

Tears poured from his eyes. He was losing her. He was losing the only girl who had ever really understood him, had ever really loved him, and there was nothing he could do about it.

Vlad bent down and brushed his lips against Snow's forehead. His tears dripped onto her cheeks, and he whispered repeatedly, "What can I do, Snow? I'll do anything. Anything. What can I do to save you?"

39

COME THE PRAVUS

THERE'S ONLY ONE THING you can do, Vladimir." Otis's eyes were dark, dark and sad and troubled in the worst way, unlike Vlad had ever seen them. His shirt was marred with blood and dirt—the filth of battle. He must have been fighting somewhere nearby and saw what had happened to Snow. Vlad hadn't seen him approach, but he was glad his uncle was here now. "You can let her die, or . . . you can turn her."

"Turn her?" Vlad couldn't believe what he was hearing. Otis couldn't possibly be suggesting that he—

"Turn her into one of us, welcome her into Elysia, make her a vampire . . . or say your goodbyes." Otis's voice was soft, but stern. The choice, he'd made clear, was up to Vlad.

"But don't I need her permission to turn her?"

"I think we're beyond following Elysia's laws tonight, Vladimir."

Vlad looked down at Snow in his arms. Her eyes were closed and her skin was paler then he'd ever seen. Even her lips, painted a deep burgundy, paled to a lighter shade as blood poured from her wound. She'd lost consciousness, which was both a blessing and a curse. A blessing because he hoped that it lessened her pain some. A curse because it robbed him of the chance to ask her if she'd rather die than be like him.

She would die. Or live out her life as a bloodthirsty creature of the night. It was up to him to choose her fate.

Entirely up to him.

"There's something you should know before you decide." Otis dropped his eyes to Snow then for a moment, his voice hushing some, as if out of respect for the dead. "She may not survive the transformation. It's possible that she will, but I have never heard of a released drudge turning successfully. Not once. Their blood rejects the transformation for some reason. You may lose her anyway, Vladimir."

Vlad ignored the blood that was soaking through his clothes. He ignored the sounds of war all around him. He ignored even his uncle's caring presence and looked at Snow, really looked at her for the first time. Gently, he ran his thumb down her cheek. Bending down, he kissed her quiet lips, swallowing his tears. He had to be strong. For Snow. "I have to try, Otis."

Otis gauged his sincerity for a moment, then, as if satisfied by what he saw in Vlad's eyes, he spoke. "Drain her, but not completely. You want her heartbeat as slow as possible, but still beating. It takes a great amount of control, but you're capable."

A flash of doubt crossed Otis's eyes. Vlad tried to ignore it, but couldn't.

"Once she's drained, you must move quickly. Bite your wrist, give her your blood. She'll cough and choke and fight, but that's a natural reaction. Be ready for it." Otis squeezed his shoulder and as he ran off to assist a young vampire fight off two Slayers, he shouted something else to Vlad, but Vlad couldn't hear him over the noise of the crowd.

Vlad lifted Snow, cradling her in his arms. He was going to save her, save her at any cost. It was the right thing to do . . . wasn't it?

His fangs slipped from his gums and he bit down on her neck, her blood splashing against his tongue. Trying to block out the incredible taste of her blood, he swallowed and swallowed again, drinking far more from her than he ever had before. She lay helpless in his arms, and he wrapped his arms around her, holding her close.

He loved Snow. And he wanted nothing more in this world than for her to survive, for them to be together, for everything to be all right.

As Otis had said, her heartbeat slowed substantially. Vlad fought the monster within him and won, withdrawing his fangs from her porcelain neck. He bit into his right wrist and held it to her mouth, watching as his blood slipped from his wrist to her tongue, until his wound healed closed again. Then he waited, and watched.

At first, nothing happened.

Then Snow lurched forward, coughing, her body wracked with violent spasms. The moment she'd shown any sign of life, Vlad's Mark glowed brightly, brighter than ever before. Snow choked and sputtered and shook. After a long time—time that was drawn out by his utter terror of losing her—she went still.

Too still.

Snow's eyes were opened, but there was no life in them.

Vlad screamed, "NO!!! Snow! Not you! Not you!"

He pulled her close and sobbed into her soft black hair. Her body was limp. Her heart wasn't beating. Everything about her that had made her Snow was gone.

She was dead.

Dead, before he could tell her that she was his perfect match in every way, that she was everything he ever wanted in a girl.

Dead, before she could experience a life full of laughter and smiles instead of one overwhelmed by pain.

Dead.

Dead and gone.

And she wasn't ever coming back.

Vlad wiped the tears from his cheeks and laid Snow's body gently on the steps. Slowly, he stood, surveying the battleground all around him. He saw Slayers staking vampires, vampires biting Slayers and ripping them limb from limb. He saw terrified citizens running, trying to get away from horrors they couldn't understand. He saw familiar faces scattered through the crowd—Joss, Meredith, October, Henry. And all he could think was that this wasn't supposed to be happening. His family, his friends, they weren't supposed to be suffering. Elysia wasn't supposed to be exposed. The Slayer Society wasn't supposed to be here.

Inside of him, something bigger and brighter and more powerful than anything Vlad had ever experienced before welled up, burning. A fiery ball of power filled with hatred and disgust and want of peace. He turned and ran up the steps of Bathory High, and as he reached the top he recalled the vision he'd experienced when he'd first drank Dorian's blood. He realized, with great relief, that he had been completely wrong about what he thought he saw in that vision. He was the Pravus—oh yes, there was no doubting that now—but he was the Pravus in a way that no one but Dorian saw.

He could kill them all. With but a single thought, he could command them all to do his bidding and die.

But . . .

As much as Vlad was vampire, he was also human. Incredible strength, amazing speed, mind control—these things were all gifts from his vampiric side. But his ability to know right from wrong . . . that was all human, and despite everything that had happened—to him, to the citizens of Bathory, to his beloved Snow—he knew what he had to do.

He was the only vampire ever born. But he had a human mother, a mother who loved him and cherished him and had given him his sense of caution, his view that deep down, people were truly good. He had spent so many years focusing on his vampire side that he'd neglected to see the many human traits he possessed. He was like Mellina in as many ways as he was like Tomas. He was a human. And a vampire.

And the Pravus.

He knew the prophecy now, knew every word of it as it raced through his veins. And his destiny was crystal clear.

Vlad faced the town of Bathory, taking in the blood and terror and fear. He lifted his arms high and with all of his being, with every bit of every part of his soul, he screamed out, "STOP!"

His eyes burned, and he knew that they were flashing brighter than ever before, just as they had in his vision. All at once, every single living being in the vicinity froze. No one moved. No one spoke.

Vlad—the Pravus—was in complete control of them all.

Every vampire, he reigned over. Every human, he had the power to protect, enslaving them with but a thought, for their own good. The prophecy was right. It was the interpretation that had been wrong. A label doesn't make something so. A label is just a word. It's what a person does that makes them who they are.

He thought of Snow, thought of her cold, pale body lying at the bottom of the steps, thought of how he'd never get a chance to tell her how he really felt. Then he whispered, "Look at me."

Every living being in Bathory complied, but still Vlad repeated his order in a tearful shout, "Look at me!!"

He pointed to Snow and said, "You've all done this. Vampires, Slayers, humans. This is all your doing. People are dying because you can't let go of your hatred for even a second. People are dying because of you . . ."

His voice dropped to a whisper. ". . . because of me."

Vlad ran a hand through his hair, brushing his bangs from his eyes. He took a moment to think, to form the words in his mind before he spoke them aloud. "Vampires, all vampires, except for my family and close friends, go back to your councils. Remember what happened here, but don't plan any kind of retaliation. Let it go. Go on with your lives."

Instantly, the vampires stopped what they were doing and walked away.

Vlad continued. "Slayers, except for Joss, go home. Forget you ever saw even one vampire in Bathory. And humans . . ."

A sigh escaped him, one filled with relief that everyone within earshot was forced to obey. "Tend to the wounded and take care of the dead. When the sun rises tomorrow, you'll only remember that an earthquake happened here, and that people died because of it. Forget the vampires. Forget the Slayers. It's over."

He'd make Henry remember, oh yes. And October and the other goths too.

He still wasn't sure about Meredith. But then . . . maybe it would make Joss's life easier to have her remember as well.

After all, it couldn't have been easy lying to her the entire time about who he was, what he was.

Vlad knew from experience.

The humans shifted around, tending to the injured and clearing away the dead. A quiet peace settled all around him, but Vlad felt no relief. He still had lost Snow. He still had lost Eddie to Em's will. He still had lost Meredith to Joss. And he still had no idea what had happened to his mother that fateful day.

Looking over the crowd, he realized that his father was missing from the picture. Moving down the steps, lifting Snow's body and cradling her in his arms, he hurried with vampiric speed across town, knowing that he would find Tomas in their house, in their home.

Once there, he placed Snow on the couch and covered her beautiful face with his mom's favorite afghan, which was now free of that smoky smell, thanks to Nelly's determination. He kissed the cloth that covered her lips and brushed away fresh tears, knowing that he would never love anyone again the way that he loved Snow.

Rushing upstairs, he stopped at the silhouette standing in the doorway of the master bedroom. Tomas's shoulders were sunk, as if he were feeling defeated. Vlad reached out, touching his left shoulder with an inquisitiveness that even he couldn't explain. "Dad?"

"Come inside, Vlad. Come inside and learn the truth." Without so much as a glance back at his son, Tomas moved into the bedroom, his eyes on the bed. The left side, Vlad noted, where his mother used to sleep.

Vlad glanced out the bedroom window as he entered the room, and said, "I stopped it—the fighting—I stopped it all with barely a thought. It's over. But . . . I can't help but wonder . . . where were you when the Slayers were attacking? I didn't see you anywhere."

"I am so disappointed in you, son."

Vlad's jaw hit the floor. "What are you talking about? Slayers were attacking Bathory!"

Tomas closed his eyes, as if exhausted from dealing with a young child's whims. "I have been infinitely patient. How else can I bring you to this truth?"

Vlad blinked, confused. He had no idea what his dad was talking about. Something inside his chest grew heavy with fear.

Tomas clasped his hands behind him and began pacing slightly. "I have lied to you, my son, but only to protect you, only to open your eyes to the truth after years of lies told to you by Otis."

Something inside Vlad's chest squeezed his heart until he thought it might burst. "What did he, and you, lie about exactly?"

"There *is* a group who supports the coming of the Pravus. It is called the Alumno and was created to do all that they could in support of bringing about the Pravus, to lay their every resource and even their lives down for the cause. But

I'm not being hunted by them. In fact, I am the group's founding member." Vlad's eyes widened, and Tomas held up his hands and hurried to explain. "You believed Otis, son, you believed every lie he spewed about our group, about how evil we are, about how the Pravus was a myth. But I assure you, this is not the case. We have an honorable cause, and you are a gift to all of Elysia."

Vlad shook his head. "I don't . . . understand. Why? And Otis—why would he think that your group is evil?"

"Jealousy, perhaps. Otis always was the jealous type."

That didn't sound anything at all like the Otis he knew, but Vlad kept that thought to himself.

"You had an unbreakable trust for the man. That is, until I planted evidence to shake that trust. Otis's hat will never be the same, I'm afraid. But it was important to instill doubt in your heart. Doubt that your perfect uncle was ever so perfect." The corner of his mouth lifted in a brief smile. "Despite what you may believe, it is the Pravus's place to right the wrongs of Elysia, my son, and to put humans in their proper place."

"But I'm human. Partly, anyway. And Mom . . ." His heart ached. "Mom . . ."

"I loved your mother. As much as a vampire can love a human. She knew her place, served her purpose. She was a good drudge. But she was also lacking in loyalty toward the end." The corner of Tomas's mouth twitched in irritation. "I was going to let her live. But then I learned that she'd been making secret plans to steal away with you in the night, and worse, to turn me in to Elysia for my crimes. Somehow, she'd contacted Dorian—the one vampire I could not possibly control or dupe. He sent his son, Adrian, here, to meet with her in secret, to investigate her claims, little good it did him."

"But Adrian . . ." Vlad rolled the name over on his tongue. Dorian's son. And Vlad had once seen his name written on a piece of paper . . . in Tomas's handwriting. "I thought Otis killed him. Otis thought that too."

"Otis was too drunk on blood that night to know what was happening. I sent Adrian a note from your mother, to meet her that night, a full day before Dorian's instruction for him to come. Adrian stole away to do so, and I used my mind control powers to help Otis to falsely recall draining him dry. After all, I couldn't have anyone suspecting that those were the charred remains of Adrian and not me." Tomas shook his head. It was sickening and frightening and horrible how easy it seemed to be for him to discuss such awful things with such a casual tone. "I had no choice, Vladimir. I bound your mother and Adrian to the bed. And once the drapes were drawn, the sun did the rest. Adrian was about as sensitive to the sun as a vampire can get."

Vlad bit his bottom lip. Hard. Until he tasted blood. Then he turned back to his father. "Who opened the drapes?"

Tomas blinked, as if he had no idea what Vlad was talking about. "Pardon?"

"Who opened the drapes, Tomas?" He didn't call him "Dad," wouldn't call him that word. He wasn't acting like a dad. A dad would've done whatever he could have to protect his son. A dad wouldn't have planned out his son's entire life as a way to lift himself into a position of power. And a dad certainly wouldn't have murdered his son's mother. He was a monster. A vile, evil, cruel monster, who deserved nothing more than pain in return.

Calling him by his first name instead of "dad" was a start, but only just.

The instant hung in the air like a hot, crackling cloud between them. Tomas's eyes darkened, as if he wasn't used to insubordination.

The sound of soft footsteps approaching distracted them both, but still the cloud remained.

Then a voice broke in. Stern, full of warning, and so familiar. Vikas. "Vladimir, you shouldn't use such a disrespectful tone with your father."

The silence returned and after some time, harsh reality hit Vlad, nearly knocking him over.

"It was you . . ." He moved his eyes, full of wondering disbelief, to Vikas. Vikas's wrist was no longer home to a Mark. It was scarred, just like Tomas's. He looked back to Tomas. His throat closed for a moment in horrified realization. Even as the words escaped him, he was having a difficult time grasping the meaning behind them. "You killed my mother. Vikas opened the drapes and . . . you both killed my mom . . ."

Vikas shook his head, clucking his tongue, and softened his tone as if trying to soothe a child. "She was just a human, Mahlyenki Dyavol. Besides, it was for the good of the cause."

To Vlad's horror, his father nodded in agreement. They

both wore the look of two people who had no idea what the big fuss was about. It ripped at Vlad's soul to see such emptiness, such selfish, horrible disregard for the most important woman in Vlad's life.

"You killed my mom!" He shoved his father, but Tomas didn't even flinch. Something about the way they were standing told Vlad he wouldn't be allowed to leave. Not until they had their say. He shook his head, his heart breaking. "You're monsters. Worse than D'Ablo ever was."

Clasping his hands behind his back, his father took on a more formal tone, like a soldier reporting details to his general. "D'Ablo's been rightly dispatched. He lost his faith, thinking he could take your place. He knew I was going into hiding, to watch you, to push you quietly from the shadows in the right direction, to wait for the proper time to claim what is rightfully mine. But he somehow lost sight of our purpose and tried to claim your status as Pravus for his own. And then there's Enrico, who'd vowed to stop at nothing to uncover any treachery leading to Dorian's death. Dorian knew of my plans, knew everything about everything, it seemed. I knew if Enrico was left to live, he'd eventually uncover hints of his son's knowledge of my plans, and I couldn't have that. Besides, I never liked him. And he was half mad, so killing him was really a charitable act."

Vlad almost gasped, but caught himself. He was shocked by what he was hearing, and immensely angry to hear it. He didn't know this man at all, and never had.

"Your mother's death was necessary because her loyalty to

me was lacking. Every boy reaches the moment when he leaves his mother behind, Vlad. I just moved your moment closer. It was easy. Like stealing and burning that damn *Compendium* so that you wouldn't grow to believe Elysia's view that the Pravus is evil. Like hiding my journal in Joss's backpack, to see how far you would go, to see if you would kill a friend. Though, in hindsight, I should have retrieved it immediately. Before that Eddie boy so cunningly stole it away. It took forever for me to retrieve it from him. The smell of his blood is excruciatingly distracting."

Vlad shook his head—his new, darker reality settling into the still horrified part of his brain. His father and his friend. They'd planned his birth and killed his mother. Everything that had ever been wrong with Vlad's life was because of them. He glared at Tomas, glared so hard he wished he could shoot lasers from his eyes and burn out Tomas's cold, black heart. "Why?"

A small smile danced on Tomas's lips. "When I left that day, the day of the fire, it was so that I could convince Em that I was dead, to give me time, time to live without the threat of a trial and wait until after your eighteenth birthday, when I knew the prophecy would be fulfilled. I was watching you, often at a distance, but always for the same reason: to watch your Pravus powers grow and take shape. The believers think that I do all that I do in order to raise you up as the Pravus. But I'm afraid my reasons aren't as simple as that. You see, D'Ablo was a fool. No one can steal your status as Pravus until you've fully developed your Pravus powers. And you just have. So isn't my timing remarkable?"

Vlad shot him a shocked glare that was bitter and full of hatred. "I will never help you. I'll do anything in my powers to keep you from gaining my Pravus traits. Anything! Even if it means my death."

Tomas merely smiled.

"You will break, my son," he whispered, that strange smile on his lips as he leaned closer to Vlad, like they shared some twisted secret. "We have our ways."

40
THE TRUTH

TOMAS AND VIKAS DISAPPEARED. One moment Vlad was standing there, eyeing his father down, and the next minute, both vampires had disappeared in a blur of vampiric speed. The second he realized they were gone, he ran as fast as he was able to, whipping through the town, on the hunt for the men who'd killed his mother for their own selfish gain.

Near the high school, he found Otis, looking lost and confused. He stopped running immediately. "Otis! Is everything all right?"

Otis shook his head slowly. He stared down the street, then up it for a moment before speaking to Vlad in a distant, distracted tone. "Your aunt. . . .Vladimir . . . Nelly, have you seen Nelly? She was just with me, and then she was gone. Like a dust storm. Just here and gone. I can't seem to find her anywhere."

Vlad moved his eyes slowly over the landscape, scrutinizing every inch of the area surrounding them. But Otis was right. Nelly was nowhere to be found.

Horror filled Vlad as his father's words echoed in his mind. *"We have our ways."*

No.

Oh no.

Tomas and Vikas had taken her, taken Nelly, and all Vlad could think was that they were going to hurt her if he didn't bend to their will.

Otis found Vlad's eyes, his filling with concern. "What? What is it?"

"My dad . . . and Vikas . . . they killed my mom, Otis. They killed D'Ablo, and Enrico too." Disbelief filled Vlad's heart even though he knew it to be true. Tomas had killed his wife, no matter how much Vlad wished that it wasn't true. Wishing a thing didn't make it so.

Otis's eyes grew wide. "What? That's quite the accusation to make, Vladimir. Are you certain?"

Vlad nodded. "Completely. I heard it from Tomas's own lips. And there's more. He's the leader of that group, Otis. The vampires who support the coming of the Pravus? He started it all."

Otis's pale face grew red momentarily, and he swore loudly in Elysian code. Vlad was very surprised to realize that he understood what Otis was saying. Even if he couldn't speak Elysian code, he was at least beginning to understand the swear words.

Otis paced for several seconds before turning back to Vlad. "I had my suspicions. For years, I wondered if Tomas was part of that group. But I couldn't bring myself to believe it. I couldn't accept that my brother, my friend, was one of those mindless, ruthless believers. You do know what this means . . . about your birth, yes?"

Vlad nodded slowly. "It means that my father only created me because he wanted to be the creator of the Pravus. It means he never really loved me or my mom."

Otis placed a caring hand on his shoulder. "We don't know that, Vladimir. But we do know that he believes so completely that you are the Pravus, the man that the prophecy spoke of, that he will do anything to further his cause. Anything. Even kill to convince you to follow his twisted path."

"It's not that, Otis. He . . . he wants to be the Pravus."

Otis shook his head, his whispered words turning bitter on his tongue. "Damn him. He'll stop at nothing to fulfill his selfish desires."

"We should run. Now! Go after them." Vlad's heart was beating a million miles a second at the thought of what horrible things might happen to Nelly if they didn't reach her on time.

Otis shook his head. "Go. Go now. I'll have to drive. I'm . . . injured, Vladimir."

Vlad followed Otis's eyes to his side, where he was clutching his blood-soaked shirt. It hadn't been soaked a moment before. Not that Vlad had noticed anyway. "Otis . . . oh my god, what happened to you?"

Otis lifted his shirt, and the sight of the six-inch gash sent a wave of nausea over Vlad, almost knocking him over. "It's healing, but it'll take time, and I can't run that fast while it's healing. Go on without me. I'll be there soon."

"Otis, you know I can't leave you behind. I want you there with me to face my father. I . . . I don't know if I'm strong enough to face him and Vikas alone."

A sleek, black car, whipped around the corner, fishtailing until the vehicle was right in front of them. The driver's window lowered and Henry grinned. "Need a ride?"

Vlad furrowed his brow in confusion. "How did you know?"

Henry shrugged. "Just had a feeling. I'm learning to trust the feelings I have, especially when it comes to saving your butt. Now are you getting in or not?"

"Otis is hurt."

Joss leaned over from the passenger seat and looked out the open window at Vlad. "I'll get in the back with him and do what I can."

Otis eyed the Slayer warily, but finally nodded. After Joss and Vlad had him safely in the backseat, Vlad explained everything: about his dad, about Nelly. But it was only after Vlad recalled a certain dream that had plagued him one night in his eighth-grade year that Vlad knew exactly where to go. After some instruction, Henry took off with a screech, barreling toward Stokerton at shocking speeds. It was the fastest that Henry had ever driven.

Henry parked in front of the Stokerton council building, and when they all piled out, including a healed Otis, Vlad wasn't the least bit surprised to see Tomas standing on the front steps, his hand clutching the back of Nelly's neck, Nelly's eyes wide and terrified, Nelly speechless.

Vlad tapped into his Pravus powers and tried to execute control over Tomas, but couldn't. Stunned, he looked at his father in confusion.

Tomas laughed. "It seems that part of the prophecy was misinterpreted, Master Pravus. You cannot control a vampire who has burned his Mark away."

Vlad pursed his lips angrily, blocking Tomas from his thoughts.

Tomas's voice was cruel. "I don't understand why you fight against fate, my son. You are the Pravus and I am your father. I will take this burden from you at any cost. Then I will rule over vampirekind and enslave the human race. It's unavoidable."

Vlad shook his head curtly as he approached. "That's not true. The prophecy says the Pravus will only enslave the humans out of charity."

Tomas pursed his lips in anger, but didn't speak.

Vlad flicked his eyes to Nelly, who looked so scared that her skin was almost as pale as Tomas's. "Let her go, Dad. Let her go. Please."

A cruel, hateful expression crossed Tomas's eyes. "You have a choice to make, my son. Kill Otis now and I will let her live. Don't kill him and I will drain her of every drop before your eyes."

Vlad looked from Nelly to Otis in shock. He couldn't

imagine either of them leaving his life permanently. Especially not by his own hand. "But . . . why?"

Tomas's voice sounded deeper, almost gravelly in tone. It sounded like he was dancing on the edge of madness. Not quirky Dorian madness. Real madness. "Because it amuses me. Now choose. Or I shall choose for you."

Otis set his jaw and looked at Vlad. "Kill me, Vlad. I've lived a long life. And if I can't live another day with Nelly, I'd rather be dead. Save her. Please."

Tomas glanced at Vlad. "If you value your aunt's life, Vlad, you'll kill your dear uncle and head upstairs to the roof, where Vikas has carefully laid out the tools we'll need to complete our transaction. If the hidden script in my journal is any indication, the final details of the ritual will be messy. It requires emptying you of both your invincibility—something that D'Ablo failed miserably at—and every drop of blood."

Nelly turned her head, though Tomas still grasped her neck, and looked back at him, her jaw clenched. "Tomas Tod, you will not hurt this boy. What would Mellina think of all of this? Have you lost your mind entirely?"

For a long moment, they stood staring one another down, until Nelly softened some, her eyes wide with sorrow, her head shaking. "That's it, isn't it? You have lost your mind. Tomas, this is your son. You gave him life, held him in your arms, fed him, clothed him. And though recent years have been from a distance, you've watched him grow into the amazing young man you see before you. You can't do this. You can't hurt Vlad. He's your son. You gave him life."

"And so it is mine to take, Nelly."

Nelly's eyes were moist with anger and determination. "I won't let you hurt him, Tomas! Mellina isn't here to defend her son. She isn't here because of you. I won't lose Vlad the way I lost her. I won't, Tomas! I won't!"

She yanked herself away from Tomas's grasp and reached for Vlad, who in turn reached for his aunt.

His eyes lit up with madness, Tomas shouted, "And I won't let you manipulate my son! MY SON!"

Before Vlad's and Nelly's hands could make contact, Tomas gnashed his teeth into Nelly's neck, draining her in seconds. Vlad froze in shock. Even his Pravus powers couldn't shake him from his disbelieving daze.

Without another word, Tomas flew up the side of the building to the roof.

Nelly collapsed.

Vlad heard the sound of her heartbeat in his ears. It slowed, then stopped before she could take another breath.

Otis followed Tomas in a furious blur.

Vlad just stood there, staring at Nelly.

His caretaker. His second mother.

Dead.

41

HONOR THY FATHER

A N INTENSE HEAT started at Vlad's toes and worked its way up his body, until every inch of his skin felt like it was being engulfed by flames. Fury washed over him like a fire.

"Don't do anything stupid, Mahlyenki Dyavol. You were created for a purpose. Serve that purpose well." Vikas was standing in the alley, one eyebrow cocked. It was clear he was looking for a fight, or at the very least, to distract Vlad from chasing after Tomas.

Vlad tried to push into his mind, to control him, to make him just stop. Stop and go away.

But he couldn't.

With a grin, Vikas held up his wrist, revealing a scar where his Mark had once been. "I burned it out of me. All of Elysia's control, gone. Even the Pravus cannot control me now."

Joss and Henry exchanged determined glances, and Henry nodded to Vlad. "We've got this guy. You go after Otis—he could probably use your help."

Joss slipped his stake from its holster at his waist and slapped the beautifully carved, silver-tipped hunk of wood into Vlad's hand. The same stake that had been buried in his chest just a few short years before. With a set jaw and a worried expression, Joss said, "Whatever you do, don't miss."

Vlad squinted up, blocking the glow of the streetlights with his hand. Otis was standing on the edge of the Stokerton council building, looking down at him with wide, panic-stricken eyes.

Vlad knew this moment. He'd dreamed it. Four years ago, he'd dreamed it. And now it was coming to pass.

Blood dripped from a cut on Otis's forehead. He wiped it away with his sleeve, smearing it across his pale skin. "Vladimir, run! Run and don't look back!"

But Vlad wasn't about to turn his back on family. He focused hard on his body and willed it upward, shooting higher and faster than he ever had before. He stepped nimbly onto the building's roof and pulled Otis back from the edge. Otis shook his head and pleaded through his tears. "Please go, Vlad. You have no idea what he's capable of."

Vlad looked across the rooftop to the shadowy figure standing there. Tomas. His father.

Behind him was the horrible table that D'Ablo had

strapped him to a few years ago, and on top of that was a large syringe and Tomas's journal.

Vlad squeezed Otis's shoulder. "This isn't your fight, Otis. It's mine."

But then Vlad was hit in the side and knocked to the ground. His knee smacked the tarred roof and cracked audibly. He winced and swore aloud.

Tomas was fast. Lightning fast. Almost as fast as Vlad.

Vlad glanced up at his uncle and saw Otis's eyes grow wide. He looked back to his father, but his vision blurred. The scene above him turned red, like blood. And then Vlad was immersed in a memory. He was no longer on the roof, but standing in a library—a familiar vision, one he'd glimpsed as one of the memories Otis had shared with him. Tomas was poring over the pages of an old book. A wall of books surrounded him.

Otis entered the room, his steps slowing, a smile on his face. "Reading, again? What this time?"

Tomas looked up, his intense focus broken by a surprised smile. "Just some old stories. To pass the time, you know. What about you? I thought you were on a plane to Siberia."

Otis eyed the book Tomas was now covering with his forearm with some suspicion. "I cancelled at the last minute. I thought we could do some hunting together. What are you reading?"

"Poetry." The lie left his lips easily, sickening Vlad.

Otis frowned and snatched the book from Tomas's hands.

"*Theories of the Pravus Prophecy*, Tomas? Why? You don't have any interest in joining the Alumno, do you?"

Tomas shook his head adamantly. "Of course not. I'm just curious."

"About what?"

"About whether or not it's possible."

The world swirled again and Vlad found himself back in the present, engaging his father. They were facing one another, Vlad with a stake in hand, Tomas with a familiar black tube grasped firmly in his palm. The Lucis.

Vlad stared at it in disbelief.

"Recognize this? I retrieved it from the council building months ago." Dark shadows crossed his eyes. "You can't fight it. I'll serve in your place, Vlad. Your memory will be raised up to a near god-like status amongst my followers. You don't want this fight. Trust me. You'd rather do as you're told."

Vlad growled, "Don't tell me what I want. You're nobody to me. Nothing. Just a stranger. Just a bad dream."

"Your partner in everything or your worst nightmare. You decide." Tomas whipped forward with lightning speed, hitting Vlad in the side and knocking him over.

Vlad hit the ground with such force that his vision wavered. Jumping to his feet, Vlad moved after his father, throwing punches and missing, the stake held firmly in his hand. Tomas gnashed his teeth forward, biting into Vlad's shoulder. Vlad cried out and backed away as fast as he was able.

Then Tomas grinned, his teeth red with Vlad's blood, and

glanced down at Otis. "Otis has been clouding your mind. So let's just clear things up for you, shall we?"

He moved forward, heading straight for Otis, a hungry, evil look in his eyes. He held up the Lucis, pointing it straight at Otis's heart.

Henry flew through the air and connected with the side of the building with a meaty smack. He fell into a Dumpster. From within the garbage, his voice croaked, "Oh, please. I've had harder smacks from my grandma."

Joss stared up at Vikas, a seemingly immortal, unbeatable foe.

Without Joss's stake, they were dead.

But at least they would die knowing that they helped a friend when he most needed them.

Vikas moved forward, a bloody, awful, evil grin on his face.

And Joss prepared to say goodbye to the world.

Time slowed.

Tomas's footsteps echoed on the blacktop. Otis's heart was beating in time with every step.

Vlad looked at the two of them, at the man who had brought him into this world and the man who had kept him safe within it, and realized that he had never been without a father—not since the day Otis walked into his life. He had a dad. One who loved him for who he was, not what he could offer.

Otis was his dad, despite what a DNA test might say.

Tomas laughed bitterly. "Your father? You'd actually think that about your uncle?"

Vlad glared and clamped down on his thoughts once again.

"Otis hasn't earned that title, my son. I've been there every day of your life! You might not have seen me, but I was there. Even that day at my funeral pyre. I was listening, Vlad. I was there. You couldn't say goodbye to me then, just as you cannot resist me now."

It was the wrong thing to say.

"Tomas!" Vlad shouted as he spun around, the stake held tightly in his fist. "Don't touch him!"

Otis flung his arm forward, knocking the Lucis from Tomas's grip. He shouted to Vlad, "Grab it!"

Time, still crawling, moved forward. Vlad stretched his arm in front of him, his fingers just brushing the end of the Lucis as it tumbled over the building's edge. A brilliant white light shot from one end, turning over and over as it made its descent.

Light filled the street. Brilliant, white, hot light that illuminated Henry as he ran toward Vikas. It was beautiful, in its own way. And Joss couldn't help but wonder if that was the light that people who'd lived through near-death experiences had claimed to see.

Joss was ready for the final blow. He released a deep breath and met Vikas's eyes.

He would watch the vampire's final attack. He would stand up and confront death with all that he had, all that he was.

But then the brilliant light tumbled to the ground, slashing through Vikas from the middle of his head all the way through his body.

Vikas fell to the ground in two distinct pieces.

Henry picked up the strange flashlight that the light had come from and turned it over in his hand. "No way! It's that Lucis thing. The thing from Nelly's attic!"

Joss had no idea what a Lucis was, but he was relieved that it had come to his rescue.

The Lucis was gone. With a furious howl, Tomas grabbed Otis by the throat.

He was going to kill him, kill Vlad's uncle, steal from Vlad one of the very few people in this world who had ever loved him, who had ever cared about Vlad in any way.

Unless Vlad stopped him.

Vlad whipped his arm forward and buried the stake deep in Tomas's chest before pulling it back again, leaving behind a large, bloody hole.

Time stopped.

Vlad's heartbeat stopped.

Then time started again. But slowly. Oh, so slowly.

The stake left Vlad's hand, parting from his fingertips and tumbling for what felt like an eternity through the air, before clattering on the floor below. The sound it made when it hit reverberated through the air, thundering in Vlad's ears.

Just as slowly as the stake had fallen, so did Vlad, dropping through the thick air to his knees. It wasn't until he made contact with the ground that he released the breath he'd been holding in—locked tight, safe, within his lungs, as if it might be his last. It came out sounding like a gasp.

A pool of crimson bloomed out from beneath his dad's body. Several small trails of blood were drawing their way outward in a spiderweb. One of the webs drew closer to Vlad but stopped before it touched him.

Vlad forced his body to draw another breath. Slow. Even. The next one came easier, but shuddered.

He'd killed his dad.

His father, creator, the man who gave him life, taught him how to ride a bike, nursed his bumps and bruises, showed him what it was to be a man, to be a vampire, made Vlad want to be just like him.

Vlad killed him. And now nothing would be all right ever again.

Tomas was on his back, one arm stretching out toward where Vlad knelt, his face turned toward his son, eyes open. But there was no life in those eyes, just as there had been no love in them moments before.

He was dead. Nelly was dead too.

He'd lost his dad all over again. His mom too. It was Vlad's worst nightmare, replayed all over again.

Tears welled in Vlad's eyes and poured out onto his cheeks, just as slowly as everything else seemed to be moving.

Alone. Vlad was alone.

And he'd never get them back. Not ever.

Warm hands closed over Vlad's shoulders. He didn't need to look up to know that they belonged to Otis. His uncle didn't speak—even without the use of telepathy, Otis seemed to understand that for some moments, there are no words.

Otis squeezed and the tears fell freely from Vlad's eyes.

It was over. Both Nelly and his mom had been avenged, and Otis had been saved. Vlad had done it all with one fell swoop.

All it had cost him was everything.

42

SAYING GOODBYE

THE FLAMES LICKED UPWARD, TOWARD THE SKY, from Tomas's pyre. The small crowd, all vampires, had been gathered in stoic silence for some time. Otis had told Vlad that it was tradition that he say something, but Vlad had no words left to speak. So Otis, ever the understanding mentor, had taken the reins and said some wonderful things about Tomas, Vlad's father, Otis's brother.

None of them, Vlad thought, had been lies. But Otis did leave out certain details. Details that were still burning like fire through Vlad's insides. He felt guilty for thinking such things, for feeling so angry and betrayed, but mostly he felt guilty for feeling guilty. He was right to end Tomas's life. He'd saved Otis—maybe even all of humankind—and avenged his mom and Nelly. He should've been relieved. He should've been even a bit proud, but he wasn't. He wasn't sure how he was supposed to feel. He just felt . . . empty.

Vampires lined up at the pyre, saying their goodbyes. It was only after the crowd had filed out, that Otis broke the silence.

"You don't have to speak, Vladimir. If you've nothing to say, you can leave him with your silence. It's okay." He gave Vlad's shoulder a caring squeeze before stepping up to the pyre himself. He was up there for a long time, and when he stepped away, Vlad noticed with great surprise the tears streaking down his cheeks.

Despite everything, Otis still mourned the loss of his friend.

Vlad couldn't help but think that Otis was a far better person than he.

Vlad watched the pyre for several minutes before approaching. The heat from the flames warmed Vlad's face and, if Vlad had any tears moistening his cheeks, they would have dried immediately as he approached.

But there were none.

Vlad's pain, at least for now, was trapped on the inside as he tried to rationalize just what had happened.

He tried to understand his father's point of view. But couldn't.

Standing there at the pyre, Vlad tried to think of the words he wanted to leave his father's immortal soul with, the words that would say goodbye forever, that would sum up his final moments spent thinking about Tomas Tod. After a long, silent moment, Vlad said, "You were wrong about Otis. He is my father. In every way that counts."

He dropped his voice to a whisper then, flicking his eyes from the pyre to the carefully wrapped body which lay to the side, awaiting burning. "Wherever we go after this life, I hope that you're there, and I hope that Mom and Nelly forgive you in ways that I can't."

As Vlad turned, he saw Otis lift Tomas's body and place it on the pyre. Vlad turned and walked slowly from his father's funeral, feeling lighter somehow, feeling right. Feeling justified.

The sun crept over the horizon then and behind him, Tomas's body burst into an explosion of heat and flames.

All Vlad could think was one word. A word he couldn't bring himself to say until now.

"Goodbye."

43
FLOWERS FOR NELLY

VLAD CLUTCHED THE BOUQUET OF DAISIES in his hand, trying hard not to crush the delicate stems and failing miserably. Nelly loved daisies. She'd tried numerous times to plant them in the flower beds around her home, but Amenti kept eating them. Vlad wondered if Amenti was adjusting to her new home at the McMillans, and if she was eating all Matilda's daisies too. He missed Amenti.

He missed Nelly.

It was raining out, but only a little. Just enough to mist Vlad's face and mask his tears. Believing in silly superstitions like rain on a wedding day bringing good luck, Nelly would've been oddly optimistic about rain on the day of her funeral.

Vlad dropped his eyes to his suit. He was supposed to be wearing it to her wedding. Not this.

People had already stood and shared their memories of

his aunt, but not Vlad. His voice, like Nelly, was nowhere to be found. As the last of the crowd filed by her coffin, Vlad stood, his heart heavy, and approached. The coffin was closed, at Vlad's request. He couldn't bear looking at Nelly's body, couldn't bear the thought of people thinking that this shell was really her, when the real Nelly was now wherever his mom was.

With a deep breath, Vlad laid the daisies on top of Nelly's coffin and whispered, "I love you, Nelly. You were a good aunt, a good mom. I miss you."

As he walked away, Otis caught him in a tight, sorrowful embrace. Vlad stood there, letting Otis hug him, letting Otis cry. But Vlad did neither.

He was numb.

44
THE RETRIAL

VLAD STRAIGHTENED HIS SHOULDERS and took a deep breath, releasing it slowly. The air inside the small room located beneath V Bar was stuffy and felt thick, but that might just have been Vlad's perception of it. He was, after all, here to face his retrial, and with it, the decision of the Council of Elders on whether or not he would live.

He was betting on dying. Everything about vampiric law, after all, insisted on it.

He just wished they'd get on with it already.

The nine council members had been whispering for some time now, but when the president turned toward Vlad, he found himself holding his breath.

Time held still.

Then the familiar face smiled, and Vlad heard words that he never dreamed that he would hear. "Vladimir Tod. This council deems that while you may not be innocent of all charges, we cannot prosecute you due to lack of information. As D'Ablo was the sole witness to your crimes and is now deceased . . . he cannot attest to your guilt. You are free to go."

Vlad searched his uncle's eyes and found only truth.

Otis smiled.

It was strange to be put on trial by his only living relative and closest confidant, but once Vikas had died of what was now being referred to as a terrible accident, Otis had opted to take Vikas's seat on the council. He was insistent, in fact, that it was time for Elysia to learn to be right and just and fair. Then, after Em had disappeared following the attempted—and failed—cleansing of Bathory, his fellow council members insisted that Otis lead them by taking her seat. To his right, in D'Ablo's chair, was Cratus—a vampire Vlad had met briefly last year.

Things were different now. Em's tyranny was no longer clouding the Council of Elders, and no one on the council—to Vlad's knowledge—had anything to do with Tomas's sordid plans to raise Vlad up as some evil being who would control vampirekind's every move. Vlad was the Pravus, and the majority of Elysia had accepted that fact. But the definition of what that meant had changed. Vlad would do everything he could to define the Pravus as a peacemaker, as a bridge between worlds.

As the council filed out, chatting casually, Vlad approached the table, where his uncle was still sitting. "So does this mean you're moving to New York, Otis?"

"Not at all. The Council of Elders only convenes a few times a year. I'd prefer to continue living in Bathory. Besides . . . I've just accepted the position of principal at Bathory High." Otis's eyes twinkled—something they hadn't done even once since the day they'd lost Nelly. It was good to see.

Vlad shook his head, chuckling. "You like going there every day, don't you? It's like you feel some kind of connection with that school or something."

"Absolutely. In fact . . . I was a priest at that church many moons ago." Something dark and strangely full of bemusement crossed Otis's eyes then, and Vlad thought back to the stories that upperclassmen had passed down to freshmen, about the vampire priest in that church who'd drained his congregation dry years and years ago, before Bathory High was a school. He parted his lips to ask if the rumors were true, but Otis cut him off with a smirk. "But that's a story for another time."

Vlad shook his head, a small smile curling his lips. There was so much more to Otis than even he knew, and now they had ages to share things together. It was easy to let go of his curiosity for the time being. After all, something was happening that Vlad had been certain wouldn't.

He'd survived his retrial.

He was going to live.

45

GRADUATION

VLAD LOOKED IN THE MIRROR AND PRACTICED his fake smile—the same fake smile he'd been practicing for months now. He'd need it today of all days. Besides, Nelly would have wanted him to smile at his high school graduation.

But there was no way he was putting on that stupid square hat until they got to the school.

"All set?" Otis peeked his head into Vlad's room. Boxes still lined the walls, but Vlad was relieved to be back in Nelly's house, even if it was only temporary, only until he started classes at Stokerton University in the fall. He hadn't been able to bring himself to visit his dad's house ever since Tomas's death, but neither had Otis, so Otis hired movers to gather their things and bring them back to Nelly's house. It was Vlad's house now, thanks to Nelly's will, and he was happy to share it with Otis, who looked anxious to get going.

"Just about. It's not like it takes much for a guy to get ready for this, Otis. You're starting to sound like Nelly." He smiled—a genuine smile—but it didn't last. His joke had brought about that look again, that shadowy, sad look in Otis's eyes. Instantly, Vlad felt ashamed. He should know better than to bring up Nelly. Her death had aged Otis, had hurt him in ways that Vlad could only imagine. Vlad opened his mouth to apologize, but Otis waved him off and hurried downstairs.

Vlad dropped his gaze to the black graduation gown he was wearing. Whose idea was it that forcing people to wear giant muumuus and cardboard squares on their heads and then parade in front of people was the way to celebrate surviving thirteen years of school anyway?

Shrugging, he picked up his cardboard hat and paused in front of his dresser. From atop the wooden surface, Vlad plucked the necklace that now held his parents' wedding rings and clasped it around his neck, tucking it into his gown. From inside the top drawer, he withdrew his secret box, and from within that, he withdrew his father's onyx ring. Slipping it onto his finger, Vlad made his way down the stairs.

He was ready. Ready to face Bathory High just one last time.

Otis was waiting for him outside, next to his crappy car. He was wearing a gray and black three-piece suit, and his infamous rumpled purple top hat, which had been recently repaired, removing all signs of Tomas's handiwork.

"Why do you wear that thing, Otis? It's not like it matches anything you own."

Otis smiled—a true, honest smile that came from the heart. "This hat was a gift to me from a young woman whom I had taught several years ago."

"But still. Why?" Vlad wrinkled his nose. He swore he saw moth holes in the purple fabric. "It's kind of an ugly hat."

Otis smiled a faraway smile, one that said that he was thinking about long ago times and happy memories. "I wear it because it reminds me of her, even if she'd long since forgotten the man she gave it to, the man who taught mythology at her college for merely one semester her sophomore year."

Vlad shook his head, sighing. It was clear his uncle wasn't going to ditch the hat, and he still wasn't sure why. "She must have been pretty special."

"She was. A shame about her taste in hats." The smile on Otis's lips spread to his eyes. "She couldn't cook either. Your aunt never could . . ."

Vlad almost choked on a gasp. "Nelly?! You knew Nelly before you came here?"

Otis nodded. "I knew it was her the moment I saw her, but if she remembered me, she never said. Still . . . I like to think the hat gave me away. I like to think she remembered the bumbling mythology teacher she gifted with a terrible hat."

A lumped formed in Vlad's throat. He could barely speak around it. "That's . . . that's really sweet, Otis."

Otis flipped open his pocket watch and frowned. "And we're really late."

They drove fairly quickly to the high school without another word. Otis had just put the car into park when he put a hand on Vlad's arm, stopping him from opening the door. Vlad raised an eyebrow. "But we're late . . ."

"This is important, Vladimir." It was Otis's turn to raise an eyebrow. "Would you mind?"

With a smile, Vlad focused, slowing down everything and everyone around them until only he and Otis could move or speak. It was like putting life on pause—one of his many Pravus traits. From the glove compartment, Otis withdrew a thin black box. He handed it to Vlad, some trepidation in his eyes. "You should have this, especially in light of recent events."

Vlad lifted the lid. Inside were a small pile of documents. At the top of the first was the word "deed." Vlad furrowed his brow. "What is this, Otis?"

"It's the deed to Tomas's home, in England. It still stands, has been perfectly preserved, in fact. It's the last place your father lived as a human, and where he spent much time while on the run from Elysia. It's yours . . ." His uncle flicked his eyes to him. ". . . if you want it."

Vlad nodded. He did want it. He'd loved his dad. Even if his dad had been too maniacal and selfish to love him back. "You'll stay, won't you, Otis? With me, I mean."

Otis smiled as Vlad brought the world back into motion. Birds once again flew overhead. People were walking by, chattering. Cars were driving down the street again. "Forever and a day, Vladimir. I'll stay as long as you need me."

A knock on the window startled Vlad, but he should have been expecting it. Outside, Henry and October were looking incredibly impatient. Vlad couldn't help but notice they were wearing matching hickeys.

Otis nodded for Vlad to go and when he opened the door, Henry said, "Where have you been? It's almost time!"

"Afraid they'll change their mind about you, Henry?" Vlad smirked.

October grinned. "He's just excited, Vlad. We all are. Stoker U!!!"

Vlad raised an eyebrow at her. "It's Stokerton University, October. Who calls it Stoker U?"

"I do."

Henry grinned and laced his fingers with October's. Vlad couldn't help but smile at the two of them. They were a great couple, good for one another in every way. October was wild and free and unique. Henry was grounded and real. And together, they were about the happiest couple that Vlad had ever seen.

They moved toward the graduation grounds, Otis hurrying on ahead—faculty was supposed to arrive a half hour before—and on the way, Vlad noticed another couple, a couple that brought a lump to his throat, a couple that he was still torn by the presence of.

Joss and Meredith were holding hands, smiling sweetly into each other's eyes. At the sight of him, Joss seemed to shrink back some, but Meredith held fast onto his hand.

Despite everything, Vlad was still extremely weirded out by the fact that they were dating.

Meredith smiled, her lips shimmering pink. "Hey, Vlad. All ready to graduate?"

"If it means never coming back to Bathory High, then yes. I was ready four years ago." Vlad sighed, a smirk touching the corners of his lips. "So . . . where are you going to college, Meredith? Stokerton U?"

"You mean Stoker U." October shrugged when everyone blinked at her. "What? I'm trying to start a trend."

Meredith shook her head. "Not for me. I'm headed for the University of California."

Vlad glanced at Joss. "You too, Joss?"

"Actually, I'm taking a break between high school and college. But I'll get there." Joss slipped his hand from Meredith's for a moment and tugged on Vlad's sleeve. "Listen, Vlad . . . can we talk in private for a second?"

Nodding, Vlad stepped to the side, away from the group, where he and Joss could talk.

Joss dropped his eyes to the ground. "I wanted to apologize for everything. The Slayers were way wrong, and everything I did to you . . . I'm sorry, okay?"

"I'm sorry, too. For everything. But Joss . . . if you keep insisting on apologizing, you'll never get past this. I forgave you months ago, remember?" Vlad gripped Joss tightly in a hug, patting his back. "Don't be a stranger, okay? And . . . take care of Meredith?"

"Of course." Joss patted his back too and as they rejoined the group, he said, "Think Eddie Poe will show up to collect his diploma?"

Vlad blinked up into the sky. "It's pretty sunny today, so I doubt it. Besides, from what I've heard in Elysia, I think he sticks pretty close to Em ever since his transformation."

October tilted her head in fascinated curiosity. She'd been asking a lot of questions about Elysia ever since Vlad told her to remember what had happened. "Are they a couple?"

Vlad shook his head. "No. Eddie's more like an annoying pet, from what I understand. But at least he got what he wanted."

"What's that?"

"To be special."

They all lined up then to walk in their caps and gowns, to parade in front of the parents and staff, and collect their diplomas. Vlad was more than ready for it.

At the sight of movement to his right, he turned his head, his fake smile morphing into a genuine one. "I thought you'd decided to sleep in or something."

"And miss my last day of high school? No friggin' way." Snow beamed. She looked so pretty, even prettier since her transformation.

"So what took you so long?"

"Sunscreen. I was ready on time until I remembered that I needed to apply sunscreen. Man . . ." She sighed heavily, dramatically. "Does it get any easier?"

"No. But at least you have company." Vlad kissed the back

of her hand, inhaling her scent. Roses. Life. And something darker now, something fitting. Snow was a vampire.

He recalled her moment of transformation, how he'd thought she'd died. But that was what Otis had shouted back to him, something crucial that he hadn't heard. *"She'll die before she turns, Vlad."*

Funny how mishearing things—or not hearing them at all—can really screw things up.

Vlad squeezed Snow's hand and turned his eyes to the stage. Meredith Brookstone, the class valedictorian, was giving her speech, but Vlad didn't really care. He'd heard those words before, full of hope and wonder at what the coming days will bring. But Vlad didn't wonder about that. He knew that whatever would come, he would face with his uncle, with his friends. He knew that whatever was going to happen, he was ready for it.

Snow beamed at him and Vlad's heart skipped a beat, almost stopping. His entire body froze with fear.

Without her even being aware of it, Snow's eyes flashed iridescent green.

Vlad gasped, not knowing what it meant, and not knowing what the future might bring.

Heather Brewer was not your typical teen growing up, and she's certainly not your typical adult now. She believes that teens are the answer to the world's problems, that spiderwebs are things of beauty, and that every occasion calls for black nail polish. When she's not dressing in black, she's dressing in black ...and counts herself lucky to be the supreme ruler of the Minion Horde. Heather doesn't believe in happy endings...unless they involve blood. She lives in Missouri with her husband and two children. Visit Heather at www.heatherbrewer.com.